THE AUTHOR

It is now nearly 40 years since John Caldwell completed his Desperate Voyage. He and his wife next travelled to America, where he graduated from the University of California with a degree in Sociology and became a social worker. A yearning for the sea soon led them to buy a 36-foot yacht, *Tropic Seas,* on which they set out with their three-year-old son, Johnny. Their second son, Roger, was born in Tahiti, and from there they sailed to the Fiji Islands and a joyful reunion with the people of Tuvutha, who had saved the author's life seven years before.

After 18 months at sea, they returned to Sydney, where John Caldwell donned suit and tie for an office job. But the sea still beckoned, and he and Mary spent two years of their spare time building a clipper-bowed ketch, which was launched with a case of beer and named *Outward Bound.* They spent a year amongst the Barrier Reef islands, survived a three-day thrashing from 30-foot waves off the Seychelles, then sailed via the Red Sea, Greece, Italy and the Canary Islands before arriving in the Caribbean. For five years they were employed there in full-time chartering, voyaging amongst islands, reefs and endless white beaches.

Struck by the shortage of palm trees, especially on the beaches of the Grenadine Islands, John Caldwell took coconut plants on most trips, planting around 8,000 in five years, and becoming known in the islands as Johnny Coconut. Coming to anchor at last, they leased Prune Island from the St Vincent Government, renamed it Palm Island, filled the swamps, cleared an airstrip in the jungle, and built a 24-room Beach Club resort, which for 16 years has been their home.

Desperate Voyage

John Caldwell

GRANADA
London Toronto Sydney New York

To Mary

Granada Publishing Limited
8 Grafton Street, London W1X 3LA

First published in Great Britain by Victor Gollancz Ltd 1950
This edition published by Granada Publishing 1985

Copyright © John Caldwell 1949

British Library Cataloguing in Publication Data

Caldwell, John, 1919 –
Desperate voyage.
1. Pagan (Ship)   2. Voyages and travels
3. South Pacific Ocean
I. Title
910′ .09164′ 8   DC122

ISBN 0-246-12708-2

Printed in Great Britain by
Billing & Sons Limited,
Worcester and London

CONTENTS

CONTENTS

Diagrams of
Pagan

Cutter PAGAN

Length over all 29'
Length waterline 25'
Beam 9'
Bowsprit 8'
Mast 33'

Length of deckhouse 9'
Height of deckhouse 2'
(no headroom)
Freeboard forward 30"
Freeboard aft 21"

PAGAN

Bunk used for storage
Cement in bilge
1000 lbs.
Keel

Ladder
Bunk
Rail
Deck line

Lead shoe
600 lbs.

PAGAN as she looked after hurricane

Main boom is secured to broken end of mast above deck for
jury mast. Broken mast is lashed athwartship to be restepped
at Samoa, which I never found. Bowsprit is broken a few feet
forward of the stem head. The forward part of the deckhouse
is smashed. The cabin ports on side shown are out. Ports on
starboard side are intact. Rails have carried away at the
deck. Sails are makeshifts recut from the original mainsail. An oar is stepped aft as a jigger mast. Estimated
speed one knot.

from side to side, and halyards flew at loose ends in the rigging — but for all that, *Pagan* rode happily out to sea.

❧   ❧   ❧

Day was gone. I was alone with the night sounds of the sea. *Pagan* pushed through the damp blackness slowly, as though feeling her way. I was straining eye and ear toward the bows for hints of land. In my lap my dainty kittens slumbered placidly, unmindful of my deep anxiety.

I drooped over the tiller, yearning for a guiding light to wink out of the black. I was lost. Three hours before I had felt certain I knew my position, but now I was steering a jig-saw course, and hoping for sight or sound of a haven where I could anchor and rest for the night, and think. The day had posed perplexing questions.

As near as I could figure I was some fifty or sixty miles off shore; somewhere near — I hoped — the little island of Pedro Gonzáles in the Perlas Islands.

It was ten o'clock at night. I was limp from hunger and from the work of practicing all day with my sails. The full long day I had hoisted and dropped sail, had maneuvered my boat on every angle to the wind, had even reefed and double reefed the sails, and had drifted and butted aimlessly over a large circle of the sea. In the end I knew my boat better, but I was left in confusion. I didn't know it well enough. Then unexpectedly dusk had swooped in. I found myself in the busy steamer channel, and grimly in need of a night of deep rest.

At dusk Pedro Gonzáles had been a blue smudge on the horizon which night quickly enfolded. Had I then used full engine with the sails, I could have soon closed in enough to make a night landfall with ease. But I held off. I had expected the breeze to build up soon after dusk and push me in just as quickly. Instead, I was becalmed on a glassy sea with sails slatting, blocks creaking, and *Pagan* rolling listlessly.

I left the sails up but put her under power and groped uncertainly forward. Suddenly the quick rush of seas came to my ear, followed by regular intervals of near quiet. I leaned closer to the night. A blackness blacker than the night reared up ahead, and soon the surf was louder.

I could see only the towering edge of the jagged isle where it blotted out the stars. Sometimes the seas, pounding against the blunt shore, sounded closer than at other times.

An outjutting of the shore loomed up ahead. I turned off, rounded it to starboard, and sighted another shaggy shadow on the port beam. I swung around and bore down between the two, hoping to stand in close where I could cast the lead in search of anchorable water.

As I crept along the seas grew louder. Close by to port was a curling line of gray surf — somehow it seemed it should be farther away.

Ahead I could see dollops of water splashing over the rocky shallows. The air was damp, as though there were spray in it. You don't acquire the mariner's instinct for imminent danger in a day of sailing! I flashed my light across the water and blinked it.

Suddenly, voices boomed from out of the black: *"No pase par aquí! Piedras! Peligroso!"*

Rocks! In a hair-raised moment I flung the tiller to port. *Pagan* jibed. Gleaming gray water flashed from all sides. I cut the engine. I raced to the mast and cast loose all halyards, clawed down the mainsail. In a trice I had, almost unknowingly, thrown the anchor out and made it fast at ten fathoms. Rocks were awash practically at the forefoot. On either beam the slush of water over shoal heads kept me on deck, heart abeat, for over an hour, as *Pagan* settled peacefully to anchor.

Mestizo fishermen rowed out in their frail *cayucos*. They swung aboard in the beam of my flashlight, grinning from stubbled faces, assuring me that my position, though precarious, was safe enough; and went away.

I sat on deck, eying the rushing water, hearing its ominous sounds — in a confused reverie. I thought back on the day filled with lessons, and I tried to look ahead to what was in store when I should be alone out on the ocean. The longer I pondered, the more I was convinced of my total inexperience for the trip I was undertaking. I didn't know my boat. I couldn't handle her. The day had shown it.

It was practice I needed, at least a week of it, if not two. I needed to work and live with my boat as I had done that day. Then I would know her, would be able to predict her behavior, could control her.

I thought of practicing in the waters off Pedro Gonzáles, using the isle as a base, and I thought of using the whole Perlas chain as a practice ground.

I flashed my light over the Perlas chart and saw in the tight-clustered arrangement of isles ideal grounds for my purpose. There were suitable bays to practice anchoring in, and there were close channels to beat through, and there were shoals and reefs and small islets to practice avoiding. In a revealing moment I decided my liking for them, and fig-

B*

ured on getting to work when daylight came. When I went below I was relieved of an unsureness that had been a part of me for days.

Now I could practice in a proper way. I could learn what I needed to know, and then sail out on the blue, easy of mind.

Throughout the day of working the sails and maneuvering my boat I had eaten little, and suddenly my stomach was squeezing and unsqueezing itself. For preparation of meals on *Pagan* I followed no organized menu. When it came time to eat I always glanced through the stores list and struck off whatever suited my mood and fancy. Then I rifled through the food lockers until I found it. I made it a point to keep a close tally on my stores, so I could readily know the exact state of my supplies.

When I outfitted *Pagan* in supplies I had the same idea you would have if you were going on a hunting trip. Hunting trips, however, are usually short-lived, whereas I had stocked up for well over four months.

When I provisioned for the trip it was a compromise — a compromise with foods I enjoyed eating, foods that were inexpensive, foods easy and quick to prepare, foods that would keep. I took aboard a gallon each of the following: rice, flour, oatmeal, corn meal, hominy grits, tea, coffee, honey, jam, oleomargarine, and sugar. The reason I say a gallon is because the only things I could find around the Yacht Club to store my staples in were a dozen one-gallon cider bottles. I couldn't afford to buy sealed containers to store food in, so I filled each of the bottles, screwed the lids on tightly, wrapped them in blankets, and stored them under my bunks. Because I had twelve bottles, I filled two with sugar.

For bread, I carried a five-gallon tin of hard, heavy sea biscuits. Housewives around the waterfront gave me a number of quart jars which I filled with dried prunes, dried apples, and dried peaches. From the ceiling of the cabin hung a huge bacon and a ham. They swayed with the roll of the boat, and freshened the cabin with a richly sweet smell.

The bulk of my food stores centered in a heavy load of canned goods — 248 tins in all, mostly large-sized cans. I liked the big cans, they were the right size for a meal; a few twists with a can opener and I had the quickest meal possible. There was everything in the selection from canned ketchup to canned fish for the kittens.

Of all my provisions, my favorite was pork and beans. Life on a boat whets the appetite and sharpens the appreciation. The simplest foods take on a zesty flavor. I didn't need, nor had I the means and time for preparing, rich, ornamental foods. My funds wouldn't allow anything more than simple, life-sustaining fare. Moreover, I was in glowing health, and had virtually no food dislikes. It was quantity rather than quality with me.

A small, low table on the port side in the after part of the cabin served as my galley. On one corner of the table was a little Primus stove — an intricate affair which worked by compressed air and kerosene. It gave a healthy flame in quick time. It made masterful fish stew.

Isthmian housewives had given me an array of pots and pans and odd tableware, no two pieces of which matched. It all amounted to an effective "kitchen," and when, on occasion, I wished to dine other than straight out of a cold can, I was able to set up an impressive formal table.

Means of storage for water had been a grave concern from the very first. One of the yachtsmen gave me two ten-gallon milk cans which I filled and lashed to the mast in the cabin. Someone gave me a ten-gallon oaken breaker, and someone else a little four-gallon oaken keg. I found a fifteen-gallon airplane gas tank in the rocks on the harbor edge. I bought six five-gallon jeep cans at fifty cents each — one I used for kerosene, and the other five for water. I bought two ten-gallon oaken breakers from the Commissary at the heartbreaking cost of five dollars apiece. From quart jars housewives gave me, I managed another three gallons which I stored in the forward bunks. When I sailed I carried a little over ninety-five gallons of water.

My fuel supply for the little Kermath marine engine consisted of eighty gallons of gasoline. There were twenty gallons in the built-in tank just forward of the lazarette. I had six five-gallon cans in the cockpit. Two five-gallon cans were strapped to the mast on the foredeck, two more were secured to the sternpost, and one was lashed to a cleat on each cockpit coaming.

Aside from the supplies of food and fuel there were other items. There were an army first-aid kit purchased from war surplus, a large cosmetic kit and other gifts such as nylons for Mary, flea powder to delouse the kittens, two brand-new suits of clothes — complete with overcoat and hat — in which to meet my wife upon my arrival in Sydney, a pneumatic life raft for emergency use, and two cheap feathers and a shark spoon with which to fish for extra food. I had a small library aboard, about twenty-five books in number, almost all of which were given me. Many magazines were brought down to the wharf for me, including comic books. The latter I

would have discarded except that I felt I could pass them off
to some appreciative native peoples along the way.

In the way of luggage aboard I had my personal belongings
packed into my sea bag — my carry-overs from the Merchant
Marine. I had seven suits of khakis, odd shirts and trousers,
shoes, and foul weather gear.

I had a number of navigation instruments aboard which
as yet I knew very little about. I was waiting to get out to sea
where I would have time enough and ideal conditions for
learning to navigate.

My total stores, according to my rough estimate upon departure, were sufficient to keep me in good supply for at least
four months. If I was lucky at fishing, as I hoped to be, or
able to collect island fare along the way, I figured I could sail
for five months. This afforded me a wide margin of safety,
since I expected to be in Sydney in just under four months.

CHAPTER III   Practice

THE PERLAS are a low, thick-wooded group seemingly at anchor in the southeastern quadrant of Panama Gulf. A scattered mestizo population of Indian, Negro, and Spanish inhabit its quaint semicivilized villages. They eke out a meager living from the uncultivated tropical fruits and vegetables, and abundant fish off the shores. Their "pueblos" lie on the leeward sides of their tangled islands and usually front small bays.

I had anchored for the first night in Perry Bay at Pedro Gonzáles Island.

The next morning early, I made sail. A brisk wind, wetted by torrents of rain, sent me east on my quest for a safe bay that I could work into and drop my anchor. Close by, in the lee of Señora Isle, I found a sandy spit and maneuvered up close to it. I guided myself in by standing on the stern, manipulating the tiller by foot, and sounding the depths, as I crept closer with the hand lead line. When I thought it fit I brought the bow into the wind with tiller hard alee, and sails luffing. I pushed the anchor off the rail and freed the chain to rattle out the hawsehole. I loosened the peak halyard and clawed in the main. I threw staysail and jib halyards loose and doused the staysail with a jerk, and teetered out on the bowsprit to pull the jib into a neat lump. I was anchored ... and it had been easy, I felt confident. I thought I would go below and enter it in the log. Then it happened: I could sense through my bare soles on the deck that the keel was thudding against something.

In the tight anchorage I had neglected to stop off the chain; it veered out full length, putting me stern first ashore. The rain poured so heavily it stood solid on the decks before it could run off. The sea gurgled with its patter. When I saw I was aground in this bleak, uninhabited little island, the rain for the first time felt cold.

The tide was ebbing speedily. Two hours later *Pagan* was on her beam ends. I sat on the top rail, drying in the new sun, trying to picture a solution. My kittens moped about my feet, wet to the skin and small as rats, echoing my hopelessness as they scratched along the canted decks.

I saw my voyage at an end where I sat. I could hear voices saying, "I told you so." I thought of my wife, and I thought of going back to Panama without my boat. I watched for hours, hoping a boat would round the bend and tow me off. The tide was coming back and the bow was beginning to waver about. She would either fill with water or ride higher on the beach. I watched the tide seep higher around her, licking and exploring. I got angry, and though I wasn't sure what to do, I resolved to fight back.

I piled much of my heavy gear on the shore with the kittens. When the bow floated, and she righted a little, I shored her up with a water barrel. The tide marched higher. I heaved tight on the anchor chain and fired up the noisy little engine, gunning it at high speed.

The tide crawled upward and I hoped it would crawl on till it floated her. I jumped into water up to my thighs and strained against the heavy sternpost. The bow was buoyant but the stern was fast in the sand.

I shifted weight from the afterpeak into the forepeak. Still no change. The tide had stopped rising — it was now or never. I put the throttle full down and jumped in again, pushing against *Pagan's* three and one half tons with every last ounce of strength.

She eased an inch, two inches — and stopped. I rested a minute and tried again. Another inch and another, then she slipped two inches. I was amazingly tired. I threw my back against the stern, pushing till my heels dug in. She stirred and slipped, then slid clear. My boat was saved.

Running aground was not my only blunder as my practice sailing continued that first week in the Perlas Islands. I made errors of navigation such as the time at dusk I mistook a sand cay off Viveros Isle for a smudge spot on the chart, and put *Pagan* bow first high and dry on it, where she lay on her beam ends for two tides before I finally hauled her out to deep water.

Then there was the time at Casaya. I saw a good spot to cast anchor for the night, just under the village, in the lee of a grassy spit, in two fathoms. Here is where I erred: in waters where the drop of tide was sixteen feet, I anchored in two fathoms!

At a monstrous hour of the night I was tipped gently from my bunk. I struggled over the sloping floor, through a jumble of strewn stores to the hatchway — then I knew. *Pagan* lay slumped over, her beam deep in the stinking mire.

All I could see was an eerie mass of shadows, except where a faint moon glinted in the morass. There was work to be done. It meant stamping about knee-deep in smelling slime

and fetching and carrying to make my boat tight against the
returning flood — and at the same time make her light so that
she would float before she would sink.

Three hours later found me naked and mud bespattered,
checking by flashlight the result of my emergency labors. I
had nailed down the cabin door. I had dogged all hatches
and ports. I had dug away from under the rail and lashed my
two purposely emptied water casks close against the bilges.
Inside I had shifted heavy lockers of food from the port side,
on which she lay, to the starboard side. Much of her heavy
gear I had carried ashore.

Later, when the lapping water licked upward on the
planks, I slogged about in the slush and hip-deep water,
straining my back as my jaunty little craft strained hers in
sucking from her fast grip as she rose to the occasion.

But the most humiliating blunder I made came off in the
bay fronting the junk lumber village of San Miguel on Del
Rey Island. I let my anchor go when its chain end wasn't
made fast to the deck and it flew out and disappeared into the
harbor as I stood there watching it. *Pagan* was adrift, heading
for the rocks. For some unaccountable reason I couldn't start
the engine. Then *Pagan* was knocking against a shallow
ledge, and that left me only one thing to do: hop in my
dinghy and tow *Pagan*, by rowing, away from the ledge. But
row as I would I couldn't fight the current, so I set up a wild
scream to the villagers for help and they came out in
their *cayucos* and hitched on, and together six boats of us
towed her off to mid harbor, where I leaped aboard, filled
my sea bag with tools, and used it for a jury anchor that
night.

Another error I made: I offered a dollar in the village next morning to the man who would dive for my anchor. Seven men pulled out onto the bay to search for it, and strangely enough, despite the fact that they were scattered in their quest over a hundred-foot circle, all seven discovered the anchor at once; and they all claimed the dollar! It was worth seven dollars to have the anchor and chain again.

Hardly a day passed that I didn't make some sailor's blunder. But the more mistakes I made, the more skillfully I learned to sail, and the better I came to know my boat.

In the end I lost my anchor. It happened in the ideally protected little basin off Saboga. A great haziness surrounds the loss of that anchor. I entered it in the log as "The mystery of the missing anchor." The mystery is still unsolved. This is how it all happened:

I made an early afternoon approach to the village. I was sighted when still well out — and boats put off from shore to meet me. This welcoming party rather aroused my vanity, and I found myself shooting into their presence with a daring maneuver or two in the offing. The Saboga anchorage is windless; I pointed in under full power, with all sail up. I saw where I could sail between two close lying boats and impress the islanders with my skill at the tiller.

Pagan was footing it fast. The stem parted water with a satisfying gurgle. I grinned beforehand over the neatness of what I would do. But in the final moments, as I bore closer, my enthusiasm for the trick fainted away and I decided too late I didn't want to do it. Sailboats don't stop with brakes, nor do they make hairpin turns that greatly resemble hairpins; at least *Pagan* didn't.

I pushed the tiller hard over and screamed inwardly for a ready response. When the natives saw my bow waver, they too began to waver. Their paddles churned the water, and instead of spreading they closed, and instead of avoiding me, they drove into me.

Or so it seemed. I couldn't see. The headsails hid everything. I felt the thud when we struck, and heard the wood splintering, and heard the swearing in Spanish.

I ran forward expecting to see one of the boats badly scarred, but when I saw them both stove in and sinking, and their occupants thrashing in the water, I didn't know what to think.

The first of the natives pulled himself aboard. His face was candid with severest pain; a pain of hugest inconvenience. The others came and stood dripping beside him, fumbling their small pouches of wetted tobacco. Then the words flew. I was cursed and ranted at as only the Latin tongue, waggled by an outraged Latin, can do it. I could only stand flat-footed and mumble.

They demanded ten dollars for each boat. It was like asking a hundred dollars for a broken shoestring. It was especially heartbreaking to me because I was down to my last twenty-five dollars, what with paying for the anchor and purchases of bananas and smoked fish and a few lopsided pearls, the only kind found in the group, for Mary.

I offered them five dollars for the two *cayucos*, and they were ready to revolt. We quibbled back and forth with our limited language, refusing to understand each other till dusk was gone and dark come. Finally they left in a huff, taking with them my little clinker-built dinghy given to me in Panama as compensation for their "hollowed logs." I gave it to keep peace in the village, and to ease my conscience.

It was that night the anchor disappeared. How it disappeared, I don't know. All I know is it was gone when I went on deck at daylight.

I made the usual preparations to sail, then heaved in the heavy chain, heavy enough in itself to hold *Pagan* in a quiet haven such as Saboga. I knew the anchor was gone when I first pulled, but I thought it had merely slipped its shackle. I started the engine and moved back and across the air-clear water, peering over the gunwale, seeing the same moss-grown rocks and coral formations. About midmorning some of the natives rowed out and helped me.

By noon my suspicions were wakened enough to suspect thievery. There was no anchor on that bottom. It was a mystery I could best settle by getting under way before something else disappeared. I readied *Pagan* to sail.

I dumped my tools back into my sea bag and made it fast to the chain as a jury anchor. I ran the sail up and shoved off for Pedro Gonzáles Island.

It was June 1; I had completed my first week of practice. I had visited bays and inlets on all islands of the Perlas Archipelago except San José, which was quarantined by the Army. I had flogged my boat through narrow channels. I had fought upwind and upcurrent in tight waters. I had sailed my boat on every conceivable angle to the wind. I had lain flummoxed in the long, recurring calms and had made errors enough to win a give-away checker game.

My confidence was sharpened. I was learning. I could say I was beginning to understand my boat. In every emergency I had got myself out of what I had got myself into. I had now the feeling of a sailor — if not the prolonged actual experience.

Through it all my sprightly little cutter had proved herself a stanch sailor. Whether on her beam ends ashore or butting clumsily into a reef, she bore an unaffected decorum and grace.

My boat could take it. I liked her. I was beginning to think of her as an individual. However, despite my liking for her and confidence in her, I couldn't move myself to make the jump off into the Pacific with her quite yet. I thought of it, but shrank from it. I needed more training. At the same time I realized I couldn't prolong the preparation much longer. Another week, or ten days at most, was all the time I could spare. I had less than four months to race the hurricanes to Sydney.

CHAPTER IV   Confidence

As my eighth day of practice hauled around, I decided to do something more impressive than "playing around in close." So the morning of June 2 saw me cleared away for a "long distance" cruise around the whole Perlas Group. With my kittens wide-eyed and capering on the cabin I stood out to south from Perry Bay.

I could, by a nearly rectangular sailing pattern, make the entire trip in a twenty-four-hour day. But I hadn't counted on the uncertainties facing the seaman in the Gulf of Panama. Between calms, which were relieved only by impotent winds, I coaxed *Pagan* at a snail's pace.

I coasted around to the south of Del Rey, past Punta de Cocos. East of Pacheca Island (the last island in the string), and with the little isle bearing west by south, I turned northwest, and prepared to heave to for the night.

It was my first night on the water. I was eager to know what my boat would do, how she would express herself with a lashed tiller all night, sailing under her own free hand, while I was below in the bunk.

I didn't know exactly what to do, so I left all sail up. *Pagan* struck a northwesterly course with the wind playing at west of north. I lashed the tiller slightly aweather and eased the mainsail. As the wind billowed *Pagan's* sails, she tended to move her bow into it. Thus, close on the wind, the mainsail luffed fruitlessly. Jib and staysail barely pulled, but pulled enough to give the slightest headway. Then at the rudder's command she fell off west of north, with sheets straining and a few ripples in the wake. Thus, backing and filling, I left her to bide her night.

Somewhere late at night I awakened to the raucous whipping of headsails, the screech of wind in rigging, and driving rain. Gusts from a squall were beating her down. Gunwale to the water, she was flying into the night.

I hadn't yet handled *Pagan* in a squall; this was my first one. To get the extreme angle out of her decks I pulled down the belligerent main. She righted, as I hoped she would, and squalls suddenly lost their terrifying reputation. One thing was important: get the mainsail down. The jib and staysail could take it.

Dawn found me west of Saboga, with a light wind bearing to northwest. I swung to a heading of southwest and crawled along a lee shore under the beam wind. *Pagan* steered herself under a lashed tiller all day with nothing untoward happening. The afternoon was especially calm. My fishing luck was in the doldrums too, because I failed to catch my mewing cats their usual afternoon fish. They fretted on the foredeck, hiding under the anchor, refusing to be friendly.

Later, though, I hooked a beamy yellowtail, big enough for all three of us. Fried fish with strips of bacon, slack-baked corn patties, washed down with coconut milk went well for an early dinner. One nice thing about the crew on *Pagan* was the lack of complaints with the food.

The day was waning. I was standing well off the southeastern tip of San José. My course was shaped easterly; Mafafa, southernmost Perlas village — a good two hours' run — was my destination. It would have to be a night approach, but I wasn't worried, now that I had some "experience." I could make it all right by rounding Punta de Cocos in time to sight something prominent in the village, then steering through the dark by compass.

Punta de Cocos is the rocky end of a fingerlike peninsula that juts southward off Del Rey. In the crook of the finger of land lies Mafafa. Once I passed round the point, I could see the village.

The enclosing dark was outsailing me to the point. In one of those reckless moments, I decided to cut in hair close in rounding Punta de Cocos. I could see, every so often, a number of growling rollers crash onto the point, where a fast shoaling ledge threw them up. Seas were piling on it suddenly and toppling onto themselves, throwing white arms of water upward. If I timed my approach carefully I could shoot past the point at the interval between rollers. If one could rely exactly on the actions of natural things, wouldn't it be a dull world?

At the moment I changed *Pagan's* angle to cross Punta's bow closely, two big combers bore down on me from abeam. *Pagan* got a deck washing I shall never forget. It came so suddenly, and at what seemed a peaceful moment, that I was overwhelmed. The mast from the hounds down was awash with spray. I froze to the tiller and watched the water scurrying over the decks — the first water I had seen there. The solid rock wall was a heave-line toss away. Another roller rammed her, and crowded aboard; this one had broken farther out and came aboard in a surge.

I thought of the engine and the mistake of not having used it.

Pagan was thrown so close to the rocks that I could see crabs clinging to them. My decks were water-loaded. When I looked out to see if I could fend the boat off, I saw the cats swimming aft along the flooded deck rails, only their heads in view, wild-eyed, pawing through the water.

Pagan was about sixty seconds from the closest fists of rock. I slung the tiller alee and grabbed the kittens, ready to toss them high onto the rocks. A counter sea rolled back from the rock face, killing the effects of the next roller. *Pagan* steadied, filled away, and pulled off a few feet. But the next sea caught her where the first had. In a smother of foam she fell back. I could see nothing I could do. Cats in hand and tiller underfoot, I waited petrified. A fourth sea boomed broadside against her, spilled over the rail, and rapped her sharply against the first line of boulders.

As the jolt ran up from the keel I was terrified lest her mast jump out and fall over me. Without looking directly at it I could see the mast was swaying wildly.

All this time the tiller had been hard down. Her bow had twisted away from the rock face and bow-on she met the next sea. As she slithered a few feet sternward, I could visualize the rudder and propeller smashed into the rocks. But somehow she lost little way. She rose to it, foundered momentarily, and battled on. With her bowsprit thrown sky-high one minute and immersed feet deep the next, she slowly pulled away from the angry cape. Her sails were pulling with all force or she would never have made it.

She slipped away to smoother water, but my eyes were

glued on Punta de Cocos, where the seas charged against the rocks, and where I had nearly lost my boat. I had brought her off safely, and I felt a flush of kinship with what sailormen call seamanship. I had saved my boat — had acted sensibly under duress.

I smiled happily to myself. At last my confidence was thoroughly built up, I was ready to go; the Pacific beckoned. I looked at the darkening horizon, beyond which was my patient wife. In the morning, I thought, in the morning I'll be on my way.

But when morning came I was interrupted at my breakfast by rapping on the deck, and the cheerful voices men have at dawn. I came up to find a rowboat of soldiers tied alongside. They were from an Army Weather Station in the same bay. They climbed aboard.

No matter what their rank, they took me for what I was — a sailor boy caught in the rush of after-war.

They were greatly interested in my boat and the proposed trip. They evinced a hearty desire to help me "get ready to go." So I decided to stay another day.

We pitched in early, the six of us; and what a job of work we did. We painted the mast and spars. We did the decks and deckhouse and cockpit in a lurid design consisting of the four colors of paint I had aboard. We oiled the standing rigging, puttied portholes against seepage, and sewed bolt ropes onto all the sails.

One, who was a mechanic, dismantled the little marine engine, and at the end of the day he explained a host of benefits performed. Something about plugs cleaned, carburetor adjusted, feed line cleared, generator overhauled, valves ground, and so on.

Another, electrically minded, wired *Pagan* so that a flip of this switch or that set her cabin ablaze with light from my engine battery. Even her running lights were wired for emergency use. The same GI by performance of his magic transformed a junk radio I had wanted to "give the deep six" into a useful instrument.

Another boy, exercising a hidden talent awakened by army ingenuity, did me an outstanding service by building a large locker, half the width of the starboard bunk and its full length, from the deck beams down. The value of this, only a boat owner can know. Another lad designed and built in a bumkin for *Pagan's* transom to stay the tall mast in case of heavy weather.

Thus, ten days after my arrival in the Perlas, I was ready to go down to sea. From jib tack to mainsail clew my little cutter was at her fighting best. Time to weigh anchor and shove off.

But the soldiers . . . there's nothing too good for a soldier. By way of thanks for their generous assistance I proposed a trip. I admit I was reluctant to do it. I wanted to be on my way to Mary. But I had to show my appreciation to the isolated soldiers.

We sailed around Del Rey's southeastern bulge to San Miguel that day. It was the bright spot of *Pagan's* life under my hand. We returned at dusk the next day to the little bight around from Punta de Cocos. *Pagan's* last service as a pleasure yacht had been rendered. From now till her ill-fated demise, her work was to be serious — and finally grim and relentless.

That night found me outfitted for sea: water breakers filled and bunged, lockers stocked, and gear lashed and tied.

There was even a supply of canned fish aboard for the kittens, a gift from the soldiers.

One thing I was convinced of — my boat could take it. Ten days of hard usage had proved that. She had a history that made those ten days possible, and made all that she went through out on the open sea possible.

Pagan was Norwegian designed and built. Her planking, decking, ribs, knees, and timbers were from the weather-tested far northern slopes. She had blunted the challenge of turbulent Scandinavian seas for many years as a supply boat for lonely Baltic lighthouses.

In 1934 *Pagan* arrived in Panama after an Atlantic passage from Poland. Aboard were four Poles ostensibly headed for Australia as settlers. They had outlived hair-raising escapes and a discouraging series of bruising gales, after which even tropical, rainy Panama looked better than the prospect of sunny Australia.

They promptly sold *Dwaja* (spirit), as she was then known, and there followed for the little gaff-rigged sloop twelve years of peaceful "harbor circumnavigation." Light harbor sails, bellied by soft harbor breezes, were bent to her spars. From Colón to Balboa she luxuriated in the peace and quiet of yacht club atmosphere. A yachting pennant swung from her masthead. Gay parties took place in her cabin. She became well known as the "original" *Pagan*, on both the Atlantic and the Pacific sides.

At some time during her twelve years' career as a coastwise and harbor playboat her sail plan was redesigned to the Marconi rig, and *Pagan* became a sharp, fast cutter. She was regarded as one of the fastest little vessels on the Isthmus. Rail down, there were few who could match her.

The boat I was to sail with was fast and sturdy, and after my numerous experiences aboard her I knew her, I had confidence in her, and so I had confidence in myself — what more could I ask?

I stepped out into the cockpit and flashed my light through the rigging and across the decks, and found everything as it should be. I was pleased. I went below, where I lay a long time before I slept, thinking into the low ceiling, glad the time had come to be going.

CHAPTER V   Sunk!

Eᴀʀʟʏ ᴏɴ ᴛʜᴇ ᴍᴏʀɴɪɴɢ of June 7 I lashed my little pneumatic raft to the base of the mast, heaved my sea bag of rocks
aboard (I had taken the tools out of the bag when they
showed rust, and substituted rocks), and sailed for deep
water. Under a hard easterly breeze, sharper than usual for
these waters, I put her immediately on a westerly course and
made for the open sea.

My destination was once again the Galápagos Islands, the
lonely volcanic group lying on the doorstep of the southeast
trade winds.

My first stop would be Seymour Island, where an army
weather station was located. That is, it would be my first
stop if the army base wasn't closed down. The last word I
had received before leaving Panama, from fishing boats recently in the Galápagos, was that the Army expected to be out
by July first. This gave me twenty-one days to make the
transit — more than enough time; I figured I could make it in
eleven days.

My plan was to haul up there for a week, check my boat
for her running and standing gear, and for her hull, then
shove off into the southeast trades and race nonstop across
the ocean to Sydney. With the hurricane season crowding
me for time, I had no alternative, unless I holed in somewhere

en route for three or four months till navigable weather returned. In case of necessity I had charts and sailing directions for likely island groups along the way. If trouble came it would be easy enough to put in for repairs or send a cable.

When the Perlas had faded from green to blue, and from blue to gray, I began thinking of what course I should steer to make my destination. I was in somewhat of a quandary about what to do, but remembering that the shortest distance between two points is a straight line, I laid a ruler flat on my chart and drew a straight line connecting the Perlas and Galápagos Islands. This line was my true course. It lay southwest. All I had to do now was to sail straight down it, and after a certain time, lo, there would be land. I soon learned that in deep water sailing theory is one thing, and actuality an astoundingly different thing!

The fresh easterly breeze began to wane by late morning. But it had enabled me to make a good offing. The Perlas were low down on the horizon astern. Off to starboard the Panamanian mainland was a thin, foglike shadow.

I whiled away the morning on the deck with my feline crew. The tiller was lashed and *Pagan* swayed gently and sailed smoothly as beam seas rolled under her. My native hat toned down the sun and my comfortable rope sandals kept my soles clean. I was stripped to shorts. About midmorning I cast out the fishing line, baited with the tail of a yellowjack I had hauled aboard the day before, and in twenty minutes I heaved a throbbing Spanish mackerel over the transom for the kittens.

They were the most antic little devils I have ever seen with a flapping fish. Hardly a day passed that I did not see them in battle with something I pulled up. The act was the same every day, but it never palled. At first they approach the fish with a cat's normal curiosity. A sniff tells it is a sort of *crêpe Suzette,* cat style. They jump viciously upon the powerful fish, growling for a tooth hold. With a violent flip the fish sends them bowling across the deck, and they scatter wild-eyed, tail flying, to the foredeck. In a moment the rich smells begin to torture them anew, and they come creeping cautiously back, innocent faced, hopeful looking. They move up beside the victim, crouch low as if to eliminate themselves, and sniff distantly, then bunch up tightly for the spring. I drop a hammer behind them — and trigger-quick they fly scampering to the bow.

They wait a moment or two, then peer wonderingly around the deckhouse corner with round, bright eyes. Down the deck they descry their quivering dinner. Once more they slink slowly, belly down, along the deck, range up beside the delicacy and sniff deliciously. Throwing caution to the winds they pounce athwartships of the fish and growl wolfishly. Like a desperate cowboy they cling for a few wild jumps and again scurry away — spitting as they go, tumbling over each other.

Patience is a game that is never taught; it is learned. Much to my entertainment these goofy little cats never learned it where fish were concerned. Right up to the day that I tearfully parted company with them, they were a riot of humor.

About noon the fresh breeze of the morning waned perceptibly. This was the first weather item recorded in my log. I was using a notebook for a log. It contained ninety pages; with a page for each day's reckoning, I figured I would just be filling it when I hove in sight of Sydney Harbor. Not knowing the proper procedure for annotating a log — if there be one — I just jotted, "June 7, 11:00 to 12:00 A.M. Wind slowing up." Thus the voyage began.

For lunch I had island fare: an avocado, the butt end of a pineapple, two bananas, and coconut milk. Tied gaily to the mast were two stalks of bananas. Rolling along the decks were coconuts, avocados, mangos, papayas, pineapples, taken from the abundant jungle before I sailed. These, I figured, would be the last fresh foods before Australia.

Often a meal was nothing more than a can of beans ripped hastily open and eaten from the tin. Meals were fancy or simple in turn, depending on how I felt and a lot of other things. Sometimes I shared the cats' daily fish, and at others it was easier to lie out in the soft sun sleeping the day away than go below for the can opener.

Later in the afternoon the lagging wind veered to northwest and suddenly stiffened, kicking up the first white caps of the trip. At nearly sundown it was stronger and had hauled around to where it blew out of the west, causing a confused sea. A scud was flying in from over the horizon. *Pagan* had a considerable tilt to her decks, and I found myself wondering at what precise moment does one decide to reef, and when one does, how is it done? I had played at reefing down in calm weather, but now, with wind beating at the bow and bow beating at the sea, it was all so different.

I went below and perused my handbook on *How to Sail*. Alas, it was designed for harbor sailors and those who haunt protected waters; not one word breathed it of the reefing ritual.

I handed my way out of the sloping cabin onto the wet

decks. I searched the low, louring clouds for a hint of the
extent of weather; nothing I read helped me. "So this is the
Pacific's stormy greeting," I thought. I looked around and
saw that the lee rail was awash; *Pagan* quivered lightly, her
timbers creaked. The wind was definitely higher; a welter
of water was surging under her, beginning to hiss and howl
in the way of mounting seas. I wasn't sure that now was
the "precise" moment to reef down, but I concluded it was a
darned good one to do it.

How to get the sail off? How steady the spar in such a
wild setting? The Indians say the best way to do a thing is to
do it. But on a boat there is a proper way. One doesn't unbend
the halyard, then heedlessly allow the wind to whip it from
hand . . . as I did. Such negligence is dangerous because
the sail spills its wind and flails wildly at loose ends. The
sail can be split right down the center, the Marconi clips
ripped from the luff, and four or five seams strained and rent
so quickly as to leave the sail in six shapeless parts in a matter
of seconds. The reason I know is that that is just what happened.

In the brief minutes that I clutched at the wind-whipped
halyard, my sail flew to spare parts. I raced to it and fought
with its threshing ends. The unruly boom swung across and
across with maddening persistence. I clung rashly to it as I
made to put the sail in stops, and in the twenty minutes or
so required to lash down the sail I must have seen each side
of the deck a thousand times. When I finished there seemed
to be more lightning than before, and the spray stung
more.

I discovered that in dousing sail I should have eased the
tiller accordingly; for now I was footing it before the wind in

all haste toward where I had used the day in coming from. In a questionable maneuver I worked her around — and suffered a few heavy slops of water as she broached. But I managed to heave her to on the starboard tack, with tiller lashed slightly to windward and with headsails aback.

I watched her point hesitantly into the gathering night. Now and then a heavy sea caromed off the bow, throwing it high; a comber curled under her, dancing her about. So this was all there was to heaving to in a storm. Child's play. Just let the mainsail blow to pieces, leave the jib and staysail up, lash the tiller aweather and hit the sack! Expensive, but simple.

As I stared into the night I began to feel a flutter in my stomach and the faintest hint of lightness in the head. I flattered myself by calling it weariness and went down to my pitching bunk. *Pagan's* cabin was having hell's merry time. There were the rattle and clank of gear gone adrift; the frantic to-and-fro race of water in the bilge; the vexing warmer temperature of the cabin; the weak whine of the wobbly cats as they fumbled about sickly. Finally the wash of angry water against the planks, gurgling suggestively as it does, became a liquid knell to whatever peace I had thought I felt.

I groped full-jowled out into the screeching night. On my knees and clinging to the shrouds, I "fed the fish."

The wind was intoning a terrifying whine to resounding crashes of thunder and sea growls, and between "feedings" I grew increasingly conscious that I was in a rising gale. More darts of lightning flashed and more wetness was in the air, smacking of heavy rain and nastier weather. The jib was bellied out to maximum. Since it was an old one I instinc-

tively felt it would soon go. The staysail was standing the
gaff; the main boom was snug in her crutch.

I stretched out in *Pagan's* lee waist and a bilious nothingness completely enshrouded me. I could think a little, and
feel a little, but beyond that I was nothing. I knew the jib was
straining; that any minute it would rip out from its fittings. She was shivering by the leech, and quaking the decks
beneath my stomach. I turned numbly onto my side and
watched the grim, hopeless match between boundless nature
and man-made trivia.

The jib shivered mightily as a man will do under a wither-
ing load. A hank parted company at the luff; there was an
intensity of already frantic motion. The aged fraying boltrope snapped, followed by a stringent rip of the sort fat boys
make when they bend too far. At the bat of an eye the hapless
sail was in tatters and its bits were whizzing off astern with
the driving seas.

I attempted to pull myself together and view more sternly
what was happening. The wind was still on the upgrade; the
sea, growing angrier, was swept into foaming windrows.
Lightning had grown to the intensity of daylight, and flashed
on and off like house lights. The air was laden with bursts of
rain. With staysail aback, *Pagan* was holding her own but
floundering. Now that I had pulled myself to, I was sensible
enough to be scared — plenty scared.

The staysail, I could tell, had reached that "precise moment" when a reef was required to save it. I loosed the halyard — but clung tightly to it and dropped the frantic sail to
where I could get at the reef points.

Reef point by point I tied in the unruly strings. Staysails
are uncomfortable members to deal with. You mustn't even

consider reefing one down in heavy weather unless prepared
to take at least a dozen buckets of water in your teeth. Then
there's the sail itself to contend with. It pounds madly
about your ears. The bow rears and plunges wild-horse like.
With all sail off, the boat rolls. And upon the foredeck
there is nothing to which you can hold. No wonder I once
heard a yachtsman refer to his imperious wife as "my
staysail."

I studied the screeching night airs before going down below, and what I saw didn't improve my seasickness. *Pagan*
had incorporated a wild roll in her behavior and the swelling
seas were beginning to bounce her about. She was falling
off before the wind; it made me wonder where land could be.

Down below, I put on my life jacket and squeezed the cats
between it and me, at my chest. Such tight quarters displeased them, so I took them out. I cut open an old-type life
preserver and removed its cork floats. To two of these I attached a string; and to the end of each string I tied a kitten,
by the hind leg. Then I went on deck and tried to feed the
fish. But I had what is called the "dry heaves." The more I
strained the worse I felt. I felt so useless I looked at everything and said "So what."

Sheets of spray whipped over the weather bow. The wind
screamed in the rigging. A raging sea was coursing astern.
The staysail had a press of wind that set her aquiver, affecting
the whole boat.

"What the devil do you do next?" I thought, and went
below. The cats were in a bewildered ball of legs and corks
and strings. I sorted them out and sat on my bunk with them
in my lap, disturbed by the noises I could hear and by my
imaginings. I remembered someone's saying, at Panama, that

the best place for a storm sail was the mainmast. I didn't have a storm sail . . . but . . .

I cut a dozen small lengths of one-inch line. Dragging out my aged spare staysail, I toted it lamely up to deck. The short lines I bent loosely about the mast. To each such "ring" I attached a clip connected to the leading edge of the sail and heaved the sail aloft with the main halyard. Because of her loose foot she strained considerably, but she did the work of a storm sail, and *Pagan* reared up and about less often. I dropped and furled the staysail, and hurried below.

The cats and I had dozed off into a questionable sleep when I was disturbed by the obstreperous beat of a rent sail. I found the little storm sail split from foot to peak, her frayed ends pointing to leeward. *Pagan*, of course, was wallowing violently.

What to do? Lightning was throwing the night into brilliant confusion. A series of squalls was lording it over us. It is said first things are worst; and this was my first storm. I was beginning to fear my little boat was heading for the port of missing ships. Such moments as these, when one doesn't know what to do next, are enough to make one vow to take up harbor sailing.

Pagan was lying in the trough of the seas. Boiling water, breaking over her beam, threatened, I thought, to turn her turtle. I hastened to unfurl the staysail — as a last resort. A heavy lump of water pitched into my ear, nearly knocked me sprawling into the dark deep. On an impulse and a fear I heaved my sea bag of rocks outboard and crawled into the safety of the cockpit and wondered what the effect would be. The bag sank but at the same time it dragged, and *Pagan's* bow swung smartly upwind.

It was deep into the hours of morning; seasickness, weariness, anxiety had chafed at my reserves. I trudged down to my
bewildered kittens — and sleep.

At close on daylight it happened. Luckily the wind had
abated — though the seas were running high — or it might
have been worse. A sledgehammer blow smote *Pagan* on her
keel. We were wrenched from sleep and flung to the floor.
The cats yowled. I jumped to my feet and stumbled before I
could walk. A rattle of displaced gear and rending timbers,
like Satan's pitchfork pounding on the cabin.

I started for the hatchway, but I was knocked flat almost
instantly. *Pagan* heeled dizzily and a dozen noises fought for
supremacy as she shuddered from the shock. In a moment
she righted, but another thump on the keel sent me sprawling again. I was sure we had run onto a sea-pounded shore.

The thought reeled through my head: "Wrecked!" I was
glad I had my life jacket on.

I groped for my cats, for I feared I would have to make
some desperate leap onto jagged rocks — and I didn't want
to leave my crew to perish in the hold. In the melee they
had dived for cover, but I fumbled upon the cork squares, so
I ran on deck, cats a-dangling.

I had expected to see the towering shadow of land leering
down upon me, and a shore of bristling rocks reaching for
Pagan's tender planks. But I didn't see this at all. Instead,
at my very feet, was what seemed the body of a mammoth
whale, its tail roiling the waters off to the right.

And on the other side another whale, only smaller, was
churning about lazily. I had heard of whales attacking small
craft — but the absurdity of it in a storm!

I was petrified lest the monster erase me with a sweep of

that broad tail. Then the outlines of "that broad tail" took a clearer shape, and I made it out to be, not the tail of a whale, but the limbs of a drifting tree. A tree whose girth was such that its lumber would have made two or three or even five *Pagans*.

Its bole lay beneath the surface, its limbs awash, and the whole of it rose and fell with each sea. Evidently making sternway in the storm, I had come backing off the crest of a wave and landed atop it. I shoved the yowling kittens below, and made to fend the obstruction off with the boat hook. My efforts against a limb were of little avail. *Pagan* was pivoted athwart it, reeling with side-to-side motions and thumping with rebounds that were too much to take for long.

Heavy rollers crashing onto the forest giant twisted it beneath the keel, exerting a shifting pressure against *Pagan's* timbers. She groaned deep in her parts with the whole-souled complaint of a wounded man.

When a dozen seas had pounded us, and the keel had wallowed an inch at a time its full length across the tree, it worked away and we floated free.

I hurried below and searched by light for seepage or hint of damage. I could see none. However, I saw something flash silvery in the bilge well, under the ladder. I strained my hand through the water till it struck something slippery, fleet, full of life. I pursued it and caught it, and tossed it on the floor boards. A squid! A live squid in the bilge! Full two inches long, a half inch around.

I immediately thought of a leak somewhere in the hull, large enough for him to slip through.

I went out into the cockpit where the bilge pump jutted up from the after end of the cabin and pumped *Pagan* dry, and, observing the bilge, I watched a determined trickle of water flow rapidly into it. Another search over the ribs and planks in the cabin, and below the water line, revealed nothing. She had sprung a leak deep in her timbers, possibly somewhere along the keel and its adjoining strakes. I decided on the moment to head for the closest land. I could only think of Del Rey.

I pumped the filling bilge dry and put *Pagan* about. Unshaking the reef from the staysail, I hauled it aloft and belayed it. I pulled my sea-bag anchor aboard. In greatest haste, and perspiring in spite of the cool wet wind, I uncovered my good jib and lugged it topside and strung it. I regretted that I had been so careless as to blow out my good mainsail. I needed it badly. Under staysail and jib she ran off before the wind, pushed helpfully by stern seas.

I put her on a course of east by south, assuming that during the day and through the storm she had slipped a little north. One part of the sky was darker than the other; the sun was rousing from its bed; the headsails, higher up, were catching the faint light. I made the Perlas Islands dead ahead.

I pumped the bilges and thought I observed that they had filled a little more quickly than before. As a precaution, I started the engine and gave her full throttle ahead. Even in the short time I had engaged the engine, the bilge had filled. I worked the pump till it sucked dry — a sound dear to the heart of a seaman on a leaking vessel. But even as I finished I could look into the well and see it refilling defiantly.

Pagan was making fast time, but it wasn't fast enough. I thought of the spare mainsail in the sail locker and what it would mean to have it flying. I started below to break it out. A disturbing sight met me: the bilge had filled and overflowed; an inch of water was standing on the floor boards.

I jumped back to the pump and pumped till I tired . . . and the bilge was dry. I stared eagerly over the whitecaps at the colorless land, and it seemed a long way off.

A half hour went by. I never took my eyes off the islands except to watch the bilge fill.

Del Rey was about eight miles distant with Punta de Cocos still farther. On the port beam San José was about five or six miles off. I must have stared too long at the land for when I looked down there were at least three inches of water washing over the cabin floor. The leak was growing.

I took to the pump and worked it at an aching pace. I changed hands several times and still water gurgled in the bilge. When at last the pump hissed dryly, I sighed and peered anxiously over the long miles to Punta de Cocos. I could hear the splashing of new water in the swaying bilge, so I took to pumping again. After pumping a seemingly over-long time, I found that I hardly gained on the rising water. And in the time taken to peer below, I had lost the gain.

I jumped to the tiller, unseized its single lashing, and changed *Pagan* to a course of due east. I was now scudding her toward San José, three miles to leeward. Once more I stood by the pump. The water inboard had risen alarmingly, its slopping had wetted down the bulkheads, and my cats, curled and shivering in my bunk, eyed the rising water dis-dainfully. I pumped furiously to outpace the water. Ahead was an open beach. At its extreme left end stood a jagged promontory behind which was a protected shore. I had no alternative but to put *Pagan* on it. I heard that seamen under compulsion had often run their craft ashore for repairs or scraping and painting.

I altered course three points to port and stood bow-on toward shore. I worked madly at the pump, afraid to look at the distance yet to go. Suddenly the motor sputtered, coughed raucously, and fizzled off to silence. I took a quick look at the engine — it was covered by water. I leaped back to the pump and worked it fitfully. I was hoping *Pagan's* momentum would carry her well in, because the tiny headsails barely pulled. Slowly, slowly the shore closed in. I jerked still more wildly at the pump, but *Pagan* was settling. Water lapped at the gunwales. Below, the cats were crying mournfully; I knew that they had been washed off the bunk.

I expected to see *Pagan* dip her rail under and sink at any moment. Then, ever so lightly, the keel scraped bottom and she steadied, losing her way. The kittens swam out the hatchway into the cockpit, towing their cork blocks. I tossed them atop the cabin and hurried to the work of dousing the headsails. Then I busied myself with making *Pagan* fast to the shore.

The decks were awash and the insides were afloat. I undogged the fore scuttle, dropped up to my waist in the hold, and fished out a two-inch hawser. This I clove-hitched to the bitt; the free end I fastened about my waist.

I grabbed the kittens and gave them a toss shoreward. They splashed about twenty feet from the sand. I dived from the bow and came up near them, and saw them as they attempted the impossible — trying to claw atop the bobbing corks. I took their corks and towed them the few feet to the beach. Leaving them to shiver beneath the cold sky, I led my line to a mangrove stump and secured it with a round turn and double half hitches.

My feline mariners, with "salt in their eyes" — which is to

say, shipwrecked — tottered weakly up the beach, weary of the sea and its vicissitudes. Suddenly they saw the towering jungle loom up blackly and glare down over them with all its silence. With minced steps and yowling complaints they swore at their seaman's lot and squatted back on their haunches to berate their wetness and fright.

I scooped up my sea mates consolingly. Poor little sea-weary blokes.

Up till now my only name for them had been "kitty." But under present circumstances a name for each naturally evolved. The little blond female I named Flotsam, and the darker tom, Jetsam. Unfortunately their name day wasn't a joyous occasion. They spent it under a bucket on the beach, out of danger, so they wouldn't stray to the jungle to become table d'hôte for a crocodile or a boa.

I sat on the damp beach and viewed the dreary picture of my boat, foundered to her scuppers on an uninhabited isle. Right before my eyes she heeled over and settled to her beam on the watery bottom. Her port rail cleared the surface, and the mast appeared about three feet away, slanted skyward at an unseemly angle. It told the story of shipwreck. Still drooping from it was the tattered storm sail.

CHAPTER VI   Castaway

THAT MORNING, seated on this unfriendly beach, and staring at *Pagan's* sunken hulk, represented for me very nearly the low point of the entire trip. I concluded it was hell to be a greenhorn.

What a laugh. "Sydney or bust," I had said when I pulled out of Panama. Now, 60 miles away, my boat was on the bottom — only 8440 miles to go! The cats seemed to sense my rancor and snuggled deeper in my lap.

I swam back to *Pagan*. It was heart-rending to stand on the sloping decks and muse over the hopelessness of the situation. I had thought I was in a bad way the day I had run aground at Isle Señora. I proved myself every inch a seaman by the foul language I used that morning. I cursed and ranted with all the invective I could lay my tongue to, and when I finished, strangely enough, I felt infinitely better.

Seated as I was on the one dry spot, the upraised beam was a familiar experience. Thus far I had almost as much sea time aboard *Pagan* on her beam ends ashore as keel-down in deep water. The trip that everyone had deprecated because it would be "too boring" was getting a little too exciting.

I had gone aground at half tide. In an hour most of the deck was uncovered and water was lapping around the keel, knee-deep. I climbed down and waded about the scarred hull, searching into her every scratch.

Under my hand the little boat had taken a considerable roughening. She had proved her mettle. It was sensible to presume that if the spunky cutter could possibly be repaired and floated, she could easily run the Pacific traverse. My introduction to sailing, at *Pagan's* expense, was easily read in her scraped and scratched under-timbers. I opened the portholes to free some of her inside water. And as the tide fell lower I submerged head and shoulders into the engine compartment to unscrew the little seacock in the curve of the bilge.

The inside cabin was a frowzy raffle to delight a junk dealer. It was a headache I refused to consider for the moment. I was interested in *Pagan's* leaks; I didn't have to go far to find them.

The garboard strake on the port side had sprung at the stem, exposing the cement-filled bilge. Much of her calking had worked out of the seams, and through this fissure mainly the seepage had come. But there were other injuries beside this. The rudderpost had been wrenched from its keel seat. A few of the planks seemed disturbed where they fitted into the sternpost and stem; and a propeller flange was bent.

I noted the defects and noted they could be remedied. From inside I searched out a hammer, screwdriver, nails, and an old shirt. I nailed the strake flush in place against the keel and into the stem and sternpost. Using strippings from the shirt I calked the seams temporarily with the screwdriver and hammer. Of necessity I worked fast. The tide would soon be flowing back. I drove myself, so she would be ready to take the water when it returned.

I met the approaching tide as I crawled from under the last of my temporary repairs. There was only time now to secure her against leak on deck: to batten scuttles, ports, seacock, and seal the companionway off.

The sea marched up the beach, encircling my boat with lapping fingers and feeling at the repairs as if to escape through them. I watched.

Pagan lifted buoyantly on the flood as she had done beneath me before. Her leaks were only a driblet of what they had been; I offset them with a few turns at the pump. At full tide, well after dark, I drew my jaunty craft as close into shore as possible and moored her tightly with her keel thumping on the steep sandy floor and the bow pointing into the jungle. Wearied with labor and anxiety, I trudged up the beach to my wailing starvelings. In all the excitement I hadn't touched food or drink all day. I was so thoroughly jaded that even the thought of going back to ferret out a can of fish for my mates from the morass aboard was an abomination. "In a few minutes I'll go," I said. When I got up to go it was daylight. The cats were gamboling about. It was a fair day; the tide was ebbing; my boat lay parallel to the beach line. The work at hand beckoned. But first . . . we were ravenous, the crew and I.

On board I found that all labels had washed off the cans. So potluck it was. I reached among the rows of cans and grabbed two. They turned out to be diced pineapple and spinach. The cats, forced to face the ups and downs of a sailor's calling, whether they liked it or not, had diced pineapple for breakfast. For me, that morning, cold spinach from a can beat ham and eggs all to blazes, and the pineapple dessert was better than any cup of coffee I had ever tasted.

For the next ten days I lived the life of a royal Bohemian. I wore not a stitch; for a hat there was my matted crown, long since in need of cropping; I had not shaved since Panama and, for that matter, I had long since vowed not to shave until I was with Mary again. Barefoot and golden browned I lay to on my little boat, mending her scarred and strained timbers for a return bout with the sea.

My food was potluck, fished cold from a can; and the selections, as they turned out, were usually monstrous. But I rounded off my diet with fruits and vegetables from the jungle. Hard by were a grove of bananas and an abundant mango tree. Farther on I found avocados and green drinking coconuts, and papayas. I responded wholesomely to the fresh foods. My work showed it, and my full sleep and my appetite and my exuberance.

I bunked in the sand under a lean-to rigged from my staysail and oars. Such sleep, such appetite, such brotherhood with life as I felt in that rustic period, I have not known before or since. There was but one thing missing — Mary. But had she been there, there would have been no haste with repairs. There would have been no repairs. . . .

During those ten days I worked long and hard. When the tide was out I strove at *Pagan's* hull with what tools I had at hand. When the tide was in and my stanch little cutter was pounded about on the beach, I pieced together and patched my battered mainsail, sewing up its three big tears, and making of it a new sail, stronger than before. In addition I patched and strengthened seams in all my sails, resewed boltropes, spliced cringles anew, and attached the hanks and slides more securely.

The job of cleaning house and stowing most of the gear

on the beach at the foot of the jungle was a day's work. It
was the work done before any other, and it left me with only
my boat to repair . . . and, as I hoped, sail out again.

The garboard planks I ripped off, plugged the old screw
holes in strake and keel, drilled anew and rescrewed them
more securely than before. I calked the seams with special
calking cotton brought along for the purpose, using a screwdriver for a calking iron. I covered the seams with lead patch-
ing full length, puttied and painted over all.

I put a lead patch down each side of the stem, overlapping
where the planks joined in . . . likewise the stern.

I thoroughly scraped and painted her down to the lead
shoe on the keel bottom. I reset her rudderpost and hammered
the propeller blade into plumb. And then I was ready to
think of horizons again.

By far the weightiest problem concerning *Pagan* was the
means of refloating her and kedging her off the beach. I had
no anchor. So I concerned myself with this matter first.

It was apparent from the beginning that I must make an
anchor of sorts since I had nothing I could use in its stead.
My sea bag of rocks was useless as a kedge; what I needed
was something that could grip the bottom offshore — something toward which I could pull *Pagan*, if I were able to get
her afloat.

I felled a scrubby tree on the jungle edge and dressed it
down to two suitable timbers — one long and thick, the other
short and thin.

The largest and strongest I used for the shank of my
anchor. Diagonally across its end I fitted the shorter piece,
four feet in length, as its arm. On the ends of the arm I nailed
long flukes that would sink into the sand no matter how the

anchor lay. Such an anchor needed no stock or ring, but it had one weakness — it floated. I remedied this by binding to it two slabs of lead sawed from *Pagan's* keel, one at its crown and the other at its upper shank.

I stood looking at the sea and my stranded boat, and estimating the distance between. My former experience of going aground helped me. In the beginning I laid in *Pagan's* bilge and on her floor boards a number of heavy stones to steady her by their weight against pounding at high tide. The strategy to float her now was: await the tide and, since most of *Pagan's* heavy stores were ashore and the stones on her floor were heavier than they, toss them quickly over. Accordingly the little craft should bob up. I could then kedge her away and anchor her. I inflated my pneumatic rubber raft to carry the kedge anchor off astern into deep water.

A half-dozen rods offshore I eased the hand-hewn anchor from the raft and watched it gulped from view. I rowed back ashore and sat beside *Pagan's* cache of stores on the jungle fringe. Flotsam and Jetsam crept into my lap, and together we watched the first investigating lips of the inbound tide nibble at the keel.

In a while, *Pagan* shifted about uneasily, thumping her beam on the sand, tending to skew around. When the tide had flooded sufficiently, I tautened the kedge line and seized its bitter end to the traveler. My boat floundered between her desire to rise and the press of the weight in her bilge. As fast as I could, I heaved the rocks over the side. *Pagan* buoyed up beautifully. I heaved on the chain, the kedge held, and off I went to anchor.

My chief concern was whether mv boat was leaking. If she

was leaking it meant I must run back to Panama for repairs. If not, I was determined to press on.

I went below and flashed a light along the planking and into the bilge. Everything was tight. Not a drop of water issued from the outer sea. When I came on deck the bow was pointing out to open water as though instinct had pulled it there and as though a prayer had been answered.

The same wicked intuition that had inspired me to sail alone from Panama now egged me on to make for the open sea.

It was late afternoon. I was anxious to be going. I pulled my rubber raft up to the transom, stepped into it, and rowed to where the tide tinkled on the strand and *Pagan's* gear lay heaped beneath a sail, and where Flotsam and Jetsam yowled beneath their bucket, the very bucket that was later to save my life. For the next three hours, I moiled with transporting the gear from the beach to the decks. At dusk I made my last trip, with the affrighted kittens staring innocent-eyed from atop the last of the stores into the blackening water.

In less than an hour I was lashing the little rubber raft under the staysail boom forward. I heaved the freak anchor aboard and secured it on the forepeak. *Pagan's* sails were spread; and billowing to a soft breeze, she stemmed out of the little bay. Something intuitive told me that this time it was real; I was on my way into the "vasty deeps" of the Pacific. Of course, I thought of returning to Panama to check my repairs. It was the wise thing to do. But when in an hour not a drop of water showed in the bilge, and when I reflected on the near month I had already lost, days, even hours, became precious in my race with the hurricane season across the Pacific.

The very fact that *Pagan* was again afloat, and making her own way, made me feel a thousand miles closer to Mary.

At midnight, when I had made a safe offing, I set the prow on a track of southwest by west, lashed the tiller, and turned in to my warm bunk with my mates.

Adventure

FROM PERLAS TO GALÁPAGOS there are 900 miles of ocean to cross. I had been told in Panama that sailing craft had taken anywhere from seven days to eternity to make it. That was about all the actual information I had.

Even men who had sailed over this vexatious stretch of water couldn't lay their finger on anything much that could help me. When they talked about it they looked off at the ocean and frowned. "Work into the Galápagos from the east," they said, "don't get west of them; you can't fight back against the trades and the current."

So that was my plan: work south till I could shape up for the Galápagos by steering into them to westward. Someone said that once I got to the Galápagos, the rest of the voyage to Australia was all "downhill." The trade winds were the thing. It was the trade winds I was after, and as vexations piled up on themselves I looked toward the trades as a salvation worth fighting to.

To limit the conditions of weather in the area between Panama and the southeast trades to such a simple word as bad or terrible is crass understatement. What makes it bad here is that disturbances are general rather than particular. No type of weather is dominant. Rather, one encounters every conceivable annoyance — not to mention their combination.

I had been in one gale, and a squall in the Perlas. And I had thought them bad at the time. But when I nosed out into Panama Gulf and farther, Pandora's box threw wide its lid and hell was a-poppin' from the start.

I didn't meet any really severe weather conditions — that is, harsh storms. But I should rather have the weather flay me a week at a time, then waft me along for a day of sailing, than do what it did.

Almost every night I was double reefed at the main and hove to. Otherwise I was in a flat calm or in a wind too gentle to enable me to make effective headway against the current. Sandwiched between these three perplexing weather habits was the unpredictable appearance of tropical squalls. Usually their only indication was the whir of wind or the cry of a rent sail.

These waters are undoubtedly the sharpest bone a sailor can have in his throat. Three uncongenial ocean currents meet here and claw at each other under the keel. There is the Mexican current dropping in from the north with its cool flood from Unalaska and the coasts of Japan. Out of the west comes the equatorial countercurrent, torrid and forceful, bringing tropic warmth and tropic life with it. Up from the Antarctic, along the South American coast, flows the cold stream called the Humboldt Current. When these varying waters meet the same thing happens that can only happen when brunette, redhead, and blonde come seeking the same man!

In the midst of these variant upsets an unsteady, one-minute-vicious and one-minute-calm, southwest wind added the final touch of mayhem. For it was to the southwest that I wanted to ply . . . straight into the eye of the wind. So I had to tack; first to south and then to west, fighting the current which was trying to suck me back to Panama — and it was succeeding at times. Some days found me hours on end in nerve-racking calms. Then a gale of wind would prod me in the ribs, causing me to heave to and fall back for most of the night. The morning would find me in a dead calm beneath a deluge of rain and rumbling clouds, or in an electric storm, the sky frightful with lightning.

On the first afternoon out I was in a rising south wind with one reef tucked in and pondering whether I should drop sail and tie in the other, when suddenly the wind dropped away to a void. Great smooth rollers ran under me and away to sternward. In twenty minutes a behemoth of a cloud swept down on me from directly behind. I could hear it talking as it came. By rights I should have doused all sail and gone below. But I was too desperate to make a few feet of southwesting. All day I had beaten to and fro across the same acre of water, into the same forceless head wind. A stern wind was a boon. I held to my hat and sat tight. The squall roared up and very crassly gave me the equivalent of a kick in the pants. In a moment I was flying before it at about seven knots! It was just what I wanted.

Imagine footing it at that clip and plowing head on into the oncoming rollers? *Pagan* was flying off the top of one into the center of another, a great spray cannonading upward and wetting the rigging to the masthead. Waves of water sluiced along the decks and spilled over the stern. A thump would herald her fall from the back of a smoking wave, and a thud would tell me that she was plowing into the base of another. At one stage I grew a little apprehensive and determined to bring her about and shorten all sail. "Nuts to it, we're going somewhere," I called out; and let her fly.

The squall lasted about forty minutes, then fell away to nothing, leaving me in a highly confused sea.

The next day I saw my first tide rip. In a moment — out of nowhere — the sea became an acreage of numberless cone-shaped bouncing wavelets. It rose and fell in an endless dance, licking at the sky with unnumbered fingers. I sat looking at something I had never seen before. It was amazing to see the uncanny epilepsy. It actually jumped aboard, but ran harmlessly out of the self-bailing cockpit. Under the keel two contrary currents had met; and redhead and blonde were tearing out each other's hair.

Another incident was unique in its way. The day had been one of weak and vacillating ladies' winds. I had used the engine several hours during the long hot day, in a futile search for a breeze. In midafternoon I gave up and decided to do with what I had. But as night drew on I found myself quite suddenly in a gale — in fact so suddenly as to be unable to pull down sail immediately. By the time the mainsail was reefed and double reefed the storm was down around my ears in earnest. Frothy seas were piling up, and *Pagan* was pitching savagely. The time had come and gone to hazard the bowsprit and doff the jib.

Staying atop a heaving bowsprit in a gale is like balancing

on a rolling barrel. Every time the sprit goes down, you
are past your knees in swirling water. About every fourth
time, you come up with water in your pockets — your vest
pockets!

You cling like grim death to the topmast stay and work at
the sail with your free hand. On a dark and stormy night it
doesn't pay to fall off. So you hold tight and work fast — but
not too fast. You get careless. That's what I did!

I had been out on the bowsprit several times in the Perlas
and I was approaching the jaunty stage. But sailboats are
marvelous devices for impressing the need of constant vigi-
lance. *Pagan*, in her own inimical way, heeled over, pitched
full down and then came up, tossing her bowsprit at the sky.
With the grace of a circus clown I floundered end over end
into the reaching dark waves.

I fought instantly for the surface. A series of seas clouted
me, knocking me sternward somewhere behind the transom.
The bumkin was a bare foot out of reach — and I knew I
must soon get hold of it, or something, or the next heavy
roller, would sweep me down wind. My fiercest swimming
was barely enough to enable me to hold my own against
Pagan's slow slog to windward. Sea water was impairing my
vision and stifling my breath. In this desperate moment I
struck something: at first I thought it the rudder edge, but
it was a pair of pants I was dragging astern to wash in the
wake. I pulled myself by them up to the rail and clung to it
for a moment while I rested.

The sea gave tremendous pulls — impressing me with its
unlimited power. In four years of the Merchant Service I
had not realized its infinite strength. From the decks of great
freighters one is on the seas but not of it. One is cradled be-

tween sturdy bulkheads of steel. One just sees the sea. When a merchant seaman gets a salt spray on his lips, it's an adventure.

As I trailed in *Pagan's* spuming wake, too spent to pull myself aboard, I learned the need for some sort of line dragging from the stern, something to grab onto if I fell over again. After I got aboard I went to the bowsprit and wrestled in the jib. But before doing so I lay on the poop, staring soberly at the retreating columns of the sea. Like brutes they ran from under *Pagan*, growling into the night. It's natural that I reflected on what could have happened. The danger for the lone sailor is what I had just escaped. I had been lucky. Next time I might not be so lucky. I felt a close part of my boat, an inseparable part of it in the battle with the hungry sea.

I wondered if I would have begun this trip had I known of the actual uncertainties to be facing me, as I was seeing them now. Yes I would, I concluded. What I was doing was fun, it had thrills. Despite the danger, I loved it. There was an appeal that every man feels — the appeal to adventure. And besides, it was taking me to the one girl in the world.

The morning of the fourth day out was like any other, except for one thing. Daylight found me standing east of south, bent slightly before the wind, making laggard time. As usual there was something untoward about the sky — but that was nothing more than I was learning to expect. I had been deepreefed the night before. To make the most of the day I had risen early and hoisted full sail. But it was useless; the wind was falling steadily off to a calm under a leaden sky.

I cranked up my talkative engine and ran her for two hours before I came upon a light breeze. It was southwest as usual and mild enough to fill my sails but faintly.

During these first five days I was in the process of learning celestial navigation which heretofore I had been too crowded with tasks to get to. While learning the celestial, I figured my daily progress by dead reckoning, using the bubbles rushing off the end of the keel as an indication of my speed through the water. So far I had estimated my gait to be a modest seven knots! — placing me approximately halfway to the Galápagos.

At 10 A.M. I found a new interest.

A great blunt-faced shark was lazing alongside *Pagan*. He eyed me with tiny pig's eyes and sidled quickly in to thwack the bilge strakes with his ponderous body.

Seeing and hearing this activity of sharks was an old story to me. Many times in the night or day I have heard them thump the planking. They do it to scratch themselves — or maybe they are vengeful. The first time I ever heard it was when I was sailing in the Perlas. It was night. I was hove-to near Saboga and down below asleep. I was awakened by a sinister thump, which shivered the boat. I bolted to deck thinking it had struck a reef, because I wasn't sure of my position. My first thought was that I had come about and run back in to shore. But mostly I thought of a reef. On deck I could discern nothing. The air was static and overcast. *Pagan* was scarcely swaying. For a long time I was perplexed. Then from an oblique angle a silver wake of phosphorus marked the track of an approaching object. At my very feet it banged into the side, scraped eerily a few feet, and slithered away. It was a shark.

I couldn't have that. *Pagan's* planks were only one-inch
oak and they were twenty-six years old. Too many back
scratchings by hulking sharks and I would be swimming in
my bunk. I broke out a spear and when the big shark lum-
bered in, I reefed it into him. With a startled twist he broke
my hold and plunged speedily. Lost: one good spear. After
that I tied a bowie knife to an oar — and when they ranged
near I gave them a tweak in the ribs with six inches of cold
steel.

But to return: the shark which filliped *Pagan's* hull that
morning of the twenty-third was a whopper. I couldn't help
but marvel at him. He was all shark. He had the swagger of
a brute bully; he was half the length of *Pagan*, and had teeth
the size of fingers.

When I saw those staggered twisted teeth I wanted them
. . . to show what I had seen. I wanted Mary to see that
crushing jawbone, to hold it in her hand.

I brought my heavy sport reel and pole on deck, and attached my largest steel shark hook. I baited it with a fat yellowjack partly gnawed at by Flotsam and Jetsam. When the
shark came near I dangled it before him and dragged it away
before he could look it over, a simple bit of classroom psy-
chology which, as it whetted him, angered him. Next time
he nuzzled it, and arrogantly swept it into his jagged mouth.

I heaved back with all the strength I had. The hook lodged
unmistakably in his bold jaw, and with the burn of cold steel
he tensed, then, slashing about with a startled suddenness,
roiling the water, sent a wave against the planking and made
off to beamward.

Threshing in agitation with his slow main strength, he
battled away from the boat, making the reel hum. When he

ended his run of sixty yards he turned on the hook and flailed the surface, gleaming silvery as he twisted in foam.

I braced myself against the lashed tiller for a ringside view of the most fascinating struggle I had ever seen.

The massive thing tore at the surface of the water, bending violently, from U shape to S shape, champing viciously. Sometimes he appeared astern, then on the bow, always with a smear on the quiet sea. He turned on his back and threshed fitfully, or spun in great full circles abeam and close aboard, followed by his pilot fish.

At one time he was more than a hundred feet down straight under me—so deep in fact I could see nothing in the limpid water. His most spectacular effort came about a half hour after he had been hooked. He had fought the line to its end, dead astern. With dorsal fin cleaving the surface he sped in fury full around the boat, threshing mightily as he went. Spray shot above him and a long wake rolled away behind him. He ended his circular run, paused a second, then sped fifty feet toward the quarter, swirled about, and raced away as though he would wrench his head off with the impending shock at the line's end. Barely before he reached the line's end he thrust himself from the water, and twisting on his back he sent a shiver from head to tail that, had the line grown taut — even if it were boltrope — would have snapped it like spaghetti. After that his defiance fell completely away. He struggled only pettily as I towed him to the rail.

The teeth I saw were unbelievable. They lay in two uneven rows, each two inches long and thicker than a pencil. They jutted at rakish angles, looked unmercifully sharp, and were wielded by a jaw mammoth enough to crush bone.

My envy of his power, coupled with the animal instincts of the victor, induced me to lean over the rail and punch him in the nose. I found it about as hard as *Pagan's* decks.

The great jaw, the jagged teeth — they were fascinating. But how to get them? My wicked intuition that all was well prodded me. Pull him aboard; cut his head off; boil the flesh away — it's simple.

Flotsam and Jetsam, with paws on the rail, could smell the fishy stench of the beast's breath and were fidgeting and mewing eagerly for a feast. I decided to pull him aboard.

First, I naïvely tried to lift him by direct pull, but only budged him scantily. He weighed hundreds of pounds. I fastened the main halyard to the gaff hook fitted in his gill and with desperate heaves dragged him an inch at a time over the transom, into the cockpit. What a monster. His head lay in the cockpit and his tail hung over the stern. He stirred faintly. I took the hatchet and buried it in his spine to end his tremors. A spurt of blood sprayed over me.

At the same moment the big body quivered violently. Flotsam and Jetsam went racing to the bow. I watched them. I heard a resounding scuffle and saw my tiller, splintered loose at the rudderpost, go flying into the sea.

All hell broke loose around me. The great shark came completely to life, threw himself in wild assault. With great sweeps of his tail and butts of his head he swept my legs from under me, almost knocking me overboard.

The great tail was pounding up and down like a sledgehammer, splintering, slamming, erasing. The gas-tank hatch disintegrated in a flash and the brazed copper tank went flat, spilling its load into the bilge. I clung to the rail, horror-stricken. The cockpit coaming rumbled, shattered, and flew at me, and if I hadn't ducked it would have gone down my throat.

In the meantime the hatchway sliding door had been popped through to the cabin floor and the rear porthole cracked. The bottom of the cockpit was giving way. *Pagan* was bouncing as though pounded by great fist blows.

I darted as close as I dared, grabbed up my hatchet, and chopped away at the heaving spine. Again he set to beating with sinuous motions. The partition between the engine compartment and cockpit screamed and split away. The cockpit deck itself broke through, the gasoline drums rumbled into the engine compartment, and the shark lay head down on the motor. I jumped in and struck again, burying the blade, and burying it again.

The destruction went on.

Pagan was being blasted apart before my eyes. I hacked with the hatchet like a wild woodcutter. I opened gashes in the head, and in the back. I had chopped his dorsal fin half away. Still he mauled my boat. I was afraid he would work his way into the cabin and rip it down or endanger the mast. I struck the harder. I went after him like a madman — blood bespattered and desperate.

He mangled the engine with side movements of his head, bending the sparkplugs down and tearing the wiring away. He fell beside the motor, threw himself around athwartships, and lying on the propeller shaft throbbed till it bent out of line. I was terrified lest he should work his way against the ribbing and smash the hull open. I lay on my side atop the engine, eased close, and notched a great hole in his stomach and lower jaw.

He jumped spasmodically. I moved after him, lost in the

bloody, death-dealing strokes. I cut his eye completely out and opened a hole from his gill to his shorn dorsal fin; still he lashed like a whip.

I sidled closer, drawing my legs up so that I could fit into the confined space, and turned more on my side to apply all my strength. Aiming for his nose — a supposed Achilles' heel — I laid it open bone and all, as far back as his front teeth. Still he throbbed dangerously. Moving closer — inches from him — I hacked into his vital stomach organs.

I was so far gone I was hardly nicking him. But it suddenly didn't matter; he gaped at the mouth and lay still. I lay for a long time beside him, watching him, hoping he wouldn't move, because if he had, I would have been in his way and too tired to shift. Everything about me was either smashed or coated red. I was caked with blood.

Before I could consider getting the battered carcass over the side, I had a few jobs to do. I had to pump gallons of gasoline, battery acid, and clotted blood from the bilges. Then I washed the gore from the decks, cabin, planking, and ribbing inside. After that I cleared away the splintered and broken lumber, piling it in the cabin.

The cockpit was a gaping hole. In the midst of it, the kittens were growling hungrily over the shark; chewing tastily with the corners of their mouths. I cut them a sizable meal and placed them with it on the fore scuttle.

Cutting into the shark's stomach, I found a motley of tragic creatures which had wholly or partly contributed themselves to his meals: two whole squid, a large Spanish mackerel, a mass of predigested small fry, the yellowjack I had baited him with, and several chunks of flesh and bone torn evidently from a very large fish.

After such a contest to subdue the shark, I considered his jawbone more a prize than ever. I cut his head off and later cleaned and scraped the bones and yellow teeth — a gruesome sight.

To heave the carcass over the side I had to cut it into two pieces and tussle with it by main strength. As to the wreckage — most of my spare time for the next two weeks was spent in rebuilding the stern.

Because of the shark I added another moral to my list: don't haul sharks aboard!

The engine was useless unless I turned back to Panama to have it repaired. As I look back now, I realize I should have turned back and put in at the Mechanical Division in Balboa for the work. In the long run I would have saved time. Too, I probably would have had a much hastier and most uneventful and dull trip across the Pacific.

The principal reason I didn't do an about-face was the state of my exchequer — it was low; only twenty-five dollars. And that wouldn't pay the docking fee. Also, my navigation by dead reckoning indicated I was making from eighty to a hundred miles a day. I expected to be in the Galápagos in a week — once there I wouldn't need an engine. The southeast trade winds, I was told, begin there, and with their power and constancy motor power is unneedful.

So I bore on, strictly under sail.

Overboard

THERE IS ONE GREAT HAZARD above all in singlehanded sailing, as I had learned, and that is, if you should topple over, there is no one to turn the boat about and pick you up. This was always before my mind, and I was forever cautious to guard against it.

The day after the shark battle I rigged a life line of about sixty feet, which I dragged astern — something to grab onto if I should fall over. Sometimes I bent a hook to its end baited with a stripping of white rag, and caught a fresh meal for the crew and me. Or I tied on a dirty pair of pants or a shirt to launder themselves in the wake. I used it also for a log line to indicate my speed. Primarily, though, its purpose was that of lifesaver in case I should fall over.

But one morning even my lifesaver nearly left me afloat on the sea.

The sun was barely up before a tumult of wind was down on me from the southwest. The sea picked up into a churlish, slapping hand, and I was banging into the teeth of it. The mainsail and staysail were reefed. I hesitated about pulling the jib, thinking conditions would abate.

Getting dunked and even dragged off the bowsprit now and then wasn't discouraging any longer. *Pagan's* bowsprit was too long — about seven feet — and very small around.

Taking in the jib in a gale was an activity for which I was never able to formulate an exact process. Never once did I doff it satisfactorily — so to the end I was practicing with it. But to get it in I usually proceeded something like this: First I crawled out and loosened the lanyard. I crawled back and slacked the halyard a foot or two, dropping the sail. Out again to snap loose a couple of hanks, pull the clew in, and pack it behind the rail at the forepeak. Slack away at the halyard again; unsnap several clips and pull in more of the sail from the grasping water, and stow it on deck.

Invariably I always left the jib to the last minute before tugging it in. Because it was clumsy to handle, it made little difference whether I grappled with it in a mild gale or a full one.

On this morning of high wind I was preparing myself for a bout with the jib by the usual cursing and swearing before-hand. When I got out on the bowsprit, I found that the turn-buckle of the stay was almost unscrewed. I twisted it by hand to tighten it, but must have turned it backward — suddenly it parted. I grabbed a handful of the sail, and hung to it as the wind filled it.

The next moment I was in mid-air dangling from the bil-lowed sail. I was fifteen feet up and the same distance off the beam. I had a death's grip on the sail luff and I was won-dering if I would be thrown too far out to swim back if I should let go. I decided to hang on.

Suddenly the sail spilled its wind and I swung inboard, crashing into the mast. Before I could think to let go I was blown back into the air again. The wind was whipping at the sail. I was being shaken back and forth as a terrier shakes a rat. Then the sail slipped loose from the stay, lost its wind, and folded as it splashed onto a sea.

The knotted halyard end caught in the block and I was towed astern. I was clinging to the stiff sail and wrestling with it as I clung; trying to gather it into a bundle, hoping I could somehow save it by gaining the deck with it. The canvas resisted stubbornly. Then the halyard slipped through, leaving me adrift: I had only the sail to hold to. *Pagan* moved away. I had the sail in a close grip, and swam to the life line astern. But sea slime and small rubbery sea animals had grown to it; and hanging to it, while clinging to the sail, was like holding on in a slippery pig contest.

I was determined to save the jib. My spare jib had been blown out in the storm off San José. The one I was fighting to save was my last. I needed it badly. A jib is a vital sail when working to windward.

In a minute I knew that fighting my way up the slimy rope with the sail still in hand was impossible. I managed to edge a few feet ahead, only to be thrown back by the wash of a swell.

I was deeply mindful of the cruel steel shark hook at the line's end. When I stopped to rest, I found that the line was slipping steadily through my hands. Not all the pressure of my grasp would counter the drag. The hook was near my feet, and threatening to snag them. I was slipping helplessly. The sea, pulling on the sail, was sliding me back and back.

The sail was bundled loosely on my stomach. I freed my hold on it and let the water devour it. I hated to do it, but what could I do?

Pagan, double reefed and heeling deeply as she pushed into the teeth of the rising wind, had a plucky look about her partly denuded spars and exposed hull as her trim lines battered the rough edges of the swelling seas, thirty feet ahead of me. She was wreathed in spray. I could hear the bow cleave the oncoming rollers.

I started the long haul up the slimed-over line from handhold to handhold, fighting each sea and the bubbling wake.

I crawled onto deck and lay watching the churning seas, crested with foam, racing away to the horizon, rumbling like trains as they went.

Lying there thinking morbidly over what might have happened, I noticed, as my eyes wandered astern with each sea, a ripple on the water's surface. I could see that it was my sail, and that somehow it was fouled with the end of my life line, and towing behind.

I gathered in the line, hoping the sail wouldn't disentangle. It didn't. When it neared the transom I saw that the shark hook had barbed the sail at the boltrope. One chance in hundreds.

I later entered the occurrence in the log as "taking in the jib the hard way."

CHAPTER IX   Malpelo Isle

Those first nine days I figured my speed by approximation. Each evening I plotted an estimated position on the
chart. It was marvelous the distance I had covered. The water
was sweeping beneath the keel at a rate of at least seven
knots, I figured. According to my dead reckoning I was hard
by the Galápagos; but was I? I wondered. Someone in Panama had said, "Don't go to Galápagos by dead reckoning; it's
suicide." I was beginning to get uneasy the day I tried my
first sextant shot.

It was a shoddy affair. I spent the day capturing the shifty
sun in terms of an angle, and working out a questionable
noon sight from a maze of figures. Late that evening, after
juggling ciphers and sights all afternoon, I arrived at a position which put me somewhere inland in Central Panama.
I gave up for the night.

On the next two days I arrived at consistent figures — but
what figures! My wearisome computations, no matter what
number of times I checked and rechecked them, came up always with the same result: they placed me only some 350
bare miles from Panama. The figures said I was near a barren isolated rock called Malpelo Isle. I refused to believe the
figures. I stuck with my dead reckoning estimate which put
me some 900 miles from Panama.

But as the morning wore on I rechecked the figures. Unfailingly they established me as somewhere near Malpelo. Finally I scaled the mast and searched the horizon, and saw nothing more than the monotonous sea. It was dirty in the southwest. A hazy curtain hung over the water.

There were birds around and they led me to believe land was near. But there couldn't be land; the Galápagos were a day away . . . unless . . . it could be Malpelo. Then, as midday rolled around, from out of the sea eased the loom of land. Dead ahead the crag floated, about ten miles off, barren, solitary, unmistakable.

This meeting of boat and sea-swept rock out on the pathless ocean came as a sort of miracle to me. For eleven days I had sailed and searched and had lifted no more than a steamer's smoke. Then suddenly figurings and jottings on a squared sheet of paper said land would raise itself across the bows now . . . and it did! The land was before me in the form of an indistinct blob of rock, small, and frothed at its base where the sea charged.

Seeing it there brought a flood of relief. Navigation suddenly became a game of fun, all the uncertainty I had felt over it glimmered, and I quickly looked upon it as simple, where for years I had fidgeted in awe at the mere thought of it.

Before I bought *Pagan* I used to think one had to know differential calculus to navigate a peanut across a dishpan. Too, I had looked at Bowditch, Dutton, and Cugle's and walked away blubbering to myself in a navigational fog. That's the way it was when I first went aboard *Pagan*. In the front of my mind was the prospective trip out onto the sea and in the back, haunting me, was my ignornace of navigation.

The devil of it was, while in port before I sailed I hadn't a spare hour to study it, the whole two weeks I owned *Pagan*. I had such a high respect for its complexities that I didn't want to put forth from Panama knowing the little I did of it, which was only visual pilotage from flying. But what could I do? Time was against me . . . I had to get across the Pacific before the hurricane season set in over the Coral and Tasman Seas. There was no time, as I saw it, to attend a fortnight of navigation school. The moment cried that I go.

When I sailed, I had exactly this navigating equipment aboard: one sextant, given to me by Captain Baverstock of Balboa. A pocket watch, exceedingly reliable. A cheap compass, that came with the boat. A hand lead line. A copy of Bowditch, given to me, though I didn't need it; I used it once — to light my Primus stove. A copy of Warwick Tompkins's *The Offshore Navigator*, $1.50, and worth its weight in gold. A copy of Hydrographic Office Publication No. 211, 90 cents. A small cardboard protractor, 10 cents. A six-inch rule, 10 cents. Good charts of likely island groups along the way, $4.00. Sailing directions and light lists for the waters I was to cross, $2.30. Total cost, $8.90.

If you will navigate, take what is listed here and sail away. When, after ten days of study and stars, you can't fix your position, turn back and take up harbor sailing, for you will never navigate. Any sensible person who can see the sun or horizon plainly can use these tools to go round the world.

ᔐ   ᔐ   ᔐ

To me Malpelo meant nothing. I was not on a sightseeing trip. But if I had been, I would not have come there for scenery. The isle is so wind-, rain-, and sea-swept that not even the guano from its host of birds will cling to it. Around its base are a few toothlike rocks. Otherwise it is sheer and uninviting. I was glad to see it for what it meant to me as a check on my navigation, but it was a setback to learn that in eleven days I had traversed only some 350 miles.

I laid my slow progress to inexperience and the host of frustrating weather conditions which had beset me. Also there was no certainty regarding the speed and exact set of the currents. But the main factor in my poor showing was the loss of the engine. The use of an engine in a calm, even for an hour, can often move the craft into an area of wind.

By nightfall I had made a good offing from Malpelo into the south. But a little later it fell calm. I dropped the main to avoid hearing it slat aimlessly and went below for the night. At daylight of the thirtieth I found that the current during the night had pulled me off to the northeast of Malpelo. The calm still held, and I fished from the deck to while away the time till a bold young breeze should whip me past the lonely rock for the second time.

Around midmorning a lusty breeze sprang up. I stood away to the west till I had cleared Malpelo, then shoved around to south and beat away toward the equator. Through the afternoon I bounded into a making wind till at nightfall I was deeply reefed and ready to heave to. Malpelo was far behind. In the face of a line squall I doused the main and put her in stops, and heaved to for a stormy night. Before I went below, out of the weather, I had what I thought to be a last look at Malpelo.

Dawn came with rain pelting the cabin like bird shot. I got up to as morbid a bit of weather as I have seen. Visibility was nil; the wind high; a lump of sea running. It was a day of perpetual dusk. Not even the ubiquitous sea birds were out. I didn't dare put up a stitch of cloth. I stayed below.

Though I couldn't see it I knew the deformed island was somewhere near. For three days now I had been in its vicinity, and I grew sober whenever I thought of my helplessness before the weather.

At noon sea and air were still unchanged, except that off to starboard I could catch the recurrent hollow boom of pounding seas. At first I thought a ship was somewhere about. But there was no blast of foghorn. After a while I realized I was falling back before the storm, past Malpelo.

Deep in the night the winds abated. I climbed out of the warm sack and showed on deck. Stars blinked in patches; the sea was still rolling in heavily; the air was both bold and weak as it is in moments of change. But it looked as if some sail could stand. I tied a reef into the mainsail and ran her up. In a few hours I passed Malpelo for the third time, looking gray in the early dawn.

The breeze freshened as the sun climbed. Late in the morning I tied in the last reefs and pulled down the jib. In the early afternoon the wind veered to a little north of west. A heavy swell set in from the south. Shortly cross seas were at work and *Pagan* was rolling and yawing wildly. Malpelo hid herself in the falling clouds. By dark I was hove-to properly.

The cats were tottering weakly on the bunk with *mal de mer*. I tucked their drooping little bodies close by me where they would be warm, and made them feel in their misery that they had an understanding friend.

The wind was backing slowly to its wonted position. Cross seas were worsening. Above the noise of wind in the rigging and rumbling of sea crests I could hear occasional proofs of seas breaking on Malpelo.

Long after I had bedded down I was awakened by the nearer crash of seas on a shore. I knew before I uncovered myself that it was Malpelo. Damn this island; wouldn't I ever get past it? On deck I reached with eye and ear into the wet night of drizzle and made the crash and hiss of the surf dead astern more or less. I couldn't risk falling back farther, so I strung up the staysail to see if *Pagan* could stand off a lee shore.

In an hour the roar was louder. It was no longer difficult to hear or make out its bearing. *Pagan* could hold her own with the wind, but it was the current that was sucking her back. I reefed the staysail and put up the double-reefed main. For the remainder of the night she held her own.

At daylight — five days after sighting the island — I found Malpelo leering at me a hundred yards down wind, and the wind was stiffening! She was directly in my wake, and reaching closer with each squall and gust. I was gravely in need of the engine. A scathing wind was on. *Pagan* had no business with sail up — still, I didn't dare take in a stitch.

At times it looked as though she might ride clear of the isle if I should drop sail and let her drift. I was tempted to back her around and risk clearing the island by running before the wind. But in such a sea I was afraid of being broached-to by veering too sharply into the wind, or pooped by shipping a wave over the stern. With *Pagan's* cockpit still not fully repaired from the battle with the shark, I didn't dare hazard it. The more I watched the jagged spire the more ominous it became.

A cold wind swept the clouds from the air. The blue dome

of the sky, across which a cool sun worked up to high noon, looked down over me as I grew furrowed at the brow. There was no need for a noon sight; my exact position was impressed on me by every minute.

I could easily have tossed a sea biscuit onto the closest rocks. The roar quite suddenly grew deafening. It's a wonder Malpelo isn't toppled right over by force of driving seas, so greatly do they slam against her. I slipped as close to her weather-worn sides as I dared, still hoping the wind would abate, or that *Pagan* would work away.

At this juncture I did the only thing I could possibly have done. But first I pushed my little pneumatic life raft off the foredeck and led it aft to secure it to the bumkin, in readiness against the moment I might need it. I tied the cork blocks to Flotsam and Jetsam and stuck them in a corner of the cockpit. Then, knife in hand, I cut the lashings and reef points away along the boom, freeing the sail, and jerked the strained canvas hastily up. It filled, and *Pagan* shivered. The lee rail went under the sea and a froth swirled against the deckhouse.

I jumped to the tiller and pointed *Pagan* as far off the wind as I could without broaching her to. She heeled more steeply and the rudder kicked. She breasted each sea jerkily. Holding the tiller was real work. Great lumps of sea bombarded the windward rail. Spray landed on the cliff face close abeam.

I knew the sail wouldn't hold long, but a few minutes' sailing would drive me far enough to clear the rocks. If the sail flew out at the seams right away — I had only one resort, the rubber raft. Flotsam and Jetsam were unmindful of my weighted concerns. They sat close together like a furry ball, looking calmly ahead.

In five minutes I peered down wind and thought that even

then I could clear the isle. Then the slides ripped from the luff of the sail. They screeched and the sail pounded at loose ends. I shoved the tiller down. *Pagan* rounded to into the wind, and fell before it. I knew she would pass close to the rocks if she passed at all. And close it was. Spray from the battered stone fell over us. It reminded me of Punta de Cocos. Flotsam and Jetsam shivered and crawled up to my lap.

The same night I drifted far to northeastward of Malpelo. At dawn the wind was still high, a lumpy sea was still rolling — and *Pagan,* under staysail and jib, was hove-to far to leeward of the horny rock. Overhead was the clearest sky I have seen on the Pacific; not a cloud showed, only a depthless blue. A fierce unvarying wind blew the full day, driving cresting seas onto the decks. I was seated in the chill cabin at work with palm and needle on the tattered mainsail. She had pulled loose at the seams, and had frayed a bit at the ends. Here and there was a rip which demanded a little attention. I noted that only the seams sewed by machine had split; those which I had stitched in at San José were good.

As I worked I thought, Why go on fighting uselessly against the fitful winds overhead and the redheads and blondes at loggerheads around the keel? Six days on one small field of water. I was for turning back to Panama, for a rest and repairs and a new start. The more I thought of doing it, the more sensible it sounded. Then my wicked intuition lulled me, telling me the trade winds were hard by, and coaxing me to push on. Mug that I am, I listened.

Late in the afternoon I completed the job and spent the time to dusk fretting before a porthole. Through the night the wind held, and only with the dawn did it moderate to where I could put on the sails and start the long beat into the wind toward Malpelo for the fourth time. All morning I worked sail and tiller. At noon I was close by the rock.

Throughout the afternoon I sailed under a halcyon sky, hoping the friendly wind would hold till the night. I was beginning to think of Malpelo as a jinx. If only I could pass out of sight of her once, my troubles would be over. As I passed her I stood at the shrouds and loathed the sight of her hornlike crags in the belated twilight. At ten o'clock, with wind still holding fair, I tied the proper angle on the rudder and called it a day.

For the first few hours of the next morning I could see a tuft of rock on the horizon astern. What an unburdening it was to imagine not seeing that grotesque shape again. Late in the forenoon, I saw again what I had not seen for eight tiring days — a landless expanse of sea.

Navigation

F OR THE NEXT FEW DAYS there were equable breezes. Old
Phoebus came out from his grizzled curtain and washed the
sea warmly. It was wonderful to be on deck all day. No line
squalls, no nightly gales, no ladies' winds. I made strange
entries in the log those days. Something about blue skies,
sunny days, warm tropical nights.

I was able in those few soft days to put the finishing
touches to the deck work on the stern. I lengthened the cockpit, by eliminating the lazarette, so that it extended to the
rudderstock, making it capacious enough, if need be, to sleep
in. Since the engine was now ballast, I lashed it down to its
bed and extended the forepart of the cockpit right up to the
hatchway. When I completed all, the stern was infinitely
altered — from the lazarette to the hatchway, it was one long
roomy cockpit.

The shark had slammed away the sliding hatchway door,
and since then I had done with a towel tacked over the opening, which I untacked each time I came out from below. This
too I repaired. I built in a pair of small, swinging doors which
opened outward, and which — so I thought in my boundless
confidence — were a vast improvement over the thick, heavy,
sliding door.

Between the engine compartment and the main cabin I

installed a watertight bulkhead. This I had wanted to do before leaving Panama but couldn't spare the time. The watertight bulkhead afforded the degree of safety I had long wanted. I am thankful I built it as sturdily as I did — it saved my life.

In only a few days after leaving Malpelo, all the deck work was finished. There was time to be devoted to the cats, to fishing, and to perfecting my navigation.

ᔋ   ᔋ   ᔋ

Navigation was done wholly by the sun. On several occasions I experimented with the moon and stars, obtaining a dusk or dawn "fix" with simultaneous sextant readings on two bodies. In the end I found it needless work, and stuck to the simple sun method.

The slow speed was ideal for navigation totally by sun. I soon narrowed my daily navigation down to less than an hour's work.

At noon I took what is called a noon sight, or meridian altitude of the sun. This established my latitude, or distance north or south of the equator. I used only the sextant with a few figures added and subtracted to come to a hasty, accurate computation.

In the afternoon — about three-thirty or four — I took a shot of the sun. From its altitude I quickly and easily (as explained by Mr. Tompkins in The Offshore Navigator) determined a line of position, at some point on which I was located. Simply be estimating my latitude, according to distance and direction traveled from noon, and applying it to the line, I had my position. Anybody can do it.

To determine my speed, I used my life line as log line. To

the end of it I connected my bucket. Tossing it over, I set off the second hand of my navigating watch, and stopped it when the line drew taut. If it took ten seconds, for instance, it was a matter of going sixty feet every ten seconds. By simple multiplication and division, I could soon ascertain my hourly knottage. But the exactness of such a calculation would depend on a steady wind. Since I was interested in a close approximation of my speed between noon and four o'clock, I usually tossed the bucket over several times and took an average of the results.

As a rule I made a point of calculating my position each day. But if I was having a good time watching the cats, or had a fish on the line, I overlooked navigation occasionally.

Around the middle of the morning each day I caught my eager cats their rations. I used my large sport reel mounted on a strip bamboo pole. Despite a limited assortment of flies to choose from, I rarely found it difficult to please the mood of the fish. My fishing equipment, aside from my sport reel, consisted chiefly of a fishing kit which came with my little rubber raft. I had a dozen hooks ranging in size from very small to large enough to catch a dolphin. There were two hand lines, a large white fly, several leaders, and two kinds of bait. I had also the three angling items I purchased in Panama: a large spinner for sharks and two smaller flies for red snappers and yellowjacks.

In these waters, rich with fish, one doesn't have to lure catches; often I made them with nothing more than a piece of cloth for bait.

As a rule I could take a delicacy from the water in an

hour's trolling, or, if caught in a calm, in only a dozen casts. Then the fun would begin as my impetuous sea mates tackled the catch. They brightened my day as they charged and countercharged their flapping victims.

What hilarious wrestling matches I have seen on *Pagan's* decks. I have seen my doughty cats tackle everything from three-inch flying fish to a nine-foot marlin, with equally heedless ferocity. A thousand times I have seen them high tail it to the bow, after a severe drubbing. In a moment they would marshal their forces, and with a technique that never varied — yet never grew dull to watch — would slink soft-footed and fierce-eyed back to the tiny war.

After gorging themselves, if the weather was favorable, they often curled up behind my homemade anchor on the bow. Sometimes they slept in the shade of the lee waist, or if the sails were furled they climbed into the folds of the stay-sail or the main. All afternoon they made pilgrimages back to the catch, thus fulfilling what ordinary house and alley cats spend a lifetime dreaming of. Though Flotsam and Jetsam often had to tolerate the horrendous emergencies of sea life, all in all I am sure they wouldn't have missed the trip for a ton of mice.

It was about this time that I noticed in *Pagan's* wake a small school of a dozen dolphin — blunt-headed, sleekly designed, and wily. I must have picked them up at Malpelo. Every day they were there idling along in the shadow of the keel or shooting out ahead of the bows, preying on the hapless flying fish or the silvery shoals of small fry. I was glad of their company and often tossed them bits of fish scraps from my catchings. They spurted hurriedly to the scraps, but remained stolid and unmoved if anything hinting of a hook showed. However, one, a little dumber than the rest, succumbed to a fly one morning.

I'll never forget the morning I caught him. I had heard fishermen describe dolphins in their death throes, but I felt their imaginations had inflated what they had seen. When I pulled my first dolphin from the deeps I saw something truly amazing. He lay there quivering and gasping deeply as I unrooted the hook. Then I saw what the fishers had told me of. Instantly his ordinarily blue-greenish color changed to blue in a shimmering wave like grain fields before the wind — then ranged between the hues of purple and gold to greenish brown, gray-brown, silvery, and finally to a startling silver, spotted with blue; then came an abrupt reversion to his familiar pastel shade.

The greatest fun of fishing these waters was that I rarely caught the same species twice. Sport varied with each catch. Sometimes I caught Spanish mackerel, albacore, tuna, wahoo, and several species I was unable to identify. These waters from Panama to Galápagos are the richest sport fishing grounds in the world. They literally teem with fish. Long ribbons of birds pounding tirelessly into the water on every hand testify to the abundance with which they are sustained.

On the surface there floated small, brownish jellyfish trailing a brown, stringlike tail. There were white dollar-size organisms floating in myriads. Several varieties of seaweed showed up. Avenues of fish eggs, from horizon to horizon, keel deep, and wide as *Pagan*, fed the fish and gave birth to fish which would be food for fish and yet would prey on other fish — life-and-death battles that I saw every day. In a handful of the water itself were dustlike particles of infinitesimal life on which shifting schools of fish, looking like sunken reefs, fed themselves. Harassing the frantic shoals of fish were packs of wolfish sharks, schools of picturesque dolphin, and the sea birds.

Every few days a great sea bat would shoot up from the depths, make a full turn, and land flat with a trenchant resound. Occasionally a shark would bump against the keel, sending me on deck with my knife lashed to an oar end, or schools of porpoise would frolic before the bow. Often I saw the geysers of whales; and once I caught a glimpse of the tall sharp black fin of the brute killer whale slicing the water.

One morning a sudden heavy soughing noise startled me at my daydreaming. Looking off over the bows, I saw a great round hump, like a ship's keel, about fifty yards ahead. It was a huge whale lazing on the surface.

The bluff of *Pagan's* onrush must have frightened him. Quite gruffly he flourished his great body in a sharp twist, and pounding the water with his wide glistening tail he plumbed. *Pagan* breasted the wave of water he set off. As we passed over the spot I stared into the greenness. And there he was, like something out of *Moby Dick*, moving in giant spirals, trailing a heavy wake of churning water and bubbles, plunging into the vast deeper darkness.

Late one afternoon, I sighted the spouts of three small whales sporting on the horizon. How many times had I seen whales similarly on merchant ships! My stolid old captains had seen them too. But to be a captain, one must be lost to the world of nature — and resigned to a world of tare and tret.

How often I had wished I was in charge of the helm. I would have visited every puzzle of the sea. So it was only natural that I should come about and run amidst the cavorting pack. Two of them plunged when I was the length of the boat away. The other, bolder, hung on. I didn't know he was asleep. I pressed the tiller down and swung up. *Pagan* cast a shadow over him. And then the bow nicked him a side blow. The sails rustled from the soft shock. In the terror of sudden awakening, he whipped out with his great fluke, flipping a dollop of green seas over the rail into my teeth. The round head grew suddenly from the lather and a snort of spray blew out of it. Then it plunged and another wave spilled into the cockpit up to my knees. Behind the stern, as I pulled away, a widening white circle eddied and shifted across the wake. Later I saw other whales, but I didn't investigate.

Another morning I hooked onto a splendid swordfish. After a tiff of two hours wherein I saw every antic the sleek swordsman of the deep could contrive, I wound him into the rail. I left him gaffed at the scupper with the grappling hook, till I was certain he was good and dead. Then I hauled him onto the boards and looked him over in detail, and made a sketch of him for the log.

From his bony falchion right back to his powerful tail which gave him the superb speed and bursts of spirit unequaled, he was a study in streamline. He was the only swordfish I caught, but after such sport, he'll not be my last.

After dissecting him and probing among his vitals, I cut myself a sizable steak and a tidbit for the cats. As an afterthought I sawed off his sword, dorsal fin, and tail. The sword, I nailed to the bowsprit end. I tacked the dorsal fin atop the cabin and nailed the flared tail to the bumkin. Salty old sea dogs have said this keeps a sailor up in his luck.

For three days, following my weathering of Malpelo, blue skies and fair winds held. I reeled off an average of forty-five miles a day. In the log I made happy entries. Considering that I had no engine, that contrary currents were opposing me, that the wind, almost hourly, died completely for a few minutes, that I was hove-down about eight hours each night — I was doing well.

Gradually I nibbled away at the distance. Sometimes I grew unfathomably discouraged. Hard, wet ropes; inclement, capricious weather; the small wearisome reef points — but most of all the desire to go faster made me gloomy. And when gloom smote me hard and the sea miles wore me down, I went below, and with my dainty crew in my lap found solace reading from among the worn letters I had received from Mary during our long separation. They chased the gloom and the wornness, and inspired me to patience.

But always there was the pleasant thought of the southeast trades. "When I get to the trades it'll all be different," was my hope. I imagined wind abaft the beam, steady dependable wind and seas running with me, no squalls, no opposing currents. I was creating a roseate paradise for myself down in the trade winds — it was what kept me going south.

The three days' respite from foul weather south of Malpelo was like a reprieve. But soon, as though these waters were taking a final crack at me before I should go dancing away from them before the trades, a thoroughly familiar weather pattern set in. There were two or three squalls a day, gale winds at dusk, and early morning calms.

Crew

THE MORNING OF JULY 8 I came on deck as usual, threw my eyes into the rigging to check on things, then gazed around the horizon at the sea. There was a fresh wind up. Off to starboard was something that made me look again. It was a dense curtain of cloudlike air, arm-shaped and bent, reaching from the sea into the clouds, and marching over the water. It was a tropic waterspout.

How many waterspouts I had seen in the Merchant Marine! How many times had I leaned on the rail peering wistfully into their mystery and wishing I was captain! And now I was captain: and I did what I always said I would do, if I saw a waterspout from my own boat. I loosed the lashings from the tiller and set *Pagan* on a track that put her straight for the center of the waterspout.

I have heard a lot about waterspouts during my time on the ships. Some have said they suck solid water into the clouds, and to put a ship through their center is to take it into a waterfall. Others have said they have hurricane winds inside. And others have said they mother a great whirlpool at their funnel-like base that can suck a ship under.

I have studied dozens of waterspouts from the rails of ships and I have always held that they were harmless. I have argued again and again that they are only large short-lived whirlwinds. And now I was going to test my arguments. I tossed Flotsam and Jetsam below, dogged the ports, and slid the companion hatch shut.

Pagan was deep reefed at the main from high winds of the night before. She crept in upon the towering dark wall of whining air. I lashed the tiller down and raced to the bow for a closer look, to see if it might not be wiser to change my mind about going on. Then suddenly the spout shifted and headed directly for *Pagan*. I ran to the mast and clung to it. *Pagan* was swallowed by a cold wet fog and whirring wind. The decks tilted. A volley of spray swept across the decks. The rigging howled. Suddenly it was dark as night. My hair whipped my eyes, I breathed wet air, and the hard cold wind wet me through. *Pagan's* gunwales were under and she pitched into the choppy seaway.

There was no solid trunk of water being sucked from the sea; no hurricane winds to blow down sails and masts; and no whirlpool to gulp me out of sight. Instead, I had sailed into a high dark column from 75 to 100 feet wide, inside of which was a damp circular wind of 30 knots, if it was that strong.

As suddenly as I had entered the waterspout I rode out into bright free air. The high dark wall of singing wind ran away. For me another mystery of the sea was solved. I shook out the reef in the mainsail, hoisted all sail, and went below to write my adventure into the log.

～   ～   ～

The next night I was hove-to — riding at sea anchor. I was slumbering peacefully: *Pagan* was dogged down tight. She had a terrific roll on, and not a stitch of sail up.

Unknown to me, my ten-gallon water breaker, secured into the starboard bilge, had chafed away its lashings. Suddenly it lurched from its position. It bounded to the floor, followed through on top of me, then careened into the port ribbing. Before I could arise, it bounded back and knocked me with it to the floor. Several times it used me battering-ram style. It jumped and rolled like something alive; there was no holding it. My weight was as nothing before it. When I rose to scramble away, it caught me at the ankles, toppling me under it, and proceeded to roll over me. I jerked my mattress from the bunk and thrust it between us. With my pillow and blankets and a life preserver I wedged it in, and trapped it between me and the bunk side. It's a wonder it hadn't broken some bones or wrenched a few joints, or for that matter it's a marvel it hadn't done extensive damage to my boat.

What had happened to the cats, I didn't know. Presently I heard their just complaints. They were part of the wedging material — certainly a job their harsh contract hadn't included. At expense to my bruised elbows and knees, I freed them, and relashed my cask.

But I wasn't the only one aboard to be severely treated by the sea's caprice. One noontime the cats and I were enjoying the midday sun. I was lolling in the cockpit and Flotsam and Jetsam were flouncing about the cabin top. They were playing cat's games on a box I was intending to paint when it dried. The wind, from southwest, was weak and unsteady, except that every now and then it bent us over gustily.

A gust of wind hit us of a sudden, knocked us out of plumb and pitched the box to the deck, bouncing the cats off the rail into the clutching sea. At first I wanted to pitch in after them and return via the life line. But the likelihood of getting both of them, or even one, was remote. I heaved my life jacket near them to mark the spot, and hastened to put *Pagan* about. Every foot I moved from the spot where they fell over was crucial. An object on the surface of the sea is well hidden at twenty-five yards. Once a seaman fell from a ship I was on. A life ring was thrown him. He was seen to grab it. By the time the ship turned about he had disappeared among the crests. Two hours we searched, in two lifeboats, with powerful binoculars. We never saw man or life buoy.

I had this in mind as I slashed the ropes on the tiller, put her helm hard aweather, and threw off the jib sheet. As she jibbed around, the sheet rings screeched across the travelers and the whole boat jumped under the blow. I sheeted the jib home, eased off the main, and bore down on the spot as I remembered it.

I ran for what seemed an unconscionably long time. Seeing nothing, I thought it meet to turn back and zigzag the area.

I brought her up into the wind and dropped her over to the starboard tack, on a reach. Standing on the cabin, gripping the mast with one hand and the glasses with the other, I scanned every drop of water. At a suitable moment I came about on the port tack and searched the crests both up and down wind. Nothing. I was lapsing into despair. Those poor little scamps, floating on an unfriendly, lonesome sea. And if they were seen, who would bother about cats?

The searchings I made on the billowy sea had a depth of compassion behind them. I made two more long tacks, covering a wide range, but the hiding sea wouldn't give them up. Hours must have passed. With last looks over the curling waters I turned to my former course. Suddenly my life jacket heaved into view aport. I felt sure I could find the cats now if they hadn't drowned, or swum too far from the preserver.

When the yellow life jacket came in view again it was practically dead ahead. But there were no cats near it. I searched the immediate water with my glasses and saw nothing. I scrutinized the top of each sea, jerking the glasses here and there to examine each unfamiliar splash. Only the impersonal sea, but no unfortunate kittens struggling on the surface. In a moment I saw why. As the jacket appeared, there they sat, atop it, blending into its unruly surface, and wailing as only lostlings can wail.

The looks they gave me, as I scooped them in, were ample clarification that they were wholeheartedly grateful. Three hours on that pulsating frothy floor had left them wringing wet and bedraggled, shivering helplessly. This, to them, at least for the moment, was the last straw.

I took them below to dry off and sleep safely in warm wool blankets.

Soon after this, one of the large variety of sea birds landed aboard *Pagan* — probably a gannet. He took a position on the cabin and regarded me airily when I came near to be friends. The first time I picked him up he vomited a mass of tiny, partly digested fish on me and jabbed at me with his long, dull bill.

Later, we became firm pals, when, after discovering he was ridden with lice, I dusted his feathers with some of the kittens' flea powder. And when I took him out of the heavy weather at night, and perched him on the handle of the tool kit in the peaceful cabin, he became my outspoken buddy. Whenever I came near him on deck thereafter he would squawk raucously — evincing his happiness at being a part of the crew — fan the air with his long wings, and nestle contentedly under my petting.

Each day he flew off a few hours to feed, but finally gave up the struggle for existence when I included him with Flotsam and Jetsam each morning in apportioning the fish I caught. But the new passenger hated the kittens. The first time they met was at a fish feed. A knock-down drag-out brawl was the result, with Flotsam and Jetsam taking a drubbing. I came out when I heard the scuffling. The kittens were spitting and arching. The sea bird was attacking them in turn, flailing them with his wings and pecking circles around them.

Thereafter I had to keep them separated.

I named him Gawky, because he was a living monument to the word. I got the idea when he toppled off the boom onto the cabin and bounced over the side when I playfully sneezed in his face.

So Gawky took his place as a boarder "on the house" along with the cats and my school of dolphin. The leader of the dolphin, a battle-scarred old veteran of thousands of successful contests with lesser and greater fry than he, I named Old Death. He didn't forage out ahead as the others did — he stayed in close, lazing under the shadow of the hull, darting out with murderous speed on unsuspecting victims, making his kills within a boat length of the keel.

One morning I saw an unbelievable thing aboard *Pagan*. I had been splicing a jibsheet fair-lead at the fish plates. Upon finishing it, I started below. And there, beside my bunk, under the chart rack, in startled quiet, was a large gray rat.

He was longer than either of the cats. His eyes, like tiny

black agates, were fixed on me; his whiskers wigwagged
nervously. Beside him a thick hairless tail formed a thin gray
wake, showing where he had turned as I startled him. He
made a motion to go, and I grabbed and tossed the first thing
my blind hand touched — my alarm clock. Glass and spare
parts flew around the tiny cabin.

I was sorry I had startled and threatened the poor devil —
"Live and let live," I thought. I figured he would be a welcome part of the crew, along with Flotsam and Jetsam and
Gawky. Out here on the high seas, in a tiny bobbing world,
what mattered it who was aboard.

It was an amazing thing — this rat aboard — when I sat
down to think it out. How and when had he come aboard?
How in all these weeks, in so small a space, had we avoided
each other? Not a sign of him had I seen. What about the
kittens — why hadn't they detected him? Where had he got-
ten his food and his water?

I jerked bolt upright at the thought of the latter. Had he
gnawed into my water breakers? I checked instantly each of
my oaken casks, turning them around, searching their whole
area. No sign of tampering.

I searched into my food stores beneath the cabin bunks, in
the lockers; and found droppings he had left behind, which
I hadn't seen before. There was no possibility of his eating
into the tins or the jars or jugs. Then, as I crawled under the
forepeak, and rummaged in the starboard bunk, I found
where all these weeks he had secreted himself.

In Panama I had stored a few items in a lemon crate, tacked
it over with canvas, and painted the covering. It was into this
he had gnawed in search of the cheese, salt pork, and prunes
inside. As to his source of water, I can only assume he licked

up my spillings during mealtime, or he licked up the over-spillings from the milk cans.

One thing I quickly learned — the kittens knew of his presence. When I brought them down, they went directly into the forepeak to stand a patient vigil at the small opening they couldn't get into. In the weeks since leaving the Perlas, I had been too busy working my boat to see the grim drama below decks.

Stowaway, so far as I can conjecture, must have come aboard when I ran aground at San José. Just possibly he had crept from the jungle into my supplies on the beach and had somehow become trapped in the gear as I reloaded it.

Judging from what is told of the sea from old, of rats not boarding an unsound ship, I was flattered by the compliment of his presence. So Stowaway, as I named him, became a part of the cruise — another mouth to feed in my little Pacific household.

Each night I placed a morsel of food and a thimbleful of water at the base of the mast for Stowaway. I wanted him to be fed and watered, so that he wouldn't be up to such rat's pranks as gnawing into my water breakers. In my spare time I sawed up and hammered together a small shelter, somewhat like a bird house. I lashed it to the mast at the floor, with the door directed forward so that our diffident passenger could come and go in secret. Though he rarely made a public appearance, he never failed to draw his rations.

He evidently felt at one with his abode because several times I caught the cats snooping around it. They had that eager look which usually possessed them when I flashed a fish under their noses.

They had many a struggle at its front door, a small round

hole. It was easily large enough for Stowaway, but Flotsam and Jetsam could get only their eyes in. What a tantalizing place for them that box became. I can still see them there, each with a fierce paw clawing through the opening, laboring like tiny lions and voicing mightily their ego and thwarted desire.

Since Flotsam and Jetsam were confirmed seamen and adapted to a regimen of fresh fish, I was surprised they would concern themselves over a mere rodent. But despite the salt in their blood, they stalked Stowaway in a fashion to do a landlubber justice.

⌐   ⌐   ⌐

And so life went . . . a succession of simple events to detract from the bane of tortuous miles. The plainest things were of the greatest interest.

Many have asked me if I was bored out there in a wooden world whose length was that of most kitchens and the width of most bathrooms. Life is never boring to me, never was, no matter where I have been. My early life was such that I was forced upon myself, when I wasn't working. I learned early to fill those hours with my own diversion.

Aboard *Pagan* I found plenty to do, even at the most static times. My main preoccupation — aside from working my boat, which took overwhelmingly of my time — was with reading. I had a varied library aboard, everything from "who dunnits" to Darwin. And I read all. Now a mystery, now a novel, now politics, now philosophy, and now poetry. The ones I liked were De Maupassant's *Short Stories*, Carey McWilliams's *Brothers Under the Skin*; Harold Laski's *Reflections on the*

Revolution of Our Time, and Will Durant's *The Mansions of Philosophy.*

Another thing I did, I spent time thinking. Often I sat for hours gazing out across the water to the sea rim, chewing mentally at whatever wished to ease into my mind.

Often my thoughts turned on my past life, and I relived completely all that had gone before. The oldest of five sons and a daughter. The loss of my father at fifteen . . . during the depression. Four years of work helping my mother support the family. Factories, mills, and sweatshops — for a boy who wanted to go to school.

Remarriage of my mother to a kindly stepfather. For me, freedom from the yoke of a large family. All I earned, my own now. But I didn't want to earn: I wanted to learn; to rise above the factory. So off I went — broke, with a ninth grade education — to college. I had no alternative. Who, at twenty, after working four years in the "open" shops of Los Angeles's south end, wants to go back to high school . . . with the kids?

Santa Barbara State College: I begged my way in and they let me stay. I borrowed money from the Dean of Men — a swell guy. I worked my way through. Played football. Class prexy in my sophomore year. What should have been my junior year was spent on merchant ships. I wanted to fly a bomber but I had a hole in my eardrum from childhood T.B. — 4F in the draft; no service would have me but the Merchant Marine.

Two years in the Merchant Marine. Twice around the world. From Reykjavik to Cape Horn. A year in the Royal Australian Air Force. Marriage — to a blue-eyed Aussie girl, the greatest event in my life. Again in the Merchant Marine, this time more than a year. The war over, Mary and I caught in the shuffle, separated by circumstances.

And now, bobbing on a splinter of wood uncertainly across the Pacific.

Some of the time I worked ship — depending, of course, on the weather. Each morning I trolled for fish. I navigated. If the cats were in a playful mood, we sported about the decks awhile. Or I had a long talk and a genial boxing match with Gawky. Many hours I watched Old Death and his boys slipping through the sea attacking the flying fish. A few hours a day I read.

Of principal importance was a letter I was writing Mary, to be mailed at Seymour Island. I added a few lines each day to it. It grew as my dreams and desires to be with her grew.

At times Mary seemed an unconquerable distance away. Soon it would be two months since I sailed from Panama. At such a rate it would take a year to get to Australia. According to my original timetable I should have been at least half across the Pacific. I would have to hurry now to outrun the hurricane season. Each day the prospect of constant trade winds pushing from behind became a brighter encouragement. Each day I found myself a little nearer them. Each day I sloughed off a few dragging miles.

With the noon sight of July 15, I pin-pointed myself at 1° south latitude and 85° west longitude; roughly 300 miles from the Galápagos. I hauled around to a course slightly south of west. From now on each day's sailing counted for the maximum. At last I was making a steady course of west. *Pagan* became a happy boat. The logbook, nearly two-thirds filled, had its first optimistic entry "12:15 P.M. Turned finally west. I can smell the southeast trades!"

The cold Humboldt Current, diverted westward by Cape Pariñas on the South American western bulge, was now helping me along. The wind had shifted into the south; a fairer face was on the sea; and a set of comfortable circumstances set in that were almost mystic in their wondrousness.

After a month of beating back and forth to a destination that lay dead to windward, such sailing as this smacked of peculiarity. But I was making time, I was killing distance, it was wonderful. Three hundred miles on the bow lay the Galápagos, athwart the equator. For the first time I eased sheets a bit, watched the life line straighten out astern in the frothy wake, and sailed as one reads it is done in books and yachting magazines.

For the next few days, I felt not a squall; not a drop of rain; not a disordered cloud. It was so unearthly serene that the cats and I bedded down under the stars in the cockpit. Even lazy old Gawky roosted out with us. He had his special position on the lashed tiller, and we rode so smoothly over a halcyon sea that not even he could fall off a perch. We gave Stowaway the cabin to himself.

In the fleet time before sighting my first land, I hastened to finish the long letter I was writing to Mary. By this time it had grown to sixty-two pages on both sides. In it was every warm thought a young man could crowd, who was in process of transit to his love, as I was. It took every bit of sixty-two pages to say what I felt. . . .

I planned to mail it at Seymour Island, a fistlike outjutting on the north end of Indefatigable, where an army weather station was located. I intended to stop only a day or two — long enough to check over the gear, and have a night or two of soft sleep; then push off.

The last 300 miles to the Enchanted Isles I reeled off in less than four days. On the forenoon of July 19, Chatham Island reared herself above the sea as a dark shadow, one point on the port bow. The first landfall; the first leg of the trip over; 1000 miles of sea behind me; 7500 miles yet to go.

CHAPTER XII   Unenchanted Isles!

ON A SUNNY AFTERNOON, I stood atop the deckhouse, leaning against the mast and peering at the northern tip of Chatham Island on the eastern rim of the Galápagos group. On Chatham lies Wreck Bay, the anchorage of the seat of the government. Ecuador owns the archipelago — the Enchanted Isles, as they are known. But I wasn't making official calls. My desire originally had been to pull straight for Seymour; and at the Army Base give *Pagan* the once-over posthaste, store a few fresh supplies, and pass on my way. But the calms, the storms, the adverse currents, the loss of my engine had thrown my timetable off, and now, arriving in the Galápagos after July first, there was no Army Base to go to. According to my information it was to be moved out by July first. However, I could see no loss in going to the site on the off-chance that the move had not yet been made.

The wind was holding at south; but it had toned in strength. My interest was taken mainly with ascertaining my set to northward by the strong current sweeping up from southward. I watched the north tip of the island, and saw it, as I suspected, shifting to south of me.

I shifted the angle of rudder, turning the bow to southward, and set myself for a broad reach that would stem me into sight of Seymour late at night — and assure me of an early morning arrival. I passed Chatham before dusk. I noticed that my driftage to northward had been considerable despite course corrections. I reset the straining tiller and went below to read.

I had a few pages to go with the "Paradise" of the *Divine Comedy*, so I wandered a few hours among pleasant words, peering out occasionally into the black. At nine I ended the mystic tale and went on deck to ponder its soul-stirring aspects. I found that the wind had petered out and *Pagan* was jolting in a confused sea. The sails were slatting and the running gear was banging as the disjointed rollers jostled her. "Bolts and shackles," a calm.

All through the night the flat air held, and the sea slapped and smacked along the bilges. I had no idea with what speed I was drifting north. Some places on the chart showed two knots; others three. There was no certainty. The chart was an issue of the British Admiralty — of excellent artisanship — but it was old, the only thing available on the Galápagos. I conjectured all the night on what my position was, on how long I had been drifting. North of my track somewhere were three small islands: Tower — Marchena — Pinta. According to the chart they were barren, waterless, seared lava. I cupped my hands to my ears, listening for the pounding of seas on rock face.

Deep in the night the sky clouded over and there were no more stellar reflections in the black water. Darkness closed down over me like a fog, and I began listening more intently. Another hour dragged past — several times I thought I heard something. Finally I shipped *Pagan's* ungainly oars, fitted them into their rowlocks on the gunwale, seated myself in the cockpit . . . and waited. *Pagan,* because of her shallow draft and low tonnage, was movable under oars; in fact, to a degree she was maneuverable. An eerie silence pervaded everything, not a whisper escaped that massive pond of reflecting water. I placed the cats beside me in their abandonship box I had built them after Malpelo. It floated. In it were provisions to do them till they could reach land. We listened with ears strained to north.

Much later a puff of wind stirred out of the southwest for a few unsteady minutes. It fell to a void before I could trim the sails. Left again alone with my imagination and the dark night, I fell into a series of wild speculations. That wind from the southwest — what did that mean? Where had the wind sat when I was reading? From the southwest? I couldn't remember having looked at the compass once during the time of reading. The lethargy of the past three days had led me to trust the wind in the south. Had it shifted? Had I actually been sailing northwest when I had thought I was sailing west?

I sat another hour, quieter than I had sat for days.

Hardly an hour later I was startled awake, by the unmistakable thunder of seas on a closed shore. I made the sound dead to west of north; about two miles off, as I could reckon. It was the din of water breaking against solid cliffs. I bent to the ungainly oars and brought *Pagan's* bow off to the east and labored her into the black night. In a short while the roar had grown considerably.

The air was dead. *Pagan's* sails slatted from side to side on each light swell, popping with a maddening persistence. Blocks rattled, sheets dragged in the sea and tossed water indiscriminately across the decks.

I was thinking of the day at Malpelo, and wishing I had a fine gale on now.

The first streaks of the new day were overdue. So I leaned more heavily on the oars. Hard by to starboard, a ragged, towering shadow was making up. At its base a gray surf was surging to and fro like heartbeats.

I could faintly observe a clear alley of escape in the weakening dark, around a hump in a bulge on the eastern coast. I pulled to clear the stomach of rock and at daylight I sat fascinated, as barely two boat lengths away the escarpment, breasting the seas rolling out of the windy south, moved away. Fore and aft, the full length of the island, great beetling cliffs, underwashed by the bristling sea, glowered on me.

My chart showed that it was Marchena Island, cliff-bound and unreceptive. I was nudging along with the current. So far as I could tell, all ahead was clear. A little to the north was Pinta, as yet not in view — small and easily avoided, according to the chart. I had only to drift around the northern tip and await a wind.

Overhead the sky had become a grizzly curtain, the sea was as smooth as a dance floor. With daylight I expected wind; but as late as when the sun first showed I was still in a void. Shortly afterward, I drifted off the low end of Marchena, only to find Pinta, twelve miles distant, lying more or less in my track. The peculiar thing was that I couldn't decide whether she was astride my path or not. One moment it appeared so, and the next it was questionable. The bowsprit, along which I was attempting to sight the island, was circling like a nervous finger.

I presently concluded that whether Pinta was in my line of

drift or not, I should start rowing. The current was shifting me toward the little isle at two knots or better.

On her southern end was an active volcano at the water's edge. It rose a hundred feet and from its blunt summit a broad column of thin smoke hung in the dour air. Its base lay in the sea; and I somehow felt that the water would be hot there. Beside it lay a shingled beach which ran onto a parched hill topped by another crater. The land everywhere had a naked, withered look. I thought of the word "dry" as I looked up the hostile slopes. Here and there was a cactuslike growth, seared gray-brown bushes, and stumpy, hungry-looking trees. Totally uninviting!

I started the rowing when I was yet a long way off, but soon wished I had started earlier. I was rowing to west because I felt it would succeed more easily than fighting the current east. There was easily eight miles of rowing to do, so I spent the first few hours at regulated long stroking. At first I judged that I would easily clear the island, and doubtless lost much valuable time when I relaxed to half-stroke.

As I drifted closer I saw a pack of seals sporting in the water. When they saw me, they stopped, with eyes showing above the water, staring from their shiny heads, looking first like boulders, then like apparitions.

One, not suspecting my dire straits, came up to offer friendship. He swam in unusually close, often ducking under the oars. I am sure we would have become great pals if I hadn't been so frantically at work. I would have loved to catch him a fish and feed him by hand. And I'm sure he was all for it.

Suddenly, I found that I was closing at a quicker rate . . . an alarming rate! I was midway across the island, and no longer in the lee of Marchena; the full current had gripped me and was thrusting me as if I were in a millrace.

Though I was clear of the volcano, I could feel its hot breath and sense its hostility. I rowed the faster, not looking up, till my arms cramped.

I looked up to gauge my progress and what I saw actually refreshed me with the terror it held. I was less than a hundred yards offshore and it was easily several hundred yards to the point of the projecting land up the coast. An impossible contest. I stroked with such wild haste that, dipping short, I missed the water altogether and flopped heels skyward onto the hatchway step. The oars went flying beamward, out of reach.

I thought of plunging in to retrieve them, but on hearing the lapping of water licking over rocks I knew it would be in vain. There were still three oars in the cabin. My first thought was to break them out; before going down I took a look, and prospects looked so grim I didn't bother to go below.

Ordinarily I'm not one to give up, but what I saw made me quit thinking of trying to save my boat. I was seventy-five yards from the pockmarked wall of lava, and hundreds of yards from the point. There was nothing to anchor on; nothing I could do. I gave up. I had to save myself.

I strained my faculties for the next thing to do. The cats. They were in their floating box; I tossed them into the rubber raft and pushed it off the rail. I made ready to cast it adrift and climb in.

Land was less than a hundred feet away. The sea was washing against it with subdued thuds, but with force nevertheless.

I stared quickly about for the last thing to do. I thought of water, food, clothes. But I thought of the fight back upcurrent with small oars to the shingled beach, and the need for an immediate start.

Then, for some unknown reason, but most likely because I was grasping for last threads, I raced to the bow and plopped my rustic anchor into the placid water. Bubbles trailed it where it plunged. It ran to its chain's end. The chain hung up and down in water empty of a chance ledge. There was nothing for the anchor to snag against. I turned to run to my raft to make away while there was still time. Then a darkening line showed on the water, ruffling it and closing in on the port beam. I hardly had time to grab the tiller before a squall raced aboard *Pagan*, enclosing her sails in shrieking arms, pressing them flat, whipping them with a faint rain.

Pagan heeled sharply to the flurry. I whooped and hollered exultantly as she worked off the now roaring shore and bit into sea room. In a scant twenty minutes — well clear of the scorched land — I rounded up to the wind and dropped the mainsail. Before tying in a reef, I pulled the pneumatic raft to the counter and handed out my despondent cats. They strode stiffly below, disclaiming for the moment the sea and its abruptnesses. I massaged them briskly in a fuzzy towel and folded them into an army blanket. To smooth their outraged humors, I took my pole to the deck and cast a singing, well-baited line off the quarter.

Gawky returned to the cabin top after having deserted us in our moment of peril. I shoved him below, out of the weather.

I made the course southwesterly, to clear the threat of other northerly island groups. I forgot about Seymour since it was back to southeast, and pointed for Albemarle, the largest and westernmost island in the group. It was my intention to make for the leeward side of the great sprawling island to rest and collect myself, but mostly to sink into restful sleep for the night.

The wind was stout and *Pagan* stemmed the tide ideally, for now we were heading south fighting the current. At dusk I noticed a gray wash of sea along an extended ledge off the north of Albemarle. It jutted out a good mile. There is nothing more frightful to a seaman than shallow reefs kicking up a growling surf.

Halfway along the ledge I could make out the cold-looking bones of what looked to be two wrecked vessels. In a foot or two of water they sat, lonely and stark, awash and helpless. They were evidently incautious fishermen who had rounded the point too sharply, or had been swept there by the current, or by one of the frequent tidal waves native to the Galápagos. I gave the whole cape healthy clearance.

The sight of the tortured hulks made me jittery. I decided not to pull into the lee of the cliffs and anchor — instead to shape a course down the northwestern shore, tack around the western point, and beat into Tagus Cove, probably on the morrow.

By now *Pagan* was much fouled on the bottom with shellfish. I was wishing I had some high tides and sandy beaches as in the Perlas. I needed to careen her a tide or so, to scrape her and paint her. I thought of returning round to Seymour where the Army might be. But I chased the thought away because of the wrecks on the point. Too, I was afraid some unavoidable delay might crop up which would jeopardize the safety of my trip. Seymour wasn't a necessity, so I decided against going there.

Floreana Island was about a hundred miles distant. I thought seriously of going there to do the hull work. The chart accredited her with a beach and sandy shore; also, there is a postbox there. In that way I could kill two birds with one stone, by doing the hull and mailing the ponderous letter I had written to Mary. Besides, doing the work alone, I could be done all the quicker and be sooner on my way.

Post Office Bay at Floreana, I had learned in Panama, is an ancient mailing station. It was created by whaling ships of old, outward bound to their hunting waters. In passing they dropped off letters to folks at home — at the same time procuring fresh water and fruits and vegetables as well as the great land tortoises (*galápagos*) for fresh meat.

If another ship happened in on the way home, she obligingly picked up and delivered the mail found staked on the beach in an old box. Today a barrel stands there. Occasionally, even now, a northeastern-bound fisherman, or in fact anyone clearing the island for the mainland, cleans it out and deposits the load in a post office in Panama or San Diego. Amazingly enough letters posted there — whether stamped or not — have been known to arrive as addressed . . . in time.

After a night of intermittent naps, and steering mostly by guess, I wound up at daybreak negotiating the strait between Narborough Island and Tagus Cove. I passed into the embayment and rounded up for the anchorage. An hour later I went below for a "nap." I slept the day out and all that night.

Post Office Bay

I FOUND TAGUS COVE an unusually snug protection — in fact ideal, except that there were no means to do the hull work. Not that *Pagan* was direly in need of it. But since I was planning a nonstop run to Sydney, I felt I wanted her clean before setting forth.

To the west of me lay more than 7000 miles of ocean. There were a little over two months before the hurricane season would set in. If I was to cross these waters in safe time, there could be no stop enroute. Therefore I esteemed it a saving in time to do the cleaning here, where I had a sufficient tide, and safe harbor such as Post Office Bay. And I could get Mary's letter, in a manner of speaking, "on its way" by the antiquated postal system. So I resolved to beat around to Floreana the next day. But first I wanted to check the standing and running gear thoroughly.

I rigged a bosun's chair to the main halyard and hoisted myself aloft. By midafternoon I had painted the thirty-five-foot mast and tightened the screws in her slide. In addition I had renewed all halyards, put up a new shroud, and painted the boom. I overhauled my main boom blocks and greased their reluctant shafts. I shifted the traveler and tried to fit it more securely, but to no avail. It had never been the same since the shark had torn it out, but it was serviceable.

By evening all was shipshape, not counting the hull and a few bits and pieces I could perform in my "off watch" hours at sea. The jaunty little cutter was straining at her tether, longing for a less peaceful element.

I had managed my time through the day with such circumspection as to even include catching a mess of fish for the cats and Gawky between chores. Gawky was getting so spoiled that he refused to go out and forage any more. But while we were anchored in the circular cove he flew out for a constitutional among the towering ledges, leaving the decks safe for Flotsam and Jetsam.

My cats, gorged and thoroughly at peace in dreams, lay curled in the folds of the mainsail. Occasionally they bestirred themselves and waddled back to their "pottie pot," a sandbox I had built for them on the fantail. After, they would saunter, as though accidentally, upon the fish, and in a manner of saying, "Oh well, there's nothing else to do," they would gnaw languidly on each of the two varieties.

After this came experiments in luxurious ways of sleeping: they sprawled on the warm decks; they relaxed in the shade of the rail; or they wandered below to the cool of the forepeak. Those cats were rotten spoiled. Heaven help them if they should ever have to go back to civilized life and table scraps.

Though I wasn't on a sightseeing tour, I was completely taken with the uniqueness of Tagus Cove. Why it isn't a famous scenic spot I don't know. It is roughly a hundred boat lengths across; shored in by precipitous cliffs. In its lofty seams, queer species of birds nest themselves and echo each other in a constant chorus. The cove is really the crater of a dead volcano with its seaward wall washed out.

Tagus is lonesome and mysterious. In her clear waters swim sharks, seals, mantas, sea lions, sting rays, sailfish, eels, and penguins. Yes, penguins. I saw a pair of them — and I have since been corroborated by a fisherman who has seen them there. They were smaller than ones I have seen in Capetown and the Falklands.

They swam beneath the keel, squirming with necks stretched, after fish. They bobbed up several times but were too busy to notice the new arrival in the cove.

Another attraction of Tagus is the arrangement of names painted in various positions over her riven surface. They run into dozens and reflect the ever-constant quest of adventure, long considered dead — and erroneously. I can remember, even yet, a score of them easily. It is obviously a tradition for boats visiting the archipelago to autograph, in some peculiar spot, the challenging walls of the cove.

I had promised people in Panama I would display *Pagan's* name in bold hull white on a prominent ledge, and I set about finding an appropriate spot.

At the far end of the cove, on its northern rim, I saw a rocky platform, behind which appeared footing secure enough to wend up onto the high ledges. I climbed into my rubber raft and rowed over with the light metal oars. From the low ledge, shoaling sharply into the water, a young sea lion waddled and dived and watched me with eyes above the water in the same way people stare at foreigners. He didn't appear frightened, in fact he climbed back onto the ledge close behind me, as, bucket and brush in hand, I began the ascent into the deformed lava clefts.

Well up, I came upon a flattened space. A few feet above it was the shapeless, barren terrain of the island. Towering over and away off to my right was a great lopped-off crater apparently burned out.

Looking back through the tight walls of the crevasse, I could see my little boat fetching snugly to her makeshift anchor. Like a peanut in a washtub, she was foil to the placid blue and gnarled varicolor of the cavernous walls.

From the corner of my eye I saw a jerking movement near my feet. A jagged spiny rock rolled over. With ghostlike mysteriousness it moved. It waddled smoothly over the rocks and then stopped as if in death. A great black eye stared blankly from its head held high, a notched tongue flicked from its jagged head. Suddenly, with the quickness of a cat, it turned and spat at me from a black mouth. The black tongue flicked again. It looked like a lizard, but more like a dragon; it was easily five feet long. It was spiny along the back, gruesomely wrinkled, had fingerlike hands and a long listless tail. It perched, not moving a muscle, glaring at me.

In all my life I had seen nothing like it. I could only remember what I had heard in Panama. Someone had said that in the Galápagos were "prehistoric species of animals."

A man named Darwin had come here once and pronounced them "different." Whatever it was he said they did, they did. I believe it; I was looking at one of the results. I wouldn't have been surprised had this thing coughed fire — I would only have stumbled more clumsily than I did. For in confusion and bewilderment my step went awry and I fell all over myself; but mostly in the bucket of paint.

The very response to fear engendered fear; and I went slipping and falling down among the sharp volcanic boulders.

I nearly landed aboard the sea lion as I ran out onto the ledge; in horror he hurtled himself into the soft water. In a fury of oar stroking I was beside *Pagan* and aboard.

No sooner on deck than the cove lost its appeal. The walls looked foreboding. What a place to be alone in! Even the cats sensed my uncertainty. They squatted in fuzzy balls, jerking their whiskers nervously.

The sun was behind Narborough; the cove was becoming a shadow; it was so still it shrieked. "To the devil with this place," I said to the cats.

Then I saw it. Beneath the keel it went, a slimy, ghostlike shadow in the paling day. The same lizard or a creature similar . . . swimming! Its arms and legs were folded to its body much as you would hug yourself. It propelled itself solely with the long tail, in a wavy motion, and it slithered with the ease of a snake. That was enough for me.

I threw off the stops from the sails, hoisted them to the full, grappled the heavy anchor chain into a lump on deck, and dumped the clumsy wooden anchor atop it. As dark crowded close, I passed from the placid waters of the sinister cove to the piling whitecaps seaward. I pointed away from the mammoth volcano of Narborough, making for sea room to the south.

Dinner that night, potluck as usual, was a can of diced carrots, gulped wholesomely from the can. I ate at the tiller, steering by foot. *Pagan* danced on her tacks to southward. Within three hours, I estimated I had cleared Narborough to southward. I trimmed sails on the port tack and filled away close-hauled into the southwest on the long leg that would clear the lower western bulge of Albemarle.

The ponderous island lies like a dividing amoeba on the meridian of 91° west. I planned to tack around her in the night, so as to catch some "shut-eye" during the broad reach to Floreana the following day with tiller lashed and sails trimmed.

The morning sun, one hour high, found me well under Albemarle. Floreana, seemingly near but far away, was a gray hump forty miles on the starboard bow. I wanted to be fetched up to the anchor by dusk in Post Office Bay. There was a current to buck, and despite a nice wind it meant a day cram-full of work at the tiller, without sleep. I crowded on full sail and settled back for a day of "yachting" along the southern reaches of the Galápagos.

Late in the day, with the last of twilight to pilot myself into the quiet harbor, I rounded its northern point and opened up Post Office Bay.

This peaceful harbor is a crescent of water about a mile deep and the same width. To the left, as I came down its central road, lay a clump of islets. Ahead a sandy beach; slightly back of it an ugly disintegrating shack. A little way along resided the famous white barrel attached to a stake. Beyond the beach grew a motley array of scraggly barren bush, and the remnants of an ancient trail with which I wasn't interested.

I dropped the hook fairly close in, and rowed ashore immediately. I hastened down the beach to the parched ornamental barrel, and inserted my bulky letter to Mary. Attached to it was a five-dollar bill by a rubber band. Five dollars from my small remaining funds was a lot; but I wanted Mary to get that letter, and if five dollars would insure it — and I felt it would — then the money didn't matter. I stood by the traditional landmark for a moment wondering if the letter would ever reach Mary. Night was crowding in. *Pagan* was a blur in the water. I didn't like it ashore here any more than at Tagus.

As I rowed out to *Pagan* I was oblivious to the dismal countenance of the surroundings or the growing cold. My mind was across the Pacific. It was also with the letter in the barrel. An unholy melancholy was on me. I was swept with the futile remorse of great desire, hindered by need of lengthy patience, and burdened by uncertainty.

I went to bed early, and silenced my quarrels with circumstances by a full night's sleep, knowing that the next night would find me rushing "downhill" to westward.

Along about noon the following day my work was finished on *Pagan's* hull. She lay careened on the short beach, partially shored up by a water cask. Her shapely hull was scraped free of marine growth and coated with the last of my boot topping. The slack tide was crawling up the planking. As the keel shifted uneasily on the hard bottom, I tested my kedge, and prayed that she would hold. In a few moments my boat was borne up, and she eased away to anchorage.

I hastily hanked on the jib and cleared all lines for the one-man scramble necessary to trim *Pagan* for departure. I took one final look around at the somber anchorage and turned peremptorily to my halyards and sheets, anchor line and tiller.

Trade Winds

By dusk of July 23, I had made a good offing from Floreana. I stood due south of the cluster of lifeless cones on Albemarle. Sometime around midnight, I expected to nose free of
the westernmost point of charred lava forms and push into the
sea stretch to westward — 3000 miles of open water to my
next landfall: the Marquesas Islands.

The wind was in the south: *Pagan* slid blithely over a be-
neficent sea. The end of the Galápagos bird squadrons bent
their homeward course around the mast and swooped away
sternward. Darkness curtained off the last glimpse of the
"ash heap" I suppose I shall ever have.

The heavens cast themselves with a measles of guiding
lights. A waning moon softened the night. The ocean un-
dulated lightly, at the behest of a fresh breeze. The spill of
wind out of the sail made my skin tingle. The night was made
glorious in the thought that I was nudging into the locale of
the trade winds: that I was starting across the big ocean to
Mary. The seas ahead of me were well known for their tran-
quillity. The current, though setting to northwest for the
nonce, would soon straighten out and shove me due west, at
an average rate of 30 miles daily, free of charge. With the
wind expected to push me at a rate of 90 to 100 miles a day I

would be amassing a daily average of 130 miles — wonderful for my purpose of speed across the ocean.

That night was the most roseate of the whole voyage. A letter was on its way to Mary, explaining all. The hull was clean, and sliding blissfully through the seas. I had gaffed a great sea turtle early in the afternoon. I would have fresh meat for three days. After that I would have dried meat — sun-dried after the style of Indian jerky — for the full passage to the Marquesas. The weather was lovely. What more, excepting the presence of my wife, could I ask?

Unhappily, my bliss was to be short-lived. I had overlooked the fact that first I would have to find the trade winds. In the Eastern Pacific, the trades don't always reach as far north as the equator. They are where you find them. In between is an airless patch known as the doldrums.

Trudging across the doldrums into the trades is a sore-footed task. When you pick up a cat's-paw for a few hours, you think you're in the trades. Then suddenly the wind elopes; and the ensuing glassiness of the sea, its silence, the boat's unending clatter, run roughshod over your nerves. A slatting sail, rattling blocks, slapping halyards, slack sheets have an indescribable nuisance value. Each calm found me drifting with the current to the north.

Not once did a fresh wind curve the sails and bend *Pagan* to her work but that I felt it was at last the trades. Again and again, however, the wind died away. In a few days I found myself north of the line. The tremendous letdown of the trades was doubly exasperating since I had expected such a sterling performance from them.

My intention had been to stay close to the equator in sailing west; to avail myself of the strong westerly current near

it. Even seventy-five miles south of the line, the extra push on
the keel slacks off a dozen miles daily. Better to go south and
lose some force of current than to stay up here in constant
calms, on a heat-reflecting sea. Reconciled to the wisdom of
a steady wind rather than a stronger current, I waited on the
next wind. It came not at once and not steadily but in falter-
ing episodes. Each time, under flattened sails and a neutral
tiller, I hauled into the southwest.

With each puff of wind I added to my southing: with each
calm I drifted back north again. The doldrums played with
me as a cat devils with a mouse. Hours on end I drifted
under spars stripped to the standing rigging, unable to bare
the monotony of flapping sailcloth and clattering tackle. I
couldn't read, I couldn't nap, I couldn't think; I could only
grope with slit eyes hour on hour for a hint of wind on the
polished water.

At the onset of a stir of air I ran up every square inch
the rigging could hold and nurtured every pulse beat out
of the sky, pushed doggedly on in search of the diffident
trades.

On the afternoon of July 27, four days out of Galápagos,
irritation aboard reached its climax when Gawky, after several
weeks of languishment on *Pagan*, suddenly soared from the
deckhouse and made a bee line for the horizon to eastward.
He departed with too much energy and determination for it
to be a routine flight. I watched him to the last, to the point
where he sparkled in the white glare, then dropped below the
horizon.

That night I made a sad entry in the log.

Still three more days ground painfully on my hopes. An
occasional sky breath teased me. I sat out the days on deck,

gnawing at dried strips of the turtle and playing at patience. Then quite suddenly the wind in a summary movement jumped out of the southeast. I eased away the sheets for the very first time and caught the breeze astern and, with way on, ran down the wind. It was a pleasure to see *Pagan* actually running off before it. I put her on a course between west and west southwest so that she would make the traverse, arriving off the Marquesas in 9° south latitude.

That night I exultantly entered the momentous news in the logbook — the first happy entry in seven days.

My noon sight for August 4, the twelfth day out, put me 1010 miles offshore — a greater distance than I had traveled in the thirty days from Perlas to Galápagos. Hereafter followed 2000 miles of the pleasantest sailing I probably shall ever experience. For days on end, the boat sailed itself. The only times I came on deck were practically of necessity. *Pagan* ran off before the wind, chasing columns of wind-pushed rollers and wind-driven clouds that never varied — in short, she sailed it as "harbor circumnavigators" do it on yacht club verandas. Life those days ran on an amazingly even keel.

At sunup I always came topside to collect the night's catch of flying fish trapped on deck. During the night the prow, slicing open the water sent them skittering like quail from the wave tops and often they flew blindly into the sails and expired in the waists or on the forepeak. Never a morning but there was at least one. If more than one were found, I enjoyed fresh fish, otherwise the hungry maws of my Flotsam and Jetsam yawned.

The flying fish is delicious food. I found them bony but worth the pains incident to enjoying their soft sweet meat.

I liked them best boiled in salt water and eaten with ketchup and crackers. They were delicious fried in bacon fat, too. Many was the time, with only one fish found on deck, I regretted having my hungry kittens aboard.

Out there I had lots of time on my hands, far more than from Perlas to Galápagos. Keeping my plucky little cutter eating at the westing was routine work of a few minutes each day. With sails curving full and the tiller lashed slightly aweather, *Pagan* floated along unheeded and free at a laughing speed. Each morning and night I glanced at the compass; at some time in the day I sauntered over the sloping deck from stern to bow and back with eyes aloft, searching out a weakness that might interfere with the peace and purpose of my little Pacific world. Here too I usually found all okay. No more work till next day.

I altered the lashings on the tiller but a very few times the whole crossing. Not once did I lower sail or reef down. The only real work of the cruise was with chafing gear on the shrouds to protect the sail from wearing through. I know there is a way of using rope yarn to make chafing gear, but being a greenhorn I didn't know how it was done and I couldn't figure out how to do it, so I ripped up my two bed sheets into one-foot strippings and wrapped them around the shrouds as a sort of padded sleeve. I bound each pad with string at top and bottom and middle; then scaled the mast and slid them up the wire where the sail chafed and made them fast to the shroud itself with line again. They did me yeoman's service; my sails right to the last were as good as the day I swung round before the southeast trades.

The weather was ideal. The days were warm and fresh, bathed by sun and the purest air. The nights were cooled by the chill current under the keel. The cool of night was a sleep-inducing cool, just enough to need a blanket and clothes on deck.

I came often on deck of biological necessity. This I took care of by use of the bumkin spread. I kept a board with a sizable hole in it on the stern. When the need arrived, I laid the board on the bumkin arms and straddled it saddle style, with the sternpost for a horn.

About the only other time I came on deck was to navigate or bask in the sun, watching the dolphin at their kill, or to play with the cats. Now that Gawky was gone, they had free run of the boat. For hours they would romp over the canvas-covered decks. I would crawl along the cabin top spying on their kittenish whims and gambols.

When Flotsam and Jetsam were out on deck, I always spent time below making friends with Stowaway. He was a most reluctant fellow, and no wonder. The kittens were in constant prowl around his abode — things had come to such a pass that I was forced to place his food and drink inside his house, so seldom was it safe for him to venture forth for it.

I tried painfully to teach him to nibble from my fingers, but with the kittens aboard it was a lost hope. He was trustless: the poor fellow had gone cynical; he was disorganized; he considered friend and enemy alike, and chose to fritter away his life in isolation.

Since I was only on deck a few hours each day, the remainder devolved to whatever suited my fancy. I perused everything from crossword puzzles to Shakespeare and Mary's old letters which I always kept in my sea bag. When I tired with reading, I pieced together the same jigsaw puzzle over and over again. For fun I turned it over and did it the hard way. These days of peace and speed were dreamlike in their constancy.

I was never bored: it is impossible for a person with an active mind to be bored with his own company. The days went too quickly. I hadn't time to do all I set out to do each morning. Besides, my early days of work had forced me upon myself, and the aloneness was something I had known before.

An average day went along something like this: I awakened usually with the first graying of dawn, inspected the course from the compass beside my bunk and went on deck to check the tiller and sails and to look for flying fish that might have landed aboard in the night. If there were two fish — and nearly always there were — I gave one to the kittens in the morning and one in the afternoon. If more than two, it meant fresh provisions for breakfast — either fried in bacon fat or boiled in salt water.

Invariably breakfast consisted of a cooked cereal. I mixed about six parts of fresh water with one of salt, boiled it on the Primus, and stirred in the cereal — corn meal, oatmeal, and such — with a heaping spoon each of powdered milk and sugar. I ate most of my meals out in the cockpit in the wash of the tropic air.

I whiled the morning at reading, at playing with my crew, at coaxing my hopeless passenger, or at watching the death chases out ahead of the bows.

Lunch was the simplest meal of the day. It was only a matter of marking an X on the stores list, then selecting a likely-looking can from the former icebox. The thing I liked about the noon meal was the surprises I often got when I opened the wrapperless cans.

In the early afternoon I napped; in midafternoon I took a sun sight and pin-pointed myself on the chart; in late afternoon I sat on the cabin peering around the sea rim in hope of a smudge of smoke or a sail. Or I sat watching the lonely, impersonal sea birds who glide their lives away over the barren Pacific wastes.

My night meal was a warm one. I fried a slice of bacon or ham and heated something from a can. There was always a pot of coffee or tea with which to wash down a couple of hard sea biscuits. Often I made a kind of stew with leftovers and a bit of salt pork or fish.

In the evening, after checking the set of the sails, and the lashed tiller, I lay on my bunk to read for an hour in the dim light of my barn lantern swaying from the overhead. When I tired, I merely pulled up the blanket and blew the lantern out. I didn't have to undress for bed; I didn't wear clothes in the tropics.

But one day I was jostled from my settled world. I found during my daily inspection that the bobstay had loosened at the stem and that the chain was dragging free from the end of the bowsprit. It was a job of the type a novice knows nothing about, but which cries out to be mended. I looked it over and started repairs with my usual trial-and-error methods. I lowered myself into the water and fidgeted and tinkered, trying to join the connections of stay and stemhead, while the rollers of the trade winds skewed me from side to side of the bow. In two hours of futile fidgeting and cursing under water, I decided to give it up.

But it was a thing one couldn't give up. The bobstay bolstered the bowsprit; it in turn supported the topmast stay; which in turn secured the mast against rearing backward and snapping off. I couldn't hazard being dismasted out on these lonely wastes. So back to work I went. It turned out to be a job more distasteful than shoveling fertilizer. Need is a harsh driver. The need to repair this impediment drove me to a merry ride, hanging onto the bowsprit and clinging to the stemhead. But working under water on the dancing object was worse. Eventually I got the ringbolt fitted into the cutter's stem . . . and dragged myself over the rail.

The jib rattled up the head stay; other sails were soon atrim and curved to the wind, and with laughing heels *Pagan* tore away to the blank horizon.

There then followed more days of peaceful sailing. *Pagan* scudded on before the southeast trades, with hardly a variation in wind and sea. Ahead, shoals of flying fish sprinted from the sea and floated away to port and starboard, slipping into the wave tops one at a time, or en masse like bird shot. And what masses of flying fish they were. I was amazed as every hundred yards, day on day, a gleaming squadron of them flashed into the sun and glided horizonward in a dozen directions.

Harassing them from dusk to dusk was Old Death and his lesser dolphin, who prowled ahead of the bow and streaked into the unsuspecting schools. For two thousand miles now, I had watched this game of stalking and hunting: a vicious circle of dog-eat-dog, among the creatures under the sea. The dolphin has a blunt, stolid face trailed by a beautifully lithe body. Along his back lies a weblike fin which ordinarily lies flat but which he flares into use in the hairpin maneuvers employed against the flying fish.

I have sat on deck hours on end watching these fascinating creatures give the flying fish the chase. Singling out a lone flyer, the dolphin will stay on his tail for five hundred yards before giving up. As the flying fish clears the water in mortal haste, his apt enemy is just behind and below. The stalk is on — a stalk of speed and thrills where a single slowing or stopping by the flying fish means death. Occasionally the dolphin sails free of the water for a twenty-foot leap to see his victim.

Spotting his game ahead in the air he returns to his element and with a few powerful thrusts rides up under him, eying him, waiting for the drop into the water. As the flying fish falls from his glide, he is set upon, and there ensues a terrifying encounter of champing teeth, flaring fins, swirling wakes, and the dolphin comes away grinning.

I have seen this tragic episode a hundred times, and only a dozen feet away. Once I saw a flying fish nipped neatly in half by Old Death. In a flash it was done — in fact with such suddenness that the fish didn't suspect what had happened. Another dolphin took him in on the run before the poor flying fish had time to realize he was already half eaten.

Once, a huge squid bolted from the water off aport and glided a hundred feet in toward *Pagan*. On plunging he espied a grim assassin close behind and threw himself, horror-stricken, twenty feet straight up into the air. The dolphin spun around and with a terrific thrust hurtled himself up out of the water. They met in mid-air: the dolphin shooting up, the squid falling. The shock of impact nearly choked the dolphin. What was left of the squid fell thirty feet away, and was gobbled up by another dolphin as it hit the surface.

Another time one of the largest flying fish I have seen, and judging his size a veteran of many a fracas with death, soared out of a wave far ahead. I watched him soar on the wind, making a clean half circle that only the wariest pursuant could follow. He slowed himself in mid-air and made to plop into an oncoming sea. What he didn't know was that he was followed: not by one, but by four dolphin, shouldering one another aside for the choice lead spot.

He settled lightly in the water. There was a rush, a flurry of fins and flukes, the chop and smack of spiny teeth, then confusion so great that it seemed the dolphin themselves didn't know which one had snared the prize.

Another day a shoal of flying fish were flushed very near the bow. As the dolphin streaked among them in their berserker way the flying fish literally went crazy. Some of them leaped straight up only to fall straight back. Others, in their terror, only stumbled along the surface, unable to break into flight. One small squadron bolted off the water straight into *Pagan's* sails. Twelve of them. Old Death and his crew often helped me out like this.

One day Old Death ran short into a small flying fish. They met face to face, then the chase of death began. I could see them from where I stood on the cabin peering into the air-clear water. The little fish skittered to his wings and soared in toward *Pagan's* beam. The gnarled old killer flashed in pursuit. He lunged into the air and struck the fish as he sailed, upsetting him, tumbling him into the sea. A scrimmage for life ensued, and the little fish got somehow into the air again. Old Death, in a rage, was close behind. Suddenly the flying fish saw he was gliding straight into *Pagan* on the beam. He wavered in flight. Beneath him was the inexorable hunter, ahead *Pagan's* hard, dry decks. He could have dropped to the water and jockeyed for a new take-off — but he didn't. He knew the outcome. I am sure the decision was his to smash his head against the cabin and drop quivering to the deck.

Not a day passed but that a number of such deathly encounters occurred an eye distance away.

On numerous occasions, when an overwhelming desire for a change from flying fish obsessed me, I sought to harpoon the dolphins; but I landed only three of them the whole trip. They are explosive energy keyed to high sensitivity. Hardly does a spear near them when they thrash away. I speared Old Death at least ten times. Each thrust into his ancient sides proved only another tattered scar, and didn't diminish his love of *Pagan's* company a jot. He followed me to the very reef where I nearly drowned.

Those of the dolphin I speared I cut into strips and dried on strings tied between deckhouse and traveler. The meat kept indefinitely if redried often enough. I alternated this with my decreasing supply of turtle, which too I had to keep drying over and over again.

During this time, about a week out of the Marquesas, I fell often in reverie . . . with the past . . . the future . . . the present. I reacted on the immensity of watery wastes by seeking an escape through thinking. Long hours out there lent themselves to retrospect and iteration. I fell to thinking of the days of crowded happiness of my romance with Mary, our courtship, our marriage. The whole panorama of unfortunate circumstances that had kept us apart but which I was now overcoming in crossing the Pacific.

I sat on the cabin, lounging under the sun and breeze, listening to the slap and smack of water against the planking, and watching the ripple thrown out by the bow. Sitting so, it was easy to think. Thoughts came uncalled for. What I thought wasn't important, but the fact that I thought was vastly important.

The morning of August 18 found me an estimated three days out of the Marquesas. My ninety-page logbook was nearly filled — I was eighty-five days out of Panama and this was just five days from the day I had expected to arrive in Sydney when I sailed. Mary was expecting me. I hoped my letter from the Galápagos had reached her telling of the upset to my timetable and explaining the new arrival date.

My sights at noon of August 20 estimated my position at 9°5′ south latitude, 138°50′ west longitude. The Marquesas were hard by. I climbed the mast often and swept every horizon for an object grayer than the clouds and stiller than the rearing seas. By nightfall land hadn't hove in sight. There were plenty of land birds around: bosun birds, gannets, gooneys, man-o'-war birds, terns. I was certain that not too far south of me was the lush tropical island of Hiva Oa I had heard spoken of in Panama. And somewhere near, probably just under the horizon on the starboard bow, was Ua Huka, and just to westward, Nuku Hiva.

That night I came on deck often to sweep the frail horizon to starboard for land and listen for the hollow boom of trade-wind seas on coral reefs. I neither saw nor heard anything, but I knew it was there.

Daylight found me under the shadow of land to the north . . . land after twenty-nine days.

CHAPTER XV   Devilfish

THE FLAT GREEN ISLAND near by to starboard was Nuku
Hiva. Back on the starboard quarter was the graying dome of
Ua Huka and distantly visible on the port beam was Ua Pou.
Nuku Hiva is the main island and port of entry for the
French-governed Marquesas Islands. I stood about two miles
south of Sail Rock on her southeast point. The wind- and
sea-laved rock was white with the foam of relentless rollers
advancing before the seasonal trades. Behind it, and blending
with it, was Cape Martin.

On Nuka Hiva's southern shore you find three excellent
harbors, Comptroller Bay, Taio Hae Bay, and Tai Oa Bay.
I idled along the coast at a wistful distance and peered into
each inviting anchorage. In my lap lay spread the chart of the
island. I explored each part I passed. I was nearly tempted to
steer into one of them.

Taio Hae from the sea is dark green, seamed with cool valleys and topped by a benevolent cloud, a valley as soothing as
fresh linen. But I wasn't on a sightseeing trip, I had no visa,
and I had no clearance papers for the port. My exchequer was
down to twenty dollars, and I had no way of knowing, if I
did go in, if I had enough money to get out.

But most important of all, I couldn't afford the time. Hurricane weather would be setting in on the Tasman Sea in less

than six weeks, and I had to be in Sydney before then. It meant hard sailing: there were more than 4000 miles of sea yet to cross. Furthermore, *Pagan* was in need of nothing. Food I had aplenty and there was three months' water supply on board.

Morale of passengers, crew, and escort was high, especially so since I was nearing 145° west longitude, the halfway mark to Sydney. Flotsam and Jetsam were thriving on the life. Stowaway, though I seldom saw him, was in fine fettle. Old Death and his mob, despite the fact that they had lost three of their number on the traverse, didn't appear to be affected by 3000 miles of day and night swimming at five knots. The whole gang was with me to a man: "Sail on," they said. So I glided along the southern extremity of the famous island that has figured so strongly in romantic literature and the lives of adventurous men in the South Seas.

Later the same day I wished I had gone into one of the quiet embayments. The mainsail halyard suddenly parted, chafed through at the peak block, and I found myself with the nastiest repair job known to the seaman, which is to say, scaling the mast to tie a splice into the becket. Throughout the voyage I had dreaded the onset of such a task. To this end I had replaced all halyards before leaving Galápagos, hoping they would last out the voyage to Sydney. The hard usage of the trades had worn the weak sisal rope through where it rode in the block.

Such a repair on the smooth waters of a basin is one thing, but in the unceasing seaway of the southeast trades it is decidedly another.

I got no farther than the hounds before I realized that what I was doing was impossible in the nude. I slid back down the swaying pole, minus a few minor chunks of flesh and smarting where I had met the mast and shrouds. I donned trousers and shirt and commenced the exhausting climb again.

This time I got well into the rigging before I encountered serious difficulties. Hanging on was a superenergetic job. I was puffing before I reached the first set of hounds. I had both legs and one arm locked tightly about the mast. With my free hand I cut away the old halyard at the becket, and barely managed to reeve the new line into the block, when I became aware that no matter how desperately I clung, I was being torn from my grip. I pulled the line through the sheave. My strength, in the maximum effort demanded to clutch the lurching spar, was deserting fast. I could hang on, I knew, only a few seconds at most. My holds were slipping, I was going.

I expected I would fall from the swinging spar and crash on the deck. The next land down wind was hundreds of miles.

It would be impossible in that sea to pass the line through the main peak block and splice it then to the becket on the topmast block. I could only hope to get safely out of the mess I had got myself into.

I made a movement to glide to deck thirty-five feet below. My leg unwound from its hold and was flung sharply away from the mast. I was thrown out of balance. My other leg followed. I was tossed against the shroud and against the mast. I could neither hold on nor work my way down without plummeting to the deck.

Below me *Pagan* looked like a canoe. Her headsails were

bellied to the wind. Each roller that passed under her counter pitched her steeply and rolled her to the rail. Up here I was looking down on first one side of *Pagan's* decks and then the other.

Unable to hold longer, I cast loose and kicked away as best I could. I fell as little boys fall from trees: completely out of control, legs kicking, arms flying. But I landed on the hard water — how it happened I don't know. Until the moment I sucked water into my lungs, I thought I had struck the rail.

I clambered on deck and lay atop the deckhouse gasping for breath.

It was evident I couldn't splice the halyard into the becket. I gave up the use of a peak block altogether and used the single purchase with one block. When I was rested, I hooked the sail on and pulled it up. It was harder to handle but it worked. *Pagan* was under full sail and showing her heels to the Marquesas.

Noon had gone. The islands were still in sight. I was resting and smarting from my labors on the mast. *Pagan* was doing her work nicely; she was shaping slightly south of west. The afternoon was passing like any other, except that I was enervated from the morning's exertions. I was sitting in the cockpit with the kittens purring their pleasant way, asleep in my lap. Slightly abaft the beam and about a hundred yards out the sea surface rippled, then it rippled again.

I stood up and watched, expecting to see a school of porpoise. The splashes and eddies drew near. Then, breaking water near by, and gliding smoothly beneath the keel, came a giant devilfish. He approached *Pagan* as though he hadn't seen her, and when he passed, he turned and slipped deliberately back, coming close enough to touch the planking, eying me with black protruding eyes. His head was the end part of a slightly humped and heavy body. His mouth was a black hole and either side of it were short armlike growths that he used, I suppose, to cram his victims into his black maw. The wide meaty wings moved with rippling motions, thrusting the tons of his weight along by the merest movements. Trailing behind him, like a life line, was a short thin tail.

The sea bat moves in utter disdain of whatever passes near him. He is remorseless in his power; confident as a peacock; more arrogant than a shark.

I wondered, as I watched him coast along, if I dared challenge him. And I did dare, because I knew that if I was careful the advantage was mine. With the experience I had gained from the shark near the Perlas, I felt I could outpoint his great weight and strength. It was simply a matter of hooking him and letting him play himself out — then I could pull him in close to the side and examine him at close quarters. This was another thing I had often dreamed of doing from merchant ships.

The size of him would necessitate a heavy line; the life line from the mainsheet traveler would do. I pulled it in and bent to it twenty feet of steel wire. I worked hastily, keeping my eyes on the huge fish as he boldly slithered beneath the keel and treaded water on the port quarter. On the end of the wire I spliced my two heavy shark hooks and baited them with a large bluefish I had caught in the morning.

This tidbit I dropped practically in the big brute's lap as he sauntered by. He deployed himself for a moment to consider it; then, with a great thrust of his batlike wings, fell on it in a rush. At the same moment, and with the same motion with which he took the lure, he plunged. I watched the line go down and come taut with such violence that the stern was pooped, and ran about three inches of water.

I watched the quiver of *Pagan's* stern and the stress against the line. I was ready with my knife to cut it away at the traveler if the strain against it threatened destruction. My idea in hooking him so was that the short line with *Pagan's* heaviness at the end would all the sooner wear him down. I was eager to finish him off and drag him to the stern where I could hack his jawbone out and add it to the shark's for Mary to see.

The line slacked for a moment, then tautened to the port side with a force that veered *Pagan* three points off course. I went sprawling into the cockpit. By main force, my boat had been stopped in her fix. She was making no headway. She merely strained where she sat. Her stern was pulled around till the wind was threatening to jibe the sail. I bounced to my feet with a decision to cut the line.

Pagan was being jerked about at will. I stepped out of the cockpit, wondering what next. As though a mule had kicked me between the shoulders, I went tossing headlong onto the lazarette. *Pagan's* decks trembled as she was jerked off course. The terror of thought gripped me; my body went cold; everything stopped. I scrambled to the stern, groping with my knife.

I heard the splintering of wood. I looked up to see the traveler being ripped away on the starboard side. It was made fast to both deck and rail by heavy screws, and yet it went as though it were tacked on. It twisted upward at a grotesque angle and bent farther as the line tightened. The strain was beginning to splinter it loose from the port rail.

I rushed to cut away the line. Something swooshed over my head. *Pagan* shivered mightily as she jibed and rounded up on the other tack; she was a half circle off course.

I looked at the sea and saw the devilfish was off the starboard quarter. He was on the surface and in his rage he was lathering the sea to a froth. His great wing tips were cleaving the surface, threshing like a wounded bird. *Pagan* was bouncing like a rowboat in a bad chop. The full weight of pull was now on the traveler where it connected to the port rail. It was now or never. I touched the taut line with the knife blade. The line snapped, unraveled, and flew at me.

There was only a swirl on the sloping wall of an onrolling wave where the devilfish had sounded into the tippled depths. *Pagan*, free of the restraint, quickly picked up speed.

I dropped the main immediately and pitched in to repair the twisted traveler and the splintered rail.

What a day it had been. As soon as the repairs were made, I was glad to get sail on, lash the tiller alee, and hit the sack, too tired to enter the day's events in the log.

∽   ∽   ∽

The next afternoon Flotsam and Jetsam added a merry note to what had been a dull day. This was one of the few days that there hadn't been a flying fish on deck for them. Also my trawling had been to no avail. My potluck meals had netted me a can of spinach for breakfast and pineapple juice with a can of corn for lunch, not a suitable substitute for catnip.

By one in the afternoon, I still hadn't caught them a fish. I was on deck pondering just what to do in such a weighty predicament. A rule of the sea reads that one's sailors should eat sufficiently. Besides, morale demanded it. My crew was on the verge of mutiny. I heard a growling and scuffling unlike anything my charges had ever engaged in before. I jumped through the companionway, whence came the fracas.

There, under the forepeak, in a deathly encounter, grappled Flotsam and Jetsam — claw and fang into our passenger Stowaway. Stowaway heaved with kickings and twistings. My young lions, with claws bared and teeth dripping, jockeyed for better bite holds. Taking each of my grim starvelings by the tail, I spread them from the would-be feast. Stowaway, bruised and minus a few patches of fur, darted to his refuge.

Flotsam and Jetsam became highly indignant that they had been denied the passenger as fresh rations, and slunk into the forepeak to continue the toothsome search.

I could feel their hurts deeply, and I wanted to do right by them. So I searched among my stores of unlabeled cans for sign of a tin of fish. The cans in the lockers and in the icebox — some twenty cans in number — gave no hint that they contained fish.

According to my stores list I had 86 cans of food stored beneath the starboard bunk. To this point, I had eaten 139 of my original 248 tins of food. When I looked, I saw a sight to set one's nerves on edge. Something was wrong. I could tell it instantly.

I had known all along that it was damp in the tight space beneath the bunk, but I had no idea that in so short a time the dampness would infiltrate into the cans. I examined each swollen, seeping tin and found all of them puffed with gas and fermented soppy liquid. Not one of the whole storage was eatable. They had putrefied to a can.

Almost I decided to put about and try to gain back against sea and current to the Marquesas. Quickly I checked through the remainder of my stores. Thus far on the trip I had devoured over half my staples. The ham, bacon, salt pork, sugar, corn meal, peaches, prunes, and cheese were gone. Of the remaining staples — oatmeal, rice, oleomargarine, hominy grits, flour, jam, and honey — there was anywhere from one fourth to three quarters of a jug of each left. I counted 150 sea biscuits, a quart of dried apples, a gallon can of ketchup, a quart of peanut butter, plenty of tea and coffee and 23 cans of food. A check on my water supply showed just under 50 gallons aboard.

Since the bulk of my food stores had been centered in the canned goods, the loss suffered under the bunk had hurt. However, on paper I shortly estimated that it was possible to extract 107 meals from the remaining supplies. I also estimated that with forty days of hard sailing I could finish off the trip to Sydney. It had to be this way: in only a month hurricane weather was due. This meant that I must ration my food, cut down to two meals a day, and eat a little less at mealtime than I was accustomed to. It was that or try to win back to the Marquesas and suffer the possibility of holing up over the hurricane season. There wasn't time to turn back; I voted to go it to Sydney in one hard sail.

I was due to pass Caroline Island, a lonely volcanic and coral atoll, in a few days. My wicked intuition that all was well urged me to press on to the little isle, to stop long enough for coconuts as an addition to my larder.

It was about this time that I began to sense a subtle change in the weather pattern. I didn't worry about it because there was little effect on my timetable — but I certainly didn't like the looks of these growing changes. They argued that I speed on, that I crowd my boat to the maximum . . . that I get to Sydney as quickly as possible.

      ◞   ◞   ◞

Overhead were split-tailed tropical birds; out forward shoals of flying fish flitted briefly, and in the wake were large sharks — all sure signs of land. On the morning of August 29 the loom of land raised across the bows, "right where it should be."

With the sun's rising I made the land — Caroline Island — to be seven miles distant, and shaped a course slightly north of South Island. On the starboard bow were a number of low mounds washed heavily by the sea.

According to the *Sailing Directions,* South Island is the main point in this tiny archipelago. There are supposed to be a few natives, a lot of fish around, and water ashore. A U.S. Solar Eclipse Party had been here in 1883, it said.

I sailed *Pagan* on a bowline for the readiest approach to the anchorage: I wanted to get done what I could before dark, so I could be on my way. I pointed up into the southwest corner of the weirdly shaped island. I donned my army fatigues and shirt; pulled on shoes and socks, the first since the Perlas; combed the salt out of my beard and hair, and took the tiller.

Not mentioned in the *Sailing Directions* is an active volcano, trailing a flow of smoke like a passing steamer. I kept the smoky crest on the bowsprit and dropped my homemade anchor in front of the reef-bound harbor. It took an uncertain hold and occasionally slipped. I found I had to keep my jib and staysail backing and filling to maintain a hold. *Pagan* rode easily, lying close under the land, catching the breeze falling from the summit.

Across the reef and over the placid lagoon I could see the shore line was planted to coconut trees. The rest was dark green jungle veering up into the heights.

Soon a sail put off from what appeared to be a small wharf. It glided over the protected bay and bounced across the thundering reef and closed in, its occupants smiling gleefully. I saluted them in as friendly a style as possible and encouraged them to moor their outrigger to my halyards.

At the helm was an old man, accompanied by his aged wife, two young men, a young woman, and two devilish looking boys and a girl. They were dark-skinned, and I am sure they were apple-cheeked under their burnt faces. They were more a Polynesian type of people — tall, brown-skinned, with long straight hair, Caucasian looking — not so squat and Negroid as the peoples I had seen farther west during the war.

They didn't know how to take me; though they smiled, they held back. I motioned them aboard in as friendly and disarming a manner as possible and indicated seating room on the cabin and rail.

I saluted each barefoot visitor with a friendly, informal handshake and nod as he stepped aboard. The men were clad in loose-fitting lava-lavas tied at the waist and extending to the knees. The two little boys were naked. All the women were robed with lava-lavas which began at the chest. The clothes of all were worn looking; they showed holes and ragged edges. I had the feeling that even these had been put on for this special occasion. Isolation showed in their faces.

The old man styled himself promptly as chief. He indicated my boat with a sweep of his gnarled hand and smiled admiringly. He spoke in a type of French unlike anything I had heard in Algiers or Quebec during the war. We quickly contrived a sort of *bêche-de-mer* centered around key words such as "boat, sea, wife, man, you, me, come, go, Australia, America" and so on. He pointed out his wife, his sons and grandchildren.

The youngsters stood somewhat in awe of me, the first white man they had seen. My blond bushy beard, growing since Panama, and by now some three inches long, alarmed them. My hair by now had cropped out over my ears, was extending toward my shoulders, and was down to my eyes in front. I tried to act in such a way as to show them I was no different from other men, except that I was luckily born white and fortunate to be partly educated.

The chief glanced below decks. Seeing no one he inquired after my crew. It was difficult to explain that I was alone and the reasons for it. Somehow I put the story across; and the men especially became quite impressed, but I'm sure they didn't believe that it was all for Mary.

In their youth the chief and his wife had lived in Papeete, the main anchorage at Tahiti. The whole group had been isolated, he explained, since the beginning of the war. When I told them the war was ended, all nodded agreeably and looked pleased, but I am sure they had no idea of who was fighting.

They fitted their mood to mine and reacted as I did. If I was amused, they were amused; if I listened very gravely to something the chief said, they in turn pondered it profoundly.

The younger men, around my age I would judge, were keen about *Pagan*. They were tall, square-jawed, with lean biceps and a spot of curled hair on their wide chests. They fingered the turnbuckles at the shrouds and the Manila halyards approvingly. I brought my sextant, compass, and pocket watch out. The watch fascinated them. The whole group drew in a close circle and emitted Oohs and Aahs when I unscrewed the back of the watch and displayed the intricate workings.

As I gained their confidence much jollity ensued — even the youngsters warmed up to me. A great happiness sprung up among us, and I forgot about my shortage of food and brought out nine unlabeled cans. As I gouged them open with the now rusted can opener, amazed exclamations went around. The old chief explained proudly, however, that many times before he had dined from tins.

We enjoyed our snack taken from the open can with our fingers. I ate the can of spinach that was opened because I was afraid their tastes might not appreciate it. They smacked feelingly over corn and beans, peaches and carrots, beets and applesauce, tomato soup and asparagus. Much dipping of fingers in various cans went on. While we ate I tried to explain the reason for my rustic anchor which one of the men had spotted in the shallow ice-clear water. It was difficult to tie up the modern conveniences of my craft with its incongruous ground tackle.

At this point a near riot occurred. The two boys, shuddering and jabbering, bolted from the cockpit and stumbled against the rail, falling onto the outrigger. The little girl and the young woman leaped across the row of legs to the foredeck, shrieking distractedly. Then from out of the hatchway into the cockpit sauntered Flotsam and Jetsam, padding sleepily, blinking at the unusual crowd.

The chief was the only one of the elders to recognize them as harmless, since the others had never seen a cat. My doughty crew was soon swept up by loving arms and such cooing and gushing went on as the kittens had never heard.

I invited the party down below decks to give them a clearer picture of my boat. Nine people make a cabinful on a twenty-nine-footer! But it was pleasant to hear voices in the little house that so long had been silent except for my voice talking to myself. I was satisfied merely to sit and listen to their appraisal of the fixtures, the portholes, the tools, the lantern, the mattress, my library, and the Primus stove. I took the stove down, pumped it up and fired it for them, and let them feel its fierce blaze. Anything to keep them talking.

When the young woman evinced interest in the milk cans, I offered her the empty one and she was pleased. One of the boys scrambled out of the cabin into the outrigger and returned with a huge black fish which he plopped on the deck for me. The old chief smiled magnanimously, and told me there were more ashore. It was about this time I decided to get rid of much of the junk that for a long while had littered the cabin. First I cleaned out my clothes locker. To each of the men and boys I tossed a pair of khaki army pants and a shirt. I cleaned out my tool case of extras I could do without. I heaved three empty jeep cans into the outrigger. I dragged out the spare lumber from under my bunk and set the boys to passing it up on deck. I gave them half my fishhooks and flies.

I could see the women were disappointed that I had not offered gifts in their direction. I fished in my sea bag and brought out several tablecloths my grandmother had crocheted for Mary. I explained to the ladies that they would make good dresses. I gave them my signal flags, which I had never used, for the same purpose. I gave them two of my four sail needles and a roll of twine. And I handed each an offering from the cosmetics case I had bought for Mary, but, as sane women should be, they were more appreciative of the half dozen jars with lids I gave them.

To the kids I dished out my magazines, comic books, and the jigsaw puzzle.

They took my house cleaning as a show of generosity and a greater cordiality grew up. They became willing to talk about their life ashore. They caught their water, they explained, from rainfall off their roofs, or trapped it from streamlets on the crater. They lived on taro, mangoes, and breadfruit from the interior of the island. They also domesticated pigs and chickens and caught sea life in the lagoon. I visualized the ordinariness of the life they must lead ashore with only a small patch of land under them surrounded by a monotonous sea.

Under safe circumstances I would have gone ashore as they invited, and, despite my haste to be under way, have relaxed for a day in their miniature village. But the holding power of the quickly shoaling bottom was precarious and *Pagan* was wantonly exposed to any shift in the weather. I pointed these things out to the group. One of the tall silent young men volunteered to stay aboard to guard against contingency. It was out of the question; it was the same as expecting me to be efficient with the intricate outrigger.

The afternoon was wearing on, the sun was well down toward the horizon, and I told the chief that I would soon be casting off. At a command from him, the outrigger, under the hand of one of the husky young men and the boys, shot over the reef and glided across the coral lagoon to the beach. In a little while it returned, lightering some water, pawpaws, breadfruit, tarl, about fifty drinking coconuts, and two small pigs and two chickens. I was overwhelmed at the generosity of an island that could ill afford to give much. My gifts, which I could easily afford, looked paltry in comparison.

I put the chickens under my bunk for the time being and turned the squealing pigs loose in the cabin. They promptly jumped all over everything. In a last-minute burst of generosity I tossed some line, some pots and pans, a can of nails and screws, an American flag, and a pair of shoes into the outrigger. These things were received happily enough, but somehow there wasn't the spontaneous reception as at first. The children especially looked at me longingly as I prepared to go. And when Flotsam and Jetsam, with paws on the rail, peered innocently and wide-eyed upon them they melted with wistfulness and no longer concealed their desire. Then I realized . . . and it hurt to think of it. I couldn't imagine *Pagan* without the kittens. They were more than a part of my boat, they were a part of my life. But still these people had precious little. I handed them into the outrigger into the happy arms of the little girl. I felt it would be cruel to deny these lonely people the company the kittens and their future generations could bring.

The time had come to go, and I must admit it weighed heavily. I knew I would soon be missing the voices, the laughter, and the warm company. It was cruel to force myself to return to the fight with the sea when here was a cool desert isle where I could put in for a rest. How many clerks, lost in a maze of office files, office routines, and the littleness of an office desk would have welcomed my opportunity?

The serious business of my leave-taking prodded me. The
sun was half under the sea. I offered my hand around the
sober circle and patted the young heads with whom I had
established a close rapport. The old man clung to my hand;
the sagging muscles of his face quivered as he passed on last-
minute advice about the weather, the set of the current, and
islands to westward. The young men looked wistful, and I
am sure that if they had been a little more bold they would
have asked to go along. Flotsam and Jetsam had found a fish
in the bottom of the outrigger, and they didn't see my preparations to go.

The last of the islanders stepped off the decks by aid of the
shrouds and settled themselves into their loaded craft.

I put my tiller over alee, shook the anchor loose, weighed
it to the hawse, and grappled it aboard. The mainsail flut-
tered up the mast; all sails bent to their work; and in a few
minutes my offing was made. I turned to wave a last good-by
to my friends and my kittens. The outrigger hadn't moved;
the islanders were standing and answering my wave. Then
growing dusk closed them in and took them away, the distance blotted out their farewell calls.

The next morning I awakened in a calm, the first I had ex-
perienced since leaving the Galápagos, more than a month
before. A little bit after daylight curtains of water driven by
high winds closed around me. At first I thought it was only
a series of squalls; but by noon I was heaved-to under storm
sail in a gale of wind out of the south. All in one day!

I spent the day in my bunk gnawing pork joints, since I
had subjected one of my piglets to his purpose the night be-

fore. That night the gooseneck broke, and I went out into the storm to wire the boom to the mast. By midnight the wind hauled around to south of east and modified. I set all sail, lashed the tiller, and made a course south of west.

After leaving Caroline Island I had a run of foul weather very like some of that I encountered on my way to the Galápagos. Always there were early morning squalls. There were occasional short calms. The wind shifted often and varied in strength. Cloud banks were heavier, wetter, and closer to the sea.

The weather was depressing. I had hoped to be making top speed over this area — instead my daily runs were lagging. I got lonesome without the kittens. I missed them snuggling in my lap when the weather deviled me. I missed their daylight capers, and when I ate the flying fish the taste wasn't the same as when the kittens ate with me.

I tried to tame the chickens, but they were disinclined to be tamed; so I ate them. The one remaining pig squealed every time I offered friendship — so he too got the pot. There were now only Stowaway and I aboard — and he was still a confirmed crank. Old Death and his boys were around but, as always, the simple things of life didn't concern them; they were concerned only with making a kill and gobbling it. Life on *Pagan* had lost the thrill of the days of Gawky, and Flotsam and Jetsam.

With the supplies I had picked up at Caroline, I looked forward with relief to the last month of the trip. Five days out from Caroline I was still gnawing pork bones and eating loads of fresh fruits and vegetables. I wanted to fatten on these perishables before my two-meals-a-day ration set in. And it was a good thing I took every available bite as I did, for

even at that moment I was on the brink of the most climac-
tic and nearly disastrous event of the trip.

The next day was Thursday, September 5, 1946 — I shall
never forget that day. It started like any other in this area.
I woke up at daylight to find a mild southerly breeze. In the
neighborhood were four squalls, and I sat at the tiller riding
between them. By the time the sun was an hour high I had
run off from under the slanting wet curtains and was reaching for the clear sky beyond and a good day's sail. I was expecting to fetch land any minute in the Suvorov Islands. I had
no intention of stopping; I merely wanted to bounce off them
as a check on my navigation. I scaled the mast a time or two,
and looked toward where the reefy group should break the
horizon.

At nine o'clock the wind palled, and soon I was slatting in
sticky air. Almost immediately a slight swell set in from — of
all places — the north. I noted this most critically and attempted to reason out the oddity. I didn't like the implica-
tions. They pointed to a wind somewhere in the north. The
weather of the past week came back to me. I glanced over my
charts, my sailing directions, my information on storms. I
knew what a northerly meant in these waters but I didn't
mention it to myself.

By noon great glassy swells were crowding upon each
other, still out of the north. *Pagan* was broached-to in their
troughs; galley utensils clinked and clanked; the boom
pounded where it was lashed; the blocks creaked and rattled.
The sky had censored itself with a deep, gray mantle. *Pagan's* unsettled groanings seemed wasted on the immensity
of the outer stillness and monotony.

By three in the afternoon it had grown darker, and, it

seemed, stiller. The heavy swells were gathering speed. They were larger, closer together, more purposeful. Off to the north an audible soughing whispered along the horizon.

Pagan's sails — except her staysail — were in. She was stripped to her standing rigging, looking nude as she rolled on that indifferent sea. I lashed the boom double secure to its crutch, clinched the halyards down, and cleared the decks. I battened all ports and hatch dogs. I nailed the fore scuttle to its coamings with heavy spikes, a precaution against deep seas boarding my decks. Down below all was shipshape: gear was stowed and lashed; lockers were packed tight and strapped down; a life jacket was on my bunk. From the bunk's edge dangled a number of short lines, to lash myself down when the need came.

On deck I sat atop the cabin . . . and waited, searching the horizon, the water, and the sky.

CHAPTER XVI   Hurricane

Cat's-paws dappled the round crests of the hurrying rollers as a light air whisked out of the north. The breeze was strong enough to steady the staysail. It had a dampness that hinted at rain and it stirred a heavy cloud to motion, which soon proved to be a squall. It came on, closed over me, and wrapped me round with wind and rain. I stayed on deck despite the wet. Inwardly I felt apprehensive; and I couldn't go below.

In a way I was wishing I had a barometer so I could have some proof of what was afoot. As it was, I was now suspecting that I was being stalked by a hurricane. But at what rate, or from what precise direction, I couldn't know; only a barometer could tell me.

The area north of the Cook Islands, where I was, has a notorious reputation for cyclonic disturbances. If there was a hurricane in the locality, there was nothing I could now do but sit tight. I couldn't counter it. I was glad I had no barometer. Knowledge of a falling glass would only have verified a foregone conclusion. As it was I could sit minimizing the unmistakable symptoms, and hope to the very last that my fears were ungrounded.

My hands were tied, there was nothing I could do to avoid whatever it was that caused the northerly swells. Conditions of the sea and weather were not such that I could move prof-

itably under sail. And I didn't want to be caught with my
sails up, so I doused them, put them in stops, and watched
and listened . . . denying every ominous sign.

I was soon encountering a series of nasty squalls, lowering
skies, and hurrying of seas. Hours later still nothing definite
could be read in the skies. I was forced to wait.

I strained at every nerve to know what was coming. I read
from every shift of wind, every lessening of distance between
the seas. I recalled everything I knew, little though it was,
of hurricanes and their peculiarities.

A hurricane is greatly like the little whirlwind which
dances along the street on a summer day, only it is infinitely
larger. Its small round center is an area of low barometric
pressure and calm air. The outer reaches of the disturbance
have a high barometric pressure. As the barometer falls you
know you are nearing the "eye" or center of the storm. Working from the outside of the hurricane, in a circular motion,
are prodigious winds which intensify right up to the edge of
the calm inner area. The whole system of terrific winds and
calm central sector is usually little more than three hundred
miles across. The duration of a hurricane depends upon the
speed it travels — anywhere from five to thirty miles an hour.

A striking peculiarity of the hurricane is that in the northern latitudes its winds are counterclockwise, and in southern
latitudes they are clockwise. Also, the portion of a hurricane
nearest the equator is generally its least violent part, the portion farthest from the equator being especially dangerous because cyclonic tracks tend away from the equator, and thus
advance across anything in its way. The thing to avoid is the

center. If you face the wind in southern seas, the center is on your left. The dangerous semicircle would depend on the path of the storm's center.

By evening the last of the squalls had passed and the worst of my fears took shape. Rain poured heavily from the jagged, lowering clouds and a mild gale-force wind set in, whipping the seas so that they charged down around me. It was no guesswork about the hurricane. I was certain that I had one right in my lap. I took my anchor below and lashed it to the mast and made a last check of all gear to see that the precautions I had made against the storm were in readiness. I unlashed the rubber raft from the mast, pushed it off the foredeck, and strung it from the stern . . . just in case.

Gray tooth-edged clouds raced past barely above the mast top. They unburdened themselves of torrents of stinging water. The wind had steadied in the north; and the fact that it hadn't changed direction in an hour disturbed me. I rigged my storm sail on the mast, sheeted it flat, and crammed the staysail below. My last move was to cinch the tiller down doubly secure. I went forward, seated myself on the deckhouse, and with arm locked about the mast watched over the bows for what was coming.

Night closed in and heavy rollers, growling a flashing gray, were the only indication that the night was anything else but wind and rain. I went below to lie in my bunk, stare at the overhead, and wait.

About an hour later, *Pagan* commenced dancing nervously. Instead of rising gently to the oncoming crests she broke abruptly into them. Instead of a quick roll before the more forceful seas, she made a sharp lurch which found her often heeled over far enough to throw me. In my bunk I was forced to grip its sides. It was obvious I was in the center of the gale winds which lie just outside the perimeter of the oncoming hurricane winds.

After a while more occasional strains shivered the boat when the storm sail cringed before the wind. The brewing hurricane was slamming with ever greater intensity. I checked the watch and saw it was just before eight. That was the last time I looked at the watch; from then on there was too much excitement, too much violent motion.

Opening the hatch doors, I peeped into the garrulous night. Hissing rollers worked with a heavy swish beneath my boat and ran growling into the blackness. The wind pursued them with the persistence of a bully. *Pagan* lay as though still; now on a hillock, now in a ravine of water . . . as yet not pitching, but rolling mightily.

She was no longer riding comfortably. Her bow was lying five points off the wind, which still persisted from the north. The port rail was under, and the windward bow was throwing spray high into the rigging, and beating into the seas. Rain was the heaviest yet. It was impossible to look straight into that wind and rain.

With the wind holding for so long from one direction, I was certain that the track of the hurricane lay directly over me. I could figure on three phases of behavior from it. The first: the infernal winds of its dangerous semicircle. The second: the lull of the hurricane's center where winds from a dozen directions send great rollers crashing into a small, crowded arena. The third, and least vicious: the navigable semicircle or tail end of the storm.

Seeing that all was well as could be expected on deck, I pulled my eyes in and closed the hatch. I braced myself against the low overhead, and flashed my light over the airless interior. For the first time I lashed myself in my bunk and waited.

Two hours later *Pagan* was slapped by severe bursts of wind and sea that rattled her like sudden earthquakes. I was sure now that I was entering the first of the hurricane winds.

At a hidden hour, sometime later, *Pagan* heeled mightily, yawed and pounded. I loosed the hitches across my chest and legs and peered into the thick weather. The storm sail had failed to hold its own in the high wind and had blown to loose ends.

It meant going on deck again. I set my sea anchor — a homemade job, rigged coming over from the Galápagos — and veered it out on a hundred feet of line. *Pagan* rounded up successfully, though she was taking heavy, noisy water over her gunwales.

Below decks I lay lashed in my bunk once more listening to every creak and groan that shot past the hollow din of shrieking rigging and rumbling seas. I could hear the churning water surging over the decks. When the heavier gusts struck, I listened deepest. I was alert for any structural defects. I had learned to know my boat by the very feel and sound of her. After sleeping for more than two months with my ears tuned to her every murmur, I knew what each sound meant and from where it came.

My great concern was for *Pagan's* twenty-six-year-old, aging, tired timbers. It was hard to believe as I lay there that night listening to the inside sounds of a small craft under extreme stress that the planks surrounding me had been spread-

ing water for those years. But *Pagan*, for all her age, was a
well-found boat.

Along about two in the morning I heard a quivering shriek
— the loose ends of a snapped shroud. It whined like something wounded. I opened the hatch and peered out. Giant
wind-whipped seas surged to port and starboard. The wind,
growing harsh and harsher, had the force of solidity.

Pagan was falling away laboriously. Her mast was describ-
ing a widening arc: she heeled to such an angle under the
heavier gusts that the mast nearly lopped off the wave crests.

She pointed in a fast glide down the back side of a moving
mountain. She plunged bow-on into the base of the next,
submerging the forepeak, and quaking under the load of tons
of green water. Pitching her bow out of the water to the keel,
she sent a rivulet rail-deep cascading along the deck and pouring over the stern.

In the deep trough formed by the hills of sea, the wind was
unable to strike; and *Pagan* righted abruptly. As she neared
the curled peak on the climb up the oncoming roller, she
once more encountered the blast. She careened before it. I
couldn't stand. Too, she was struck by the thundering wind-
driven comber which broke in a heavy continuum atop each
hurricane swell. It was then *Pagan* pounded most. Her
bow was pitched up as though dynamited, and she yawed
wildly until heavy seas, boarding her, weighted her down
so that she wallowed clumsily, her lee rail out of sight.
Then she would shake herself free of her load and go
reeling down the back side of another great, rolling swell of
water.

The broken shroud — the forward one on the starboard
side — was flailing like a whiplash. It cried the danger to my

thirty-five-foot mast jolting at the storm blackness with only one shroud holding it on the starboard side.

The wind snatched my close-fitting watch cap from around my ears and threw it into the venting clouds. In a second I was drenched to the shoulders by flying spray.

I stared into that disjoined sea and saw instantly the uselessness of my life jacket. I stripped it off.

Before jumping on deck I bound a heavy line around my middle, and made it fast to the handrail on the deckhouse. I awaited a moment when the decks were water free and leaped out of the hatchway, closed it, jumped into the windward waist, and lay flat, facing up deck. The prying fingers of the wind caught the loose folds of my shirt, filling it at the front, tearing away the buttons, and ripping it down the back and sides. It hung by tatters. My full strength was required to lie flat on deck. I didn't dare stand into that wind, or even sit. When I looked into it for a second, I could feel my eyes depress; I could feel my hair whip against my cheeks.

I had strung a life line above the rails — from the bow to the shrouds and to the sternpost. Two more life lines lay strung on deck from the forward bit along each waist to the rudderpost. These latter lines had double knots tied in every two feet: and to these I clung each time a swirling sea charged along the deck.

I pulled myself ahead a few feet and locked myself, feet and hands, around the knotted line. When the decks spilled themselves of eddying water, and when for a moment I could expose myself, I freed my waistline on the handrail, moved it forward a length, and slid up under it. Movement was slow. It had to be. Thus I worked my way to the starboard shrouds to examine the damaged member.

I found that the turnbuckle on the after shroud had loosed. The shocks of the mast, reeling in a wide arc, had been absorbed by the forward, weaker shroud, weakened in the encounter with the devilfish, and it had parted.

The mast was held only by the one shroud, and it wasn't tight as it should have been, since the turnbuckle had unscrewed. The load on it was terrific. It couldn't sustain that tremendous load for long. Each time *Pagan* pitched her heel clear of the water and twisted over into a flat beam roll, the mast looked as if it would jump out of its stepping. I could feel the timbers in the deck beneath me crawl.

I tightened the turnbuckle as well as I could by hand. But it wasn't enough. The single shroud couldn't hold out alone. There was only one desperate move I could make to save the mast: loosen the forestay at the stemhead and bend it to the chain plate as a jury shroud.

As the next heavy sea went crashing around my shoulders and over me, I made ready to loosen my body line and fasten it a few feet ahead so that I could snake my way to the bow. I moved slowly and carefully across the open deck. Between seas I shifted my line from one secure fastening to another — and more than once, but for the line, reaching green waters would have snatched me over the stern.

Scrambling from the mast across the fore scuttle to the bitt was a risky business. It was then that I was clinging only to the deck lines, having nothing to which to attach my waistline. I watched the seas overspilling the rails, and timed the intervals . . . then jumped. I made it. The seas growled unhappily and continued to be unhappy, sniping at me as I worked. I loosened the forestay as quickly as possible and, gripping it fiercely, slithered back to the shrouds.

I lay on my back on the blown decks working with only my hands and forearms in the wind. I took my time; thought carefully over each job before I did it. When I finished, *Pagan* was bolstered by full shrouds and I was eased of mind. The decks, aheave and awash, didn't seem so bad with the mast safely held. The job completed, I made the gross error of sitting up to check it. An explosive wind bent me to a helpless angle. A flurry of bubbling water lifted me bodily and bounced me against the deckhouse and into the shrouds, then whelmed me over the rail onto a churning sea.

The line was around my waist, fortunately. The pull of the sea spun me upside down, wrenched at me, and tore. *Pagan* submerged her rail and I found myself clawing in a surging froth, closing my throat against the water. I was hard against the hull, being slammed against it, one minute under water and one minute not. A heavy sea dropped down on *Pagan* too perpendicular to be climbed. I saw it curl over, towering before me. *Pagan* had just heeled obliquely, throwing her windward rail high. I was yanked from the water, and had it been possible to stand in the wind I could have walked down the hull. Above me I could see the curling lip of descending water.

My tiny craft, caught between sea and wind, sank bodily beneath the impact of her decks. I was glad I wasn't on the open deck, as the flood engulfed the bow and rolled heavily against the bulkheads.

Another drink of salt was choked down me as the boat was dragged by main force before the ungovernable sea. My arms and legs were thrown at will. She sidled and broached about as though she would wallow and founder.

The high strain of fighting back had pared my strength

away in a few short minutes. I was choked with water in lungs and stomach, and flopping against the hull had set my head to spinning. I was giving it up, I knew it, but I couldn't resist longer; the thing was I didn't want to resist longer. I could see *Pagan* close by and I could see the gray loom of seas, but I couldn't reach toward one or lean away from the other. I relaxed. I became part of the sea. I could hear the singing siren.

Pagan's white hull was only a foot or two away, looking like a high wall. I wanted to touch it and climb over it. I closed my eyes, wondering what would happen next. A dollop of seas whirled broadside onto *Pagan*. I struck the rail and floated against it. The deck tilted steeply; I slipped somehow inboard and brought up against the deckhouse. *Pagan* came out of the hollow between the seas cringing before the winds.

I knew immediately that I was safe on board. I remember vomiting the water I had swallowed, and tugging faintly at the hard wet knot on the handrail. The next thing I knew I had toppled through the hatchway, had somehow closed it, and had tumbled in a heap on the cabin floor. I was too sick and weak to care what happened next. For long hours I rolled to and fro on the floor knocking against the bunks as *Pagan* tilted high. Finally I crawled into my bunk and bound my lashings over me.

Dismasted

W<small>HEN</small> I <small>AWAKENED</small>, it was daylight.

I didn't waken because I had slept enough, or because the daylight had caught my eye. Not forty-eight hours of sleep would have been enough. Not a searchlight could have disturbed my profound sleep. I wakened because of *Pagan's* sudden change in behavior. Her pitching and rolling became suddenly beyond what I had ever felt before. She inclined to flatness on both beams; and pitched so high that it seemed incredible she didn't jerk her keel off.

I thought at first my boat must be turning over and over. But I could see the overhead remain near where the overhead should be — and I tried to explain to myself what was happening.

Most perplexing was the absence of the storm's noises. I had passed out with the hurricane shrieking in the rigging. Now, aside from the wash of water in the bilge, a pounding on deck, and an occasional swish of sea, there was little else . . . strange.

The combination of quiet and violence scared me.

Unbinding my lashings, I wavered to the hatchway, barely able to keep off the plunging bulkheads. I opened the hatch doors a foot and pushed my eyes above the cabin. I saw a vast circle of foam upshot with rearing cones of water . . .

but not a breath of air stirred. There were no rollers or combers as such, only peaks of water shooting up and falling away flatly.

Instantly I knew I was in the lull of the hurricane; which is to say, the airless central circle around which revolve the cyclonic winds. Pushed into this diabolic arena were thousands of wind-churned seas from countless directions to collide and intercollide.

I don't know how to explain it, unless I suggest that you visualize yourself on a crag, surrounded by numberless other such, then, at a given signal, they resolve themselves to liquid and each sets upon the others as would hunger-crazed beasts.

As far as I could see, great pyramids of water bolted masthead high from the sea surface. Here and there great cross seas crashed into them, dispersed, re-formed, and crashed again. *Pagan* lay to her scuppers beneath a constant deck of water. Her sea anchor was helpless; she danced to all points of the compass, her mast scoring the water on either side. Suddenly she was high and suddenly she was low.

Nausea assailed me. The sickening surge of the boat, and the unstable watery sight, set me to vomiting. I couldn't hold myself up longer.

I stumbled into my bunk and lashed myself down. I realized that I should get up and pump the bilges; also plug the broken porthole — but I was too dead sick to move. I couldn't even brace myself against the lurch; I just lay there, rolling against my lashings.

All morning my head spun as the jaunty craft threatened to fall apart. Not once could I sleep, even fitfully. I lay listening to the noises. I was nervous to distraction as to what could happen to my boat in this constant, violent rough-and-tumble.

Early in the afternoon I nosed into the outer circle of the hurricane. Once again the rigging dinned with the howling winds. This time the wind had shifted into the south and my bunk was on the windward side. One inch of tired oak plank-ing — only a span away — stood between me and disaster-crested seas. Most of the time I was tilted high in the air with the other bunk below me at the bottom of the slanting deck. Water was overtopping the decks and sloshing through the smashed porthole. It wet me down, refreshed me, eased the seasickness a bit.

I was still strapped in my bunk. The seasickness was paci-fied by the more consistent motion of the boat. Now that the wind set upon her again, there was a system in her wild be-havior that was kindred to my experience.

From where I lay, I could hear the bedlam of wind in the rigging, could feel my boat wince before each header. The furiously whipped seas were snarling across the decks like packs of wolves. Because of water slopping through the port-hole, I got up and stuffed a pair of pants in the opening. I realized that while I was up I should go out on deck and cut free the boom, which, flying at the end of the topping lift, was smashing at the stern end. Also the bilges needed pump-ing. But, remembering my narrow escape on deck, I reasoned that the threat of boom and wet bilges was naught compared to the risk of venturing in the open. I remained in the safety of my wet bunk and tightened the lashings over me. Again I waited . . . listening.

The process of riding out a hurricane in a small boat is terribly nerve-racking. It's the sense of futility you feel in the face of imponderable odds. The hurricane is supreme master; you are its trifle — a cork in a tempest.

There is only one safe way to ride out a hurricane on a small boat: flat on your back lashed in the bunk with ports and hatches dogged, and everything strapped down. But lying there strait-jacketed to a mattress is depressing: you always wonder what's going on in the rest of the boat. You wonder if somewhere a leak is breaking, or a repair needs attention. To keep the boat under constant examination is too bruising a job: the prospect of overseeing things on deck is taboo, positively taboo. So I passed the long jolting hours in my bunk . . . waiting, and determining *Pagan's* condition from a distance.

The fact of *Pagan's* years, the fact that she still had her original wood — this was the reason I listened the more intently. She was too old to be bucking up to a hurricane and this thought was cropping up all the time. Another concern which accosted me was my life raft.

It had been trailing astern since the start of the hurricane. When I was last on deck I had caught a glimpse of it, wallowing to its gunwales in the angry froth. But that had been during the lull when I was sick. I could only hope it was still there. If not, I had nothing to escape in, if trouble came. I thought of going to the deck to look for it, but I didn't figure it was worth the risk. There was nothing I could do if I needed it but go out and look for it; if it wasn't there, well . . . that was that.

How many hours I lay there straining at my lashings, waiting for some indication that the storm was abating, I don't know. Night came. More hours dragged. The hurricane was twenty-four hours old. It labored on to somewhere near thirty.

The same violent jerks of the boat, the same roaring wind, crashing sea, clatter of dislodged gear, and slosh of a water-filled bilge!

In the wee hours of the morning of September seventh — after two days of storm — hard luck struck. My first recollection that something was amiss came when *Pagan* broached to and refused to round up into the wind. Great seas were ramming against the beam and combing athwart the decks. She scudded before each tumbler, creaking loudly and inclining more than usual. She lunged as though filliped by a mammoth finger. It was punishment beyond what my boat could take for long.

I unbound my ropes and took a look outside. It was the same wild world as ever: a sea blown to windrows, heavy curlers boarding the decks, volleys of spray flying around my ears, *Pagan* yawing at the will of each disjointed sea and wind.

I could tell without seeing that the sea anchor was gone: evidently chafed at the bobstay. I was thinking of something I could use to replace it. Somehow my boat must be made to face up to the wind. Only a sea anchor could make it do that. With *Pagan* rolling and pitching eerily it was impossible to make one. What was worse — there wasn't time to make one; an hour of this and *Pagan* would break up. To prove my point a swelling billow with a smoking mane sent us lurching on our beam ends. I acted quickly.

There was my rustic anchor lying on the cabin floor, lashed to the heel of the mast. If I heaved it over and let it drift out to chain's length it should drag enough to hold the bow into the wind. It was worth the try. I groped for it in the dark. I wrapped it in the jib, and bound it on the outside with the sheets to make it act as a decent drag. I tied my life jacket to the flukes to prevent it from sinking; and made ready to heave it out of the hatchway into the sea.

The decision to go out on deck was hard arrived at. But I had to go. In some way I got the anchor into the cockpit and crawled in beside it, lying low under the wind. I heaved it overboard, clinging to the bitter end of its line. With just my eyes over the coaming, I watched it float forward. I had now to secure the line to the bow. I waited a long minute before facing the open decks. As she lay, *Pagan* was in a position to pound herself apart, broad-on to the breaking seas.

The windward bulwarks wore an uninviting look; so I jumped into the flooded lee waist. So long as I was alee of the cabin I could crawl. I had to be careful; the rail on the starboard side was gone, carried away by the flood. There was nothing to hold to if I should be washed outboard. When I edged out ahead of the deckhouse into the wind, I lay flat on my face and snaked my way. All the time a line was fast to my middle and connected to a stanch object. In addition I was gripping the knotted line strung over the deck.

I was afraid that heavy seas overrunning the gunwales would raise me so that the cyclonic fingers could roll me overboard. But I made it safely to the stemhead and fastened my waistline to the bitt. At the same time I hitched a hasty bowline with the anchor line to the chain leading from the chain locker. As quickly as possible I slipped back to the safety of the cabin. *Pagan* was yawing badly. If the anchor dragged more slowly than the boat, the bow would fetch up to the wind. I hoped she would answer soon.

Just then the most severe shock of all rocked her — a gust firing point-blank. Piles of water rambled roughshod athwart her to the height of the portholes. She heeled to her beam ends, and creaked loud enough to hear above the storm sounds. In abject terror I fled below.

Another roller struck her more heavily than the other. For a moment the beam planking became the deck under me. The rattle of loosened gear filled the blackness of the tight cabin. Before my little world could right itself, it shivered again beneath an impact. And a moment later again. This time the sea hurtled over the starboard quarter; she had been turned half around by the force of the sea blows. At the same moment a resounding snap of solid timber impinged on every sense of my body, froze me, stopped me short. The mast! I could tell by the feel of the wounded boat.

I knew what a broken thirty-five-foot spar could mean. I staggered faultily toward the companionway. Something heavy pounded her by the stern. Another heavy sea had hit her. Just then — and exceeding quick — the stout little doors dissolved into a sheet of gray. With black suddenness a lump of water shot at me. In the wink of an eye I was sledge-hammered back the full length of the cabin, rolling, twisting. When I stopped falling I was under the foredeck, sitting waist deep in rushing water, surrounded in dark.

In front of me was the heel of the mast. On one side were my mattress and blankets, where they had washed with the sudden inflooding. On the other were the sails, where I had stowed them. In my lap, pinioning me and fighting me, was a fifteen-gallon water cask, swept loose from its lashings. I was helpless to push it away. The surge of the knee-deep water forced it one way and another, against the mast or my chest. In either case it was still in my lap. When *Pagan* pitched, throwing her bow down, the water rushed me, and knocked me flat and covered me.

Pagan took another roller across the stern. More water poured through the companionway. The water rose to my chest and raced to and fro faster in the pent space. I was knocked under more often. It was harder to sit back up.

Pagan's interior was a welter of attacking wavelets. It was like a tomb; it was frightening. With an ocean to drown in I was drowning inside my boat. I fought to get at least on deck. To be licked off by the wind and sea was more fitting than perishing under deck beams, hundreds of miles from a safe shore.

A providential movement of the barrel enabled me to sidle from under it and struggle from beneath the forepeak. The cabin was a nightmare. It ran thigh-deep to water. Three quarters of my gear was adrift. The locker doors were gaping, and their contents were dropping into the brine. The lockers themselves, caught by the shifting water, were in the process of ripping from their fastenings.

I wavered through the morass and clambered into the brimming cockpit. Its coamings were gone, but I was protected from the wind when I lay low. *Pagan* was rounding up nicely to the drag of the anchor; I could tell by the feel she was plunging into it dead ahead.

The mast had snapped; that was definite. I could see it wrenching at the dark sky. I could feel it nearly jerk the planking off at the chain plates, and I could hear it stomping on the foredeck, threatening to break through the deck. The heavy pole was held up by the shrouds and stays. It was trying helplessly to fall. Each pitch, each roll, each twist, endangered the life of my boat. And lying there in the flooded cockpit I could see it all, and I could see there was no alternative but to chop away the shrouds and free the big spar to topple into the sea.

A hatchet was ready to hand in the cockpit. I bellied along my system of life lines, tying my waistline ahead of me as I went. The decks were still awash, and the wind still in high glee. Lying on my back I hacked at the now slack, now taut, wire shrouds. Eventually one cut through; it went singing into the dark obscurity. I chopped away at the other. The stress of the wavering mast would have snapped it, in a little time, without my hackings. It suddenly parted. The high, heavy pole slammed away to leeward and splashed onto a sea.

I cringed against the deck when it went and heard rumbling and splintering after it fell.

Without a mast the little craft lay more comfortable, less affected by the powerful winds. She no longer beat into it, but rose with it, and kept an evener keel. I crawled back close beside the cabin and crept through the breach in the coaming into the cockpit.

The cabin below was a bog. My boat was terrifyingly close to sinking. Water was the depth of hip boots, and was solid from the watertight bulkhead to the bow. Only the fact of that water-resistant wall kept her from foundering by the bow or stern as the water surged fore and aft with each upward lurch and toss of the bow. She had to be pumped out before more seas should crowd aboard her.

But how to pump her out? My bilge pump was aft of the cabin and connected to its overhead. Its position was vulnerable to the wind. I dared not expose myself by using it. But *Pagan* had to be emptied . . . somehow.

There was only one recourse: the bucket. I lowered myself into the hip-deep swirl and fished around till I found it. I commenced the awkward bailing. I braced myself against the carlings or clung grimly to the hatch coaming, while wrestling with the bucket. I bailed till I felt green in the face; and bailed on.

It was easiest to stand in the center of the cabin and heave the water into the cockpit, and when the boat rolled, the cockpit emptied through the splintered coamings into the scuppers. But when it pitched, some slopped back into the cabin. Also the forepart of the deckhouse was smashed in from the felling of the mast, and some big water came in occasionally. The three portholes to windward were out. But by a steady sweat I could gain on the threatening water.

The seasickness of earlier in the storm began creeping over me again as weariness set in. After hours of bailing the floor boards were visible. I took time to plug the dripping portholes and stow a few soggy items of gear in suitable corners. Then I dipped and poured till the boards showed dry.

I ragged my watered mattress onto my bunk and prepared to fall onto it. The floor rose sickeningly as *Pagan* spun before a bank of water. She was pushed off her heading till she lay stern-to, before the seas. I leaped atop my bunk as the first seas crowded aboard and roared around the decks. Braced against the deck beams I watched the floor fill to ten inches of water — an hour's fast bailing and, tired as I was, a heart-breaking sight.

Another sea had at her and more water spilled through the companionway. I bolted out into the overflowing cockpit, hiding under the wind. A third sea overran the transom, licking at me, nearly forcing me back into the cabin. After that *Pagan* broached to and appeared to be coming about into the wind.

I was safer down below bailing than sitting out in the wind.
I lowered myself into the watery hold and fished for my
bucket. I filled and poured for endless hours. There was no
consciousness directing my work — I bailed blindly and
dumbly and unfeelingly. In fear of further swampings, and
in completest indifference, I jettisoned anything and everything that came to hand. My mattress went by the board; also
blankets, tools, dishes, canned food, coconuts, clothes, water
breakers, sails — all that encumbered my bailing.

I was fighting for my life in hip-deep water, lightening my
boat. Any moment I expected her to dip her stern into a sea
and go under. I was fighting to lighten her before that sea
came — if it was to come. There was no such thing as bailing
just water alone, I bailed whatever I scooped up in the bucket;
and I scooped and bailed till it was an effort to lift even the
empty bucket.

When I could no longer think or even hope — for I hadn't
eaten, or drunk, for two days, or slept — I collapsed on my
bunk boards. I slept as I fell. And I slept where *Pagan* rolled
me. I wasn't lashed down.

I was totally jaded, sick, and numb. I put myself in *Pagan's*
hands. I was aware of nothing. I never knew when the hurricane ended. Maybe it was an hour before I came to aware-
ness or maybe half a day . . . or a day . . . I can't know. I
only know that I sat up, and that it was strangely quiet, and
that *Pagan* rolled easier than she had done in days.

She was shifting on a light seaway. Outside it was dull
and gray, but calm. The horizon mewed lightly in the direction the hurricane had gone — the adaptable sea was already
composing itself for the friendly sky on the opposite horizon.

CHAPTER XVIII   Jury Rig

F ROM THE TIME I had collapsed on my bunk boards, while the storm was yet on, I slept twice around the clock. I wakened but once in that time for a couple of hours, at an unholy hour of night, to bail out twenty inches of water in the hold. How it got there I didn't know. It hadn't dawned on me that my boat was leaking. I had thought the flooded cabin was caused from a swamping while I slept. But outside there was calm. There were no seas to jump aboard. I was tired, still too tired to reason things out, so I fell again on my hard, wet bunk boards. But now I was aroused from my deep slumber by water slopping over me again.

The floor was flooded. It was dawn, and I was rested. I went on deck for the first time since the storm to pump the bilges, and to see what my boat was like.

Pagan lay in a flat calm. Smooth-crested swells of the after-storm passed under her. The sky was blue and tranquil — here on this wide field of the sea was little to indicate, for one with Olympian eyes, that a violent hurricane had recently passed under *Pagan's* near-derelict hulk, heaved into view out of a sea valley onto a glassy roller.

It gave me serious pause just to stand and look.

What I saw was a monument to chaos. A dismasted boat is a naked sight; but one in the condition that *Pagan* was in —

battered and bruised, limping as if wounded — is a heartbreaking sight for a seaman. I walked to the bow and stood
looking back over the scarred decks of the little ghost ship.
She no longer creaked and rattled from tackle and spars. Her
tackle and spars were down, and dragging in the sea with her
rigging.

The bowsprit was gone, snapped at the stemhead. There
was barely a rail on the boat — only slivers and stubs. The
staysail boom was gone, its fastenings broken at the bow. My
carefully laid deck canvas was peeled away where it had been
caught between wind and sea. The forward end of the deckhouse was caved in, evidently by the mast and the charging
seas. The splintered stub of the mast, a foot high, where the
stick had twisted off, was the most unreal sight of all. Only
one porthole was whole; all others were stuffed with an array
of clothing.

Back aft, the cockpit coamings were broken away. The
companionway doors were gone. For the second time Pagan's
tiller had been torn off, despite the double secure lashings I
had applied before the storm; this time by the boom hurtling
at the end of the topping lift. The bumkin was snapped off —
this too by the clublike boom. But most representative
of the hurricane's damage were the raffled trailings of
Pagan's rigging in the limpid water. They hung from the port
side and trailed astern like tufts of matted hair, clutching
the mast, the broken boom, the bowsprit, and splinters of the
bumkin.

She had lived through the storm and stress, and I was glad.
I tried to depreciate the extent of damage; but somehow my
observations weren't convincing.

My little life raft was still floating astern, partly submerged.

Later I learned that one of its compartments had been deflated, probably in altercation with the boom.

The hold had all the earmarks of an Augean stable; a chowderish mixture of the thousand and one articles of gear I had tucked away in corners, which only an inimical sea could fetch out. It was a fearful sight: a quagmire, one to discourage a battery of janitors. Tools, articles of clothing, oilcans, loose line, crippled fixtures, strips of bedding, shoes, and splintered lumber lay intertwined where they had wrestled during the storm.

The sea was quiet as seas are in the calm, and as I looked out over it, it seemed more quiet than it had ever seemed before.

My main concern was to see *Pagan* under sail as speedily as possible. Before I settled to my work, my thoughts turned to food. For three days and nights I had not eaten; I was ravenous. I found a quart can of tomatoes and a coconut in the debris and broke into them with the hatchet. After gulping them, I looked for water.

My water breakers, I soon found, had all slipped their bungs, so that the water was either spilled or polluted. But strapped to the carling on the starboard side was a small keg of "emergency water" — four gallons. All I had aboard. "Plenty," I thought, and took a deep drink. It would last me to Samoa, what with coconuts and other liquid foods that I could dig out later from the mess in the cabin.

I went on deck and pitched into the work of rigging *Pagan* to sail. This, it seemed to me, was the most important consideration at the moment. There would be plenty of time later, when *Pagan* was once more fitted out and running before the wind, to clean up below and take stock of food, water,

and my position. For the nonce it sufficed to know, by re-
calling my last determined position before the heavy blow,
that I was somewhere in that lonely stretch of the Pacific between the Cook Islands and Samoa; exactly where would be
easy to determine when I sought out my navigation equipment and took a sight. Before the sun was fully up I had
pulled the mast inboard and lashed it obliquely across the foredeck. I intended to carry it thus to Samoa where I could have
it restepped and continue my trip.

The broken thirty-five-foot mast, weighing several hundred
pounds, was far too heavy and clumsy for me to set up alone.
I thought of cutting off its lower twenty-five feet and stepping that, but even that much, I knew, would be too cumber-
some to handle. I was looking hard and stretching my imagination hard to conceive from *Pagan's* derelict woods something suitable for a mast.

There was the better half of the boom. I fished it in and
trimmed it for an abbreviated mainmast. It was small, hardly
fifteen feet. It was all I had. My plan, devised fitfully as I
went along, was to rig *Pagan* as a yawl. A yawl, roughly, is
much like what *Pagan* had been as a cutter, except that a
small mizzenmast is located just behind the tiller. Rigged as a
yawl she would have a good spread of sail, and would handle
easily. I wanted a spritsail, so I cleared away the remainder of
the old bowsprit and reset its larger half, but without a bobstay.

The former shrouds, cut shorter with the hatchet, I used
for the new standing rigging. I made my connections at the
head of the new mast directly to the main boomdale, using
"U" bolts. I sawed out a hole in the deck in front of the broken
stump of the mast. The fore side of the stub I shaved flat

with the hatchet. I did the same to the after side of the boom, and knitted them together with two heavy bolts and strong lashings. I wedged in the new mast securely at the deck hole. To tighten the stays and shrouds properly I used the heavy turnbuckles at the chain plates.

Thus the storm-ravaged boom afforded a twelve-foot mast, carrying a ten-foot-high trysail. By midday I had rigging up that could hold a mainsail, staysail, and jib.

About this time of day I knew *Pagan* was leaking. The bilge had filled since I had pumped it at dawn, proof, even to a green horn, of a leak. I pumped the bilge and went below. I spent an hour looking for the leak, pushing through the gear-piled floor and into the mess of the forepeak, and finally decided it was somewhere below the cement-filled bilges where I couldn't see it or reach it. There was nothing I could do but pump the bilges hourly and hope the seepage wouldn't grow.

All afternoon I cut and sewed miniature sails from my weather-worn mainsail. For the mainmast I made a trysail ten feet high and seven feet long. She was hoisted on the boom-dale block and belayed at the staysail traveler. One-inch line spliced around the mast served as rings. I sewed each ring into the luff. This sail worked loose-footed, clewed up to an oar stock which I pared down for a jury boom.

I worked the pump from time to time, gushing out the estimated twelve gallons of water that was seeping into the bilges every hour. As I pumped I eyed the full circle of the horizon in hopes a ship might break over it. The hourly pumping, I felt, was a job that in time could grow distasteful, but since I was only some 400 miles from Samoa, by rough guess and assuming that the hurricane had not carried me far from where it found me, I wouldn't be at it long enough to matter.

Staysail and jib were considerably smaller than the mainsail, looking like pillow slips when they filled away. I sheeted the staysail to the chain plates, and the jib to the bitt. By dusk I had three sails in the wind. An occasional bubble showed in the wake. I lashed the broken tiller so that I made a course, according to the star, of due west. As yet I hadn't found my compass, but I didn't worry about it because I knew it was somewhere in the mess below. The important thing at the moment was to get sail up and way on.

Dark was drawing in. I pumped the bilges with a hundred quick strokes. Rifling in the hopeless tangle of the cabin, I came up with a can of peas. It was the first bite since dawn — I had been so busy.

When I had eaten I went on deck. Night had closed in. I sat on the cabin for hours watching the four winds, flashlight in hand, waiting to give a signal. At a late hour I hit the sack — or what I called the sack. I slept on my bunk boards, folded in the one blanket which I hadn't "deep sixed" during the confusion of the hurricane. This was only a temporary arrangement; I figured I could tolerate it till I lifted Samoa.

Daybreak found me out in the fresh morning air shaping my last oar into some semblance of a mizzenmast. A mop handle served for the boom. I had to build on to the splintered remains of the bumkin in order to sheet the new addition.

I used rope to rig it, and set my shrouds and topping lift from a masthead knot tied and nailed in a groove at the peak. It was stepped just aft of the steering post, going through the deck and bedding in the sternpost.

By noon the jigger was sheeted home and carrying wind.

Pagan was converted from a cutter into a yawl, and was limping down wind at an estimated one knot. For the time being I held her on her westerly course, "rail down" for Samoa. The next job was to get the cabin shipshape, take account of the food and water, find the navigational instruments, and grope after my position on the sea.

Before my cleaning job was finished that afternoon I learned some sobering facts. These facts so set me back that I lay awake many long hours that night. I learned, first of all, that I was completely without navigational instruments — not even a compass. Secondly, that I was practically foodless. Thirdly, that the only fresh water aboard was the four gallons in the emergency keg plus a quart of battery water I found in the hold.

On my bunk, in a thin weak line, lay the miserably few articles of food and comfort I had found. There were a bottle of ketchup, two unlabeled cans of food, and a coconut, my total larder!

I could recall that during the hurricane I had heaved many articles out in a frantic haste to lighten my boat — and as I heaved, I realized that items of food were going by the board. But never had I realized I was so completely tossing out my food stores. Further, I had not realized that my jugs and jars, in which were capped my precious staples, were being smashed and their contents mixing with the sea. In the desperateness of the hour there had been no time to so thoroughly think out the possibilities and probabilities of my actions.

Beside my scanty food supply lay my sextant, or rather what was left of it. It had once been a fine precision instrument, but now it was a twisted piece of junk. The index mirror was broken off completely. The telescope was gone. The alidade was bent at a rakish angle and jammed so that it couldn't be moved. The arc was rippled beyond any dreams of repair with means at hand.

Close by lay the compass — what was left of it, that is. The glass was smashed and the precious liquid had spilled. The guts of the instrument were lost in the disarray of the cabin, and it was the more useless in that it was torn from its gimbals, and they weren't to be found.

During the day I found no charts, no *Sailing Directions*, no Light lists; not even my carefully kept log of the voyage. These articles I always kept in the chart rack beside my bunk. When the cabin filled, the rushing water had licked them out.

The tidying process disclosed considerable damage to the interior of my boat: The icebox, lockers, galley, sink board, chart rack, ladder, and floor boards had been torn from their fastenings. They were a mass of amorphous lumber. The crushing weight of the twisting water in the hold had chewed down all my fixtures except the stout bunk.

There were few exceptions to this destruction. Built into the forward wall of the deckhouse, high up, was a small elongated cabinet; of all the inside furnishings it alone was dry. In it were twenty cartons of cigarettes, which I was taking to Mary's dad, some matches, and my navigation pocket watch. The cigarettes were useless because I have never smoked, and near the cabinet, on the starboard bulkhead just under the portholes, there clung the bookshelf; in it a frowzy mixing of wet pages and crumpled bindings.

Pangs of uneasiness set in. I tried to recall every important tenet a seaman should know for such times as he is lost on the sea, and foodless and waterless. Once, during the war, I was in a lifeboat for a short while. But it had been infinitely different from this. There had been the company of twenty men. We had a regular food and water ration, handed round by the old scoundrel, our captain. And we had our officers, with gold braid enough to defy the devil, to inspire us. The greatest difference between the lifeboat and *Pagan* was that in the lifeboat we knew we would be rescued. The Army and Navy were looking for us; so we enjoyed ourselves teasing the sharks and regretting we couldn't feed them!

That night on *Pagan* I detailed for myself a strict regimen to be followed to the letter. Food and water were to be carefully doled. I suggested a pint a day water ration and a few nibbles of the food, something to take the edge off hunger. With Samoa so near, I wouldn't be sorely pressed. A matter of two weeks' discomfort, then port, and the luxury of refitting my boat for the last leg of the voyage. The date was September 9 — five days since the start of the hurricane.

I was lost, that was definite. Five days ago my position, according to memory, had been 13° 21′ south, 162° 40′ west. I had then been a bosun's roar from the Suvorov Islands, a low, nearly barren, uninhabited coral reef. After a long calculation I figured I was somewhere south and west of the Suvorovs, somewhere under their lee. Not close enough to bother or to risk looking for them. Better leave them be, I thought. Do the safe thing, go on west to Samoa.

I guessed the distance to Samoa at about 400 miles. To be on the safe side I put it at 450; actually it was 480. I estimated my progress with sails at twenty-five miles per day. And from what I remembered of the Pilot Chart, there was a current push of from zero to twenty miles per day on the keel. I conservatively planned on five miles a day help from the current, which would jump my daily coverage to thirty miles.

By simple arithmetic, I supposed that in sixteen or eighteen days I should come upon Samoa, provided I was in the right latitude. If I wasn't, then I would pass by it into landless westward waters. The closest sizable land if I missed Samoa was Fiji, some 600 miles to the southwest. I made up my mind not to miss Samoa, to press every faculty of boat and man to find it. Rigidly rationed as I was in food and water, and at my slow speed, I didn't dare miss it.

I determined to be as circumspect as possible with my steering; to keep a ready eye for all signs of land and commerce on the sea; especially to husband very closely every morsel and drop of my edibles. There was to be absolutely no physical exertion, aside from pumping out. If my body was to stand the gaff of a sixteen days' fast, there must be a minimum loss of energy, with plenty of sleep and rest. Also I must attempt to add to my meager provisions; I would fish, and perhaps catch sea birds.

I thought grimly on each possible precaution that would lengthen the supply of food over the next eighteen days. Before me sat the two cans of food, the bottle of ketchup, and the coconut.

Since I had worked the whole day and was tired, and my body was in pressing need of nourishment, I decided to bolster my flagging flesh and spirits with one of the cans of food. Doing so was contrary to the strict ration I had set for myself, but I needed backing up after three days of grueling work. Maybe I was short on resistance and couldn't face up to the ration; but I like to think there was a real need for that can of food. It would take at least a can; my body felt the need of two or three cans. I hatcheted one of the cans open and found it to be peas. I took them out into the cool night, to dine on the deckhouse, to eat and watch for a chance light. They were delicious beyond belief; there was a sweetness and delicacy I never knew peas could have. I chewed them to a fine gruel before swallowing them, remembering Captain Bligh's advice to his starving men in their open boat.

The night was fresh. Stars were on the march across the heavens, leading *Pagan* west. I checked and steadied the tiller. The bow was set on a planet just off the end of Scorpio, giving a nice westerly course. When the planet should fade below the horizon, I could use the Southern Cross, keeping it on the port beam. A spanking breeze welled up from the south. The mast was bent slightly from plumb. I was making good my thirty-mile-a-day clip. I pumped the bilges, took a last look at the unbroken horizon, and went below.

Sitting on my bunk, I had a light nip of water before hitting the sack. I thought that the best method to conserve water would be to drink only when thirsty, and then just a sip, but taking care never to consume more than a pint a day. With that ration I had water for thirty-two days. I fitted the bung to my precious keg of water and rolled in for the night.

Lost

THE FIRST THING I did next morning was search out all my medical supplies. I had many cuts and abrasions, and skinless knuckles and joints. I wanted to get them healed before hunger began taking its toll. I salved, and patched over, my dozens of cuts and scratches.

My next move was to take steps to plan out my navigation; to somehow keep a record of my position and my progress along the track to Samoa. I scratched out a makeshift chart on the floor of the cockpit showing the sector between the Marquesas and Australia. I etched the islands in from memory and remained fully aware when I finished that my work wasn't exactly accurate.

On the chart, as closely as I could figure it, I drove in a nail to represent my position, intending each day to shift the nail as I made to westward. Thus, on entering my second day under full sail, I tapped the nail in at a point a little to the south and slightly to the west of the Suvorov Islands. And, since I had no calendar and in order to keep up with the passing days, I managed a kind of calendar that consisted of X's on the wall — knifed in just above my bunk below the porthole.

My fishing kit I never found. But I ran onto two hooks, and some line. I found, too, a small packet of fish bait. It was salted pork strippings. I baited a hook and fed it over the stern, keeping the line fast to my little finger.

For the first time since the hurricane I noticed that Old Death and his voracious boys were still with me. It was heartening to see them; now I had a mobile food supply. They were having difficulties in orienting themselves to the slower speed of the boat. Before the hurricane, when I had sailed faster, they were able to advance at a more favorable clip upon the unsuspecting schools of flying fish, but now the flying fish were able to observe my approach from a distance, and scatter. Despite this handicap my faithful dolphin never deserted me; nor did they trust me, keeping a discreet distance to avoid my spears and ignoring my baited hooks.

Happily, the hurricane had not pitched all my books from the bookshelf just above my bunk. There were nine volumes with which to shorten the hours to Samoa. I spent most of the morning reading. One hour I gave over to a nap. Other than pumping out, and searching the horizon, I did nothing. I avoided the deck in the heat of the day, but as the afternoon waned I came out to enjoy the fresh breeze and see to the steering. At the same time I made a check of the sails and my jury rigging. Everything looked okay.

I remembered that it is a good idea for those living in thirst to bathe the body with salt water. The pores drink in the moisture, and a little of the parched condition is thus comforted. I slipped over the stern and dragged in the wake to my neck. The cool water was delightful, laving over me with soft fingers and washing away my uneasiness. After ten minutes I climbed aboard, refreshed, and dried in the sun and wind.

As yet I had eaten nothing during the day. An intermittent gnawing walked hobnailed around my stomach. I decided to open the ketchup and have a taste — enough to take the edge off hunger. Working the cap loose, I took a strong suck from the bottle. I replaced the cap and leaned the bottle against the curve of the ribbing. The sight of it tormented me, set my juices to working, so I shoved it beneath my bunk.

By dark, I hadn't caught a fish. I drew in my line. I pumped the bilges and lay down. My system for working the pump varied in the day and night. During the day I came up to pump out every hour. This gave me a chance to search the horizon a dozen times a day. At night I pumped out as often as the noise or splash of rising water awakened me, which was every few hours.

When I arose to greet the sun and found my belly gnawing I went seeking another swallow of ketchup. I found the ketchup bottle empty. I remembered taking a suck in the deep of the night, and that's all I could remember. It must have been deeper than I realized, and it was regrettable, but the ketchup was gone. . . . I didn't worry about it. For breakfast I rinsed out the bottle with a part of my morning's water ration.

My hook was over the transom as soon as I could put it there. I sat reading on my bunk, jiggling the line tied to my finger. I dwelt constantly on the remaining can of food and the coconut. I wondered about the can. I guessed at what it could contain, and the more I guessed the emptier my stomach grew.

Hunger pains irked me all morning. Finally I thought, "Why be hungry when there's food around?" I grabbed the hatchet; and in a few minutes I was downing a can of sauerkraut. I thought as I ate, What an unreasonable thing to be hungry when there's food around.

The coconut lay on the foot of my bunk.

I was still hungry. My stomach was squeezing and un-squeezing itself. I put the coconut out of sight. But I thought of it constantly. I brought it out, smelled it, shook it, and heard the teasing rustle of coconut milk. I put it back. My throat and mouth turned wet with the possibilities of a bite of the soft white coconut meat. I went on deck, but soon concluded the sun was too hot.

Down below I got the coconut out and sat staring at it, fascinated. "Don't eat it," I said, "be reasonable." "Reasonable my eye," I replied, "if I were reasonable, I wouldn't be here." "It's all the food you've got for eighteen days." "So what."

Ten minutes later I was smacking over the last white morsels of the exquisite coconut meat. My careful plans for apportioning out my food had gone glimmering. What did it matter; I was full and happy. I had no worries. If there was no food, there was no food . . . and that was that. Better to eat and be at peace than stalk and fret over a morsel. My spirits rose. "Tomorrow I'll catch a fish."

I went on deck and basked in the cool afternoon sun. In a while I dropped over the stern and rinsed my body in the fresh sea. After, I went below and read till dark. About seven o'clock I pumped the bilges for the last time that day, had my nightcap — a bare sip of water — and turned in.

All the next day I sat expectantly at the end of my line. Noon came; I had a small drink. It tasted sweet. Dusk came on, dark closed around. I pumped out, went below, and had a small drink that I called dinner. I turned in sorely disgusted. I didn't even bother to haul the fishline aboard: it lay strung out through the hatchway and over the transom dragging in the sea astern, still twined about my finger.

In the middle of the night, I was raised from sleep by something nearly jerking my finger off. Instantly I realized it was a fish and went bounding to the deck, hauling on the line as I ran. From under the transom I pulled a rather life-less-looking fish. When I took the hook from him, he just lay there breathing heavily. Suddenly he flipped himself about with quick snaps and, because there was no rail, splashed into the sea and swam merrily away.

I was stupefied. I turned my light onto the black water but could see nothing. The excitement of possible food had restirred the hunger movements; the sudden disappointment made me sick. I called myself onto the carpet and raked myself over the coals. When I realized that cursing and fuming was using up my reserves of energy I went below and fell into a miserable sleep that lasted through the night to the dawn.

I put fresh bait on the hook. The old bait, of course, I ate. It was pork rind processed chemically. It was tough and salty and had a peculiar ironlike flavor. But it was delicious. It set my digestive juices to flowing and soon all the devils of hunger were tormenting me. For hours I sat brooding over the packet of bait, saying no, and denying the growing call of my emptiness. And I knew there would be no respite from it as long as there was a crumb of food aboard. I decided to have just one of the thin strips of bait. "Just to suck on," I said. By noon, not unstrangely, all but one of the strippings of bait was gone.

I sat and stared at it. It was beautiful to my eyes — I put it aside and tried to forget it. Soon I was back, fawning over it, pondering its destiny. As bait on the hook its value was in-estimable; yet, on the other hand, it could just happen that a fish might steal it, and I would have neither fish nor bait. The fate of the strip of rind became of huge proportion. I carefully weighed its future, thinking deeply on every possibility. Then . . . saying to myself, "a bird in the hand. . . ." I placed the rind on my tongue, and soon I was sucking on it happily. That settled that problem.

But it made me feel better to eat. When the food was gone I relaxed, read, and thought of the good time I would have in Samoa. Water, not food, is the important thing in starvation. This I knew. As long as I had a few sips of water each day, I knew I could survive to Samoa. I was rigorous with my water, knowing that my very life depended on it. I never drank more than a pint a day and I always staggered my drinking through the day and night so that I received its maximum benefit. But eatables . . . I gulped them on sight.

During my life I have achieved ideal health. I knew my body could stand any physical rigor within reason. To go without food for long periods isn't a great test for the human body. So I didn't worry if my impulsiveness resulted in a temporary hardship. The thought of Samoa only two weeks away braced me up.

I caught the same fish again. The moment he tugged at my finger, I bolted to the deck, bristling with sudden hunger. I pulled him quickly over the stern and dropped him in the cockpit. Before he could take a first breath I was on him.

I fell chest first over him, smothering him with my weight. Very gradually I eased off and clutched him with both hands. I felt as the lion feels with a fawn under his claws. The fish's baleful eyes watched me as I beat the life out of him.

I fetched him below; and less than five minutes after being hauled from the deep he was cleaned and scaled. With his insides gone there wasn't much to him. He was a common variety of triggerfish, blackish brown, about eight inches long and half as wide; his head made about third of his body. Under my bunk was the faithful little Primus stove, and miraculously enough it fired up. I scraped the rust out of the skillet.

I was at a loss as to how to cook my catch. I couldn't afford the water to boil him, and I couldn't use salt water for its effect on my thirst. There was no grease for frying. Then I remembered the jar of vaseline in the medicine kit.

After drying the fish, I coated him liberally with vaseline and dropped him into the hot frying pan. As he sizzled and popped beneath a cloud of smoke, I rolled him over. When he grew seared looking and soft, I cut the fire and pinched at him with my fingers. In a few minutes there were only a few bones to identify what had twenty minutes before been a fish cavorting in the sea. I kept the bones for breakfast.

The next day dragged by with nothing more exciting than the hauling of the wind from south to southeast. My line was still dragging astern, but there had been no bites. Hunger ravaged my stomach like tank treads. I had been saving the vaseline in case I caught another fish. As dark closed in, and my stomach cried out, I cleaned the jar with my finger and licked it dry. It was greasy and probably contained little or no nutritional value as fat; but at least it quieted the hunger call.

A morning soon after I wakened with greediest hunger because all night I had dreamed of feasting and gorging. I sipped my morning water ration, which only tormented me. I went to the medicine chest, and before I could caution myself I ate the only jar of Vicks. And that afternoon when the devil harried me again, I squeezed one of the two tubes of boric acid down my throat. I saved the other tube and a can of tooth powder for the next day.

I spent the afternoon thumbing through the only magazine aboard — one that had lodged on the bookshelf. As I turned over each page it was the same thing — food. Mammoth advertisements showing food in its most toothsome manner. Great roasts and salads, sandwiches and desserts, stews and cocktails. Hunger cramps started. Each page tortured me. I jumped up and with one sweep tossed the magazine far out on the green water. I felt better.

The next day I mixed half the tooth powder with water, and drank it as a potion. It had a pleasant aftertaste but it made me flinch when it went down. By nightfall, still no fish.

Prospects for the next day looked good. There was half the small can of tooth powder, and the other tube of boric acid compound. I bedded down that night unutterably hungry.

Then came the worst night of all. A night of food dreams. A night of ghosts in the form of chocolate cakes and steak dinners. Through the long hours I writhed between waking and sleeping, and at last I wakened finally and found myself champing at my blanket. I jumped up and fumbled hurriedly into my medicinal supplies. I came out with the last tube of boric acid, squeezed it into a blob on my fist, and smeared it into my mouth. Then I slept.

With morning I suddenly remembered my shipmate, Stowaway. I hadn't seen him since the hurricane, and strangely, I hadn't particularly thought of him. The little house I had built him was gone; it evidently went by the board during the storm.

I remembered Stowaway as I had seen him last, just before

the hurricane, sleek, fat, and beady-eyed. I grew aquiver with
the thought of the nice stew I could make of him. I began
a detailed search of the boat, which took me into its every
nook and cranny. For hours I crawled and squirmed into
impossible places. By noon I found no trace of his recent existence aboard. I had torn away all the inside planking and
ripped up what floor boards were left. I had also lowered myself into the watertight stern section and probed through it
with my flashlight. I finally had to admit that my long-time
buddy had been washed overboard.

But the search hadn't been entirely fruitless. I found several
articles that I could use. There were a chamois cloth, an army
shoe, a box of pepper, a tube of lipstick and a jar of face
cream left from the cosmetics I had planned to take to Mary,
a small box of tea, a bottle of shaving lotion, a bottle of hair
oil, and a tiny jar of fish eggs for bait.

I opened the fish eggs to put fresh bait on the hook. I
baited it and intended to screw the cap on the jar. To explain
what I did next is impossible; there is no explaining it, it
just happened. Before I could get the lid on the jar, I had
gulped the eggs. There was only the empty jar in my hand,
but hopelessly little comfort for the valuable mouthful I had
downed. . . . But they were gone; so I didn't have to worry
about how to resist them.

My hunger went unchecked. When I napped in the
afternoon I fell into eerie food dreams. I had to get up, I
couldn't sleep. I turned to my limited food resources and
experimented with them. I chopped the chamois cloth into
tiny fragments, spilled them into a strong tea made from my
ration of water and some of the tea I had found, and boiled
them for ten minutes. This I seasoned heavily with pepper,

a half can of tooth powder, and a generous dash of the shave lotion. To give it an interesting taste, I tossed in a fistful of salt water and a part of my can of machine oil.

The result was a stew that made my eyes burn and my nose revolt when I ate it. Since the chamois had been used to strain gasoline, it gave the brew a distinctive zip. I ate half of it that afternoon and deferred the rest till the next day.

I got up as on any other day and started out the battered companionway. What I saw on the sternpost paralyzed me. It was a sea bird. He sat there looking absent-minded and wriggling his tail feathers. I could sense his fatness and I was eager to have my hands on him in a death grip.

Instantly I was the primitive beast stalking his prey. I knew I couldn't creep upon him, close enough to pounce on him, unseen. I thought of crawling near and clubbing him, but the mizzen was in the way. Then it occurred to me to spear him. There was my fish spear. Spear in hand, I eased into the cockpit and each time his eyes were away from me I slid a foot nearer. Six feet from him, I dared not go farther. I posed my weapon, took a deep breath, took nervous aim, and jabbed. It was a clean stroke impaling him at the breast.

The bird was one of the small variety of tern which tolerate the Pacific wastes. Defeathered and cleaned he weighed out something less than a pound. The vaseline was gone, so I coated him with machine oil and put him on the fire.

It was a wonderful breakfast. I smacked over the thought of it for the rest of the day. At night when I had failed to get a fish and no further birds had landed aboard, I brought forth the small handful of bones left from the morning feast. Each bone I gnawed and crushed and sucked, then sprinkled it over the side.

The next morning I quaffed off the last of my devilish
brew. It made my hair crawl to smell it. It had soured in the
night, so I downed it quickly, not wanting to lose its liquid
value. Later I became queasy, and lay hove-down with a
fever that night, unable to bail out. By morning the water
had risen to my bunk top. I realized I had better make some
effort to get afoot and pump out, or the decks would soon be
awash.

I got up and stood in the knee-deep water. There was nothing to eat. I looked up hoping there would be a bird as on
the morning before. There was nothing — only the limitless
whitecaps. I drank my ration of water for the day. It made
me feel better. I pumped for an hour, lowering the water to
the bilge. The growing morning heat was robbing me of my
moisture. I lowered myself over the stern and dragged along
in the gentle wake. It refreshed me and I came aboard strong
again.

I finished the dreaded job. It left me so tired that I went
below to bed. I slept several hours but awakened with fitful
pangs of hunger. There were only the face cream, hair oil,
shaving lotion, lipstick, and army shoes aboard. I sifted
through them for something edible.

I took a nibble of the lipstick and found it not too bad.
Cutting the red lump loose from its holder, I broke it in two
and swallowed each lump. However, the lipstick didn't relieve
my hunger. I opened the jar of face cream, and before I knew
it had crammed the unctuous mixture down my throat. It
left an oil taste in my mouth for hours and made me slightly
squeamish, but the inner twistings ended, and I was at peace.

I slept till past high noon and went on deck to work the
pump. The effects of my semistarvation were beginning to

tell. I began for the first time to labor at the pump. Also, I felt a greater inclination to sleep, and a general drowsiness, and I was aware of a slight fogginess in the head. I had lost some flesh, my arms were thinner, a few ribs showed, and my knees were somewhat knotty. My waistline grew more fashionable every day, it was smaller around than I would ever have had occasion to imagine it could be.

All I thought of was food. Every waking hour was dedicated to it, and every sleeping hour. I recalled great meals where I had sat to table in the past and eaten hugely. And I dreamed of tables in the future where I would sit for hours and glorify food.

While I was pumping I noticed splashes emanating from the life raft astern. It had a shallow layer of water in its bottom, and from there they came. When I took a close look I could see that some sort of fish was trapped inside and attempting to swim in the insufficient water.

Flipping about helplessly was a delicious looking flying fish. He had evidently leaped inside and now he was trapped. He was easily eight inches long. I picked him up and admired his shimmering beauty with drooling glances. I was estimating how tasty he would be fried in machine oil. "But first," I thought, "I'll just have a nibble of his tail."

I bit his tail off and ground it up exuberantly, bones and all. It was savory beyond description. Before I quite understood what I was doing I had devoured the whole fish and was picking scales out of my teeth. All I could remember of the fish was the slightly bitter taste about halfway through.

The fresh meat put me in a scintillating mood. My spirits soared and I felt that I would come on land any minute. By my arithmetical calculations I was hard by Samoa. The

Manua Islands should be appearing presently. Maybe in the
night the loom of them would rear up on *Pagan's* bow. I
decided to rise as often as possible in the night to pump out
— and look for them.

I rose often in the night and searched, but nothing broke
the monotonous dim horizon.

Morning found me on deck at the crack of dawn, straining my eyes across the bows. I climbed the mast and peered
ahead; but when the little spar groaned beneath my weight,
I clambered down. The horizon offered up nothing to en-
courage me. But the ocean did.

Just under *Pagan's* counter I espied three triggerfish —
new arrivals from near-by land, I suppose. I broke out the
spear and set to work. Kneeling on the stern, I sighted down
the spear shaft and struck. My first thrust was awry. I tried
again and again, but learned that striking at so small a target
with a single barb isn't easy. Eventually I nicked one of them
and he limped off astern. I never saw him again.

The other two played wary and sought the protection of
the keel. To draw them out I dropped bits of wood on the
water which they sidled out to investigate. Peering over the
stern, I stabbed them as they sauntered out, and again when
they hurried back.

In time I nicked another of them and he too fled sternward, not to reappear. I realized if I was to get the last one
I must make a spear with more than one barb.

Dusk was coming on. I was exhausted and ravenous. There
was nothing to eat except shaving lotion and hair oil, and an
army shoe. I wasn't desperate enough to stomach those, so
I had a last look for land, pumped the bilges, and slipped below for the night — hungry.

The day's exertions had been too much for a peaceful sleep. Food dreams haunted me . . . hamburgers, "Cokes," hot dogs, chocolate sundaes whirled through my mind, causing me to pitch and toss. In the middle of the night I dreamed I was chewing a juicy chicken bone and shouting for more. I awakened, and there I sat bellowing into the black night for more chicken.

A foot of water covered the cabin floor. Outside was the persistent noise of the sea as it lapped against the planks. I got up to do the pumping — an hour's work.

Before dawn I awoke with hunger's sharp stitches in my stomach. I couldn't sleep. The recurrent thought of the spear I had to make was badgering me. In the end I arose early, and began to work at it. I made it from one of the oars given me by the Perlas Indians. I cut the oar blade off square a foot from the tip and drove four nails up grain. Pounding the head of each nail flat, I filed them sharp and into some semblance of a barb. I pared down the oar blade to coincide with the handle, and my spear was ready.

At daybreak I was perched on the stern waiting for old "wobbly fins," as I called him. The triggerfish swims very leisurely and with a lackadaisical flourish of his large fins. In a short time he sauntered out into the rising sun. My first strike missed cleanly. He reared back to note the cause of the disturbance around him, exposing himself broadside. It was a shot I couldn't miss.

Soon he was frying on the fire, smoking like a coal burner. I had to fry him in hair oil since I had used the last of the machine oil on the bird. I ate him so fast it made little difference what he was fried in. And I ate him as I fried him, head, scales, fins, and all. Usually I saved the bones for the next meal, but when I finished there were no bones.

The policy on *Pagan* was rapidly becoming: when there is food, eat it; when there isn't any, forget about it.

With the acquisition of food, I burst into liveliness again. I felt optimistic about land and expected to see it by noon. There were a few signs to indicate its presence. Flying fish were more in abundance than at any time since the hurricane, and Old Death and his boys were giving them a merry chase. Several sea and semi-land birds were in the air, hovering over the voracious dolphin, swooping on the flying fish. And astern, their wicked pointed fins jutting menacingly up from the dark water, was a school of leering sharks.

I stood before the mast all day watching each new cloud. Right up to dark there was a landless horizon. With the ship making so little way I wasn't afraid of beaching myself in the night on something I couldn't see before dark. I pumped the bilges and went below.

That night I had a bad case of "channel fever," the nervous anxiety that plagues the seaman the night before arrival. I slept fitfully and, when I dreamed, I had nightmares. I wakened once shouting "Land ho," and rushed out on deck expecting to see it. Before daybreak I was perched at the mast, watching for a sail or a cone of land.

Light of day brought no gray shadow that could be called land. There were the usual birds of the past few days — and more of them, it seemed.

Two in particular showed the keenest inquisitiveness about *Pagan*. They flew up within a dozen feet of the stern, hovered for a moment, then broke away into a slanting curve that brought them back again. I could see that if I had a weapon, I could knock one of them down as he poised in flight. A bow and arrow, it flashed across my mind, would be just the thing.

I crept below, and after a considerable search decided to rip out one of the oaken deckhouse beams for the bow. It was nearly an hour before I had broken the heavy timber out. Outside, the prying birds were still slanting across the stern, and in fact, now that I was below, they appeared to be easing in a little closer. In another hour I had sawed the beam, chopped it, and whittled it into something resembling a bow. The arrows were easier to fashion. I simply sawed strips from a pine plank, wired a nail to the tips, and prepared to shoot them untufted. I strung my bow with a strand of wire left over from the shrouds.

With an arrow fitted to the string I waited, and watched for the moment when I could shoot. I was standing just inside the cabin, prepared to fire through the companionway. When a bird soared in and hovered a moment, I let fly, but missed. I had many shots and was heartened by an occasional glancing blow or near miss.

The birds grew chary. By noon I had lost nine arrows and the birds were no longer coming quite so close.

Nails — especially after the extensive repairs I had made — were scarce. I made a few more arrows, and during the afternoon I fired twelve, my total supply. Hunger pains and exhaustion, the long hours of nervous anxiety, were beginning to tell. What was worse, there were only a few more nails for arrows, and these were in the foreward hatch where I had nailed it down in preparation for the hurricane. I pulled them and made more arrows. Soon I was shooting at the ungainly frigate birds again.

My aim was getting erratic. Then, unexpectedly, one of my shafts connected. A head shot: he folded limply and tumbled into the water a few feet off the beam. There were pointed fins just to sternward or I could have dived the short distance to retrieve my kill. I pulled the rubber dinghy up, hopped in, paddled to the limp feathery ball, and even as I was stepping aboard *Pagan* again, I was ripping out handfuls of feathers.

Food for two days in a row brought a Christmas-like spirit to *Pagan*. My optimism soared. I would sight land by the next morning; if not, by noon; and by nightfall enjoy dinner at the Naval Station in Tutuila. I also thought of a scheme for making a slingshot from rubber of the life raft. It would be simple enough to knock down a dozen birds in the time it had taken with the bow. That night I had a rosy dream instead of the usual nightmare.

The next morning, after looking fruitlessly for land, I set to work on my slingshot. I wanted to knock down a bird or two to sustain me through the day till land came. After extensive practice in making such boy's weapons as a youngster, doing it now was a pushover. In little time I was ensconced in the cockpit with my new weapon and a small pile of nuts, unscrewed from the engine.

Soon I was getting an occasional shot, but not doing well, because I was overearnest. Moreover the large frigate birds which make easy targets were gone, only the smaller terns were around. They flew faster, were smaller. About eleven o'clock I winged one. He landed off a good way, too far to chance a retrieve in the dinghy; but when I came about and beat up toward him, he took off and limped along to eastward. It was tough luck, but there were plenty more around.

Sometime in the late afternoon I sent another plummeting into the green sea. I jibed ship and flew toward him; but he too got away.

Along about five o'clock I gave up. I poured a few pans of sea water-over my body to moisten the dry, dying skin. I pumped the bilges, had a last look for land, and shuffled below. I was dead tired and thoroughly disgusted. The thought with which I went to sleep was, "Tomorrow there will be land, I hope."

The next day was overcast and dull. Overhead, for the first time, floated white bosun birds, short-winged, long swallow-tailed, plummeting from time to time like falling bombs into the sea. They were new on the scene and they were land birds. I had seen them from the Perlas Islands all across the Pacific — and always I had seen them near land. It is said the bosun bird hovers within sight of his land. I watched them float, collapse their wings and tremble downward, and as I watched my hopes for a quick approach to land grew.

Somewhere close was land. The birds bespoke it. I followed them, studying their every movement for hours. Not a hint, not a clue did they drop of where land might be. And there was no trace of land on the horizons . . . until, in the afternoon, dead ahead, it welled up from the sea. I could barely distinguish it in the haze, but it was land, I knew it was land. I raced toward it exultantly. Land after sixteen days of near starvation! I found myself clinging to the mast, shouting and singing. Then it happened. What I had thought was land went racing away along the horizon, changing its shape as it went, and hiding itself in the thick air. I had been hoaxed by a cloud; but I wasn't discouraged, land was near.

The bosun birds were still flying overhead "in sight of

their land." I wished I could see with their eyes. I wished
I knew what they knew. Somewhere near was land. There
were gannet birds in the air and varieties of land terns, besides the bosun birds and the ever-present sharks loafing
patiently around the stern. But where was the land? How
close, how far, in what direction?

I searched the horizon for hours, trying to penetrate the
overcast air. Land was overdue; I should have sighted it two
and even three days before. By calculation I had passed it. I
consulted the figures of my guesswork navigation. If I were
making thirty miles a day; I should be near, or past, land. The
nail, marching to westward over my chart, was sticking up in
the center of the Samoan group. On the bulkhead, above my
bunk, a lengthening line of X's leered at me. I changed my
figures from thirty miles a day to twenty-five — and still I
figured I should be near enough to sight land . . . if it were
there. I decided to wait another day before taking action. I
went out on deck.

A grizzly mantle completely censored the sun. The wind
during the night had been steady from the northeast. Its
habit, in this area, was to veer steadily from the south over
a space of days to the northeast, then suddenly haul back to
south and start the cycle anew. There was no way, with the
sun blotted out, to know the set of the wind, whether it had
changed or not. I certainly didn't want to run before it, with
it on my starboard quarter, if I didn't know its direction, especially if it was out of the south. I last remembered it on the
starboard quarter giving me a westerly course. According to
the stars it had been — then — somewhere in the north quadrant.

The sea swell indicated no change in wind direction. I

decided to play it safe, and doffed all sail but the tiny jib. The work tired me. I went below and slept an hour and came back.

Floating high up were the bosun birds. Their very presence teased me and tantalized me. Land for them was but an hour's flight. I thought of the closeness of land, and of the possibilities of finding it soon, and thought on the deep dishes I would eat. It made my stomach crawl, and I forced it out of mind.

Pagan drifted under a heavy sky. It was painful to have a wind and not to be able to sail; it was worse than being in a calm. But midafternoon hunger was crucifying me. There were several shoes around, only one of which was of undyed leather — an army shoe. I stared at it dejectedly. It smelled like you-know-what; but it was food. I cut the upper part away from the sole, and started chewing its tongue. It was too tough even to be dented. Army shoes are tough customers. I soaked it awhile in salt water, taking it out occasionally to beat on the end of my bunk for "tenderizing." Greasing one sizable piece with hair oil, I fried it, but it only turned black and stayed just as unchewable. Finally I boiled the whole shoe in my precious water ration. I didn't boil it long; as soon as evaporation began to tell on the water content I cut the fire. The soup had an inspiring taste, but the leather was still unbearable. In the end, I cut it into strips, and though I still couldn't chew it, at least I could get it down, and that's all that mattered. I went to bed that night with something under my belt.

Don't eat leather if you want pleasant dreams. For unending hours I writhed in the grip of nightmares about food. I was in a mammoth grocery store running berserk among corridors of food. I wakened in a labor of sweat only to drift back to my horror dreams.

Sometime late that night when I pumped the bilges I caught a glimpse of Canopus, and joyfully established the wind in the south. My hunch had been correct. The wind had shifted. Had I sailed with it on the starboard quarter, I would have been sailing northeast. I trudged to the deck and strung up all sail. Once again *Pagan* was making a bowline to the west.

A wan sun hidden intermittently by mountains of heavy clouds arose and flashed pale beams on a mass of land at the bowsprit end. I watched it closely for a suspicious minute, then I was sure it was land. When I saw it loom up, I nearly went crazy. I jumped up and down on the cabin top and giggled like a child. Grabbing my bucket I ran onto the stern and indulged in a hasty salt bath. The land was closing in at an amazing rate. I dried myself cursorily. Valleys in the land were visible. I went below to get dressed. I donned a suit of khakis, a hat, shoes, and combed my beard.

Coming on deck, I noticed that the land had changed not only its shape, but its direction — in fact, it wasn't land at all, it was a cloud, it was going straight up. I watched it ascend in dejected silence. My heart slumped down to my shoe bottoms. If my body hadn't needed the liquid so badly, I would have wept.

That afternoon, I ran out of nuts to use as ammunition. Everything had been stripped from the engine and its fittings. There was the thousand pounds of cement in the bilge used as ballast. I chipped out a dozen suitable pieces, but by dark had had no success with them.

That night was the grimmest aboard *Pagan* since the

hurricane. Flashlight in hand I sat for hours in the cockpit studying my makeshift chart of South Sea waters scratched in the wood of the cockpit floor. According to my figures I had far overshot Samoa. The next land to westward was the Hoorn Islands, the exact position of which was unknown to me. But to the southwest about 600 miles lay Fiji — some three weeks' sailing time.

It was two days since I had eaten anything substantial. A dread decision was in the balance: go on looking blindly for Samoa, or head south, while there was still time, and connect with the wider area of the Fijis. Covering a wide swath as they do they offered a broad front that would be easier to find than Samoa — but the big thing was to get there; to go for three weeks on two weeks' supply of water, at a half pint a day. It was a decision to be weighed, to be thought on.

If my assumptions were correct, I was somewhere approximately northeast of the Fijis. Unless I headed south soon I would miss them altogether and have to struggle on to the next land, the New Hebrides Islands, over 500 miles from the Fijis. I pondered over the crude map, measuring distances, weighing possibilities. Finally I decided to look one more day for Samoa.

The sleep of that night was woefully unsound. I dreamed I was wrecked on a beach; and I was happy. There was a huge gray whale stranded there. I grabbed him by the tail and started devouring him alive as I had done the flying fish. And I awakened clawing and growling at my bunk boards. It was just as well, the bilges needed pumping.

Before daylight I was atop the deckhouse peering past the wind-filled jib to the landless horizon. It was my twenty-first day under the jury rig. All that day I sat on the fore scuttle, rising often to search across the bows. Overhead were the bosun birds, gannets, land terns, and man-o'-war birds, screaming down on the flying fish scared up by Old Death and his raiders. Land was somewhere, but where? The only times I went aft was to pump the bilges. I kept a daylong vigil that came to naught. As dusk, then dark, closed in I did what seemed the only reasonable thing to do. I stepped aft and changed the angle of rudder, by directing the splintered remains of the tiller to leeward. The bow hauled in upon the southeast breeze and stopped in the south. "Fiji or bust," I said, as I lashed the splintered stub and trimmed the sails to hold me on a new course.

From that moment onward the tenor of my situation changed. I was no longer, as I had led myself to believe, temporarily under duress; I was in a position of extreme indefiniteness about everything. I wasn't even certain that if I did head south I would be able to find the Fiji Islands. It all depended on how far west I had sailed in search of Samoa. It depended on whether I was sailing at a rate of twenty-five miles a day or thirty — or more or less than that — regarding which I had no way of knowing. It depended on the westerly set of the current — that is, its speed. It depended on whether or not I could face another twenty-one days of fast. It depended on whether there were any intervening reefs — and the Fijis are notorious for hidden offshore reefs. I could take a wild stab in the dark and hope for a safe landfall, and that was all.

My most burdensome concern was the weather. Like a sword of Damocles the threat of a destructive hurricane hovered in the offing, I was moving in a widely known cyclonic track, with the hurricane season under way at that!

Pagan couldn't outlive another hurricane, and I hadn't the strength to fight the ruinous winds or bail the boat out for prolonged hours. I closed my mind to the likelihood of any such event, and concentrated solely on the dubious trip ahead and the bout with starvation — the first round of which was over.

The bow of my boat was in the south; I worked the heavy bilge pump for the first time on the new course. I looked off across the stretch of hostile water, took account of my crawling speed, listened to the grumble of hunger in my stomach.

Then an urge struck me that penetrated to my very warp and weft, so I followed it. In such circumstances what else remains to a man but that last unfailing resource, the Great Captain — the Captain of all ships. I bent to my knees reluctantly; for in the last months my sins had been monsters.

From Perlas to Galápagos, and from Galápagos on west, I had uttered such curses as I doubt have ever been heard over the keel of a ship. In every squall, gale, calm, cloudburst, and contrary current, I had unloosed a flood of invective to shame a mule skinner. But more than that . . . in the height of my extremities I had profaned God Himself. On many an occasion I became so bold as to defy Him, deny Him, and swear I would profess atheism all the rest of my life. I even invited Him on deck — man to man — anything but the obstructing persecution of the elements, anything but the slow crawl when I wanted speed.

And now, lost, foodless, without instruments, I humbly bent my knees to the deck and laid my folded hands upon the cabin. With eyes raised I read off a most heartfelt forgiveness and piteous appeal to *Pagan's* real Captain.

CHAPTER XX   Foodless

I SAT IN THE COCKPIT searching my rough-drawn map of the Southwest Pacific. I was pondering the sea stretches I would be crossing and guessing upon the advisability of what I was doing. There were still a few birds from land beating about. I was still sure that land was close, but to go on searching over a trackless sea when *Pagan's* speed was nil, and with food gone, water dwindling, and the next land 600 miles away — no, I couldn't afford to risk another day in vain search. The broad Fijian chain of islands was findable. My only safe recourse was to go there, and take that lesser of two risks.

I had a predominant guide, since the Dog Star Sirius, in its east–west march across the heavens, drives directly over the center of the Fijis. It was my plan to go south till I was under Sirius, then west till I struck land.

There was a beam wind from the east casting up a light chop. *Pagan* sailed easily; now and then she slopped a little water over the rail. The spray for the most part kept me below in the dark cabin.

Toward late afternoon, I remembered a mosslike growth on *Pagan's* leeward side that had grown during the long traverse from the Galápagos. I would have eaten it before now but I was in doubt as to its effects.

I went on deck and examined it closely. Its color varied

between light and dark green, and it was hairlike, growing about an inch long in several spots. I scraped off a fistful of it and squeezed out its salt water. I pushed a part of the salty grasslike wad into my mouth and chewed and swallowed it. It tasted the way grass should taste, sprinkled with salt. It didn't ease the hunger but it eased the mind.

I thought of the half bottle of hair oil and took the weedy stuff below. With a light sprinkling of the oil — and a stretch of the imagination — it had a saladlike taste. But when I had eaten the grassy bit, I found the hunger still gnawing. It wouldn't be quieted.

There was nothing more to eat except the moss. I scraped some more of it from the hull, dripped the last of the hair oil over it, and chewed it down. *Pagan* was foodless. I sipped the last of my ration of water for the day, pumped the bilges, and settled in for the night.

I waked with the worst hunger pangs yet. The moss, without hair oil, was unbearable, but I ate enough of it to quiet my hunger callings. However, in a while they came again and devils tormented me all morning. By afternoon I couldn't stand it longer. I wanted just a bite, just a chew of something to cheat hunger of its grip.

There was a last pair of shoes, but when I chewed on a corner of leather the taste and smell of dye sickened me. I turned to my belt. I took it off and sat holding it in my hands. It was genuine cowhide; I had owned it for years, had worn it in college and all through the war, had worn it through four shipwrecks. Sentimental attachments swelled within me, and I put it back on. There was only my wallet: of kangaroo hide, a gift of Mary's father. Starvation overcame sentiment in its case, and I emptied its contents into my shirt pocket. As with the army shoe, I boiled it, pounded it, cut it into strips — they lasted through the day and the night.

I was sitting on deck just at dawn watching as always for that point on the horizon from which the first birds would come. A small white sea bird, flailing the air with long wings and shrieking loudly, slanted across the bow from what could have been any direction and circled in for a close view of *Pagan*.

I flipped a single cement chunk toward him, more as an afterthought than a serious intent. Bird and rock miraculously converged. A puff of feathers flew up, and the victim plummeted into the sea like a crippled plane, a bare thirty feet from where I stood.

Unlashing its lines, I threw the helm hard down. *Pagan* rounded to, veering into the wind and bearing down on the wad of white. I scooped thé downy creature inward.

What I did next has been unbelievable to me ever since. Crazed by the thought of food, but more crazed because I had food in my hands, I tore the head from the body in one motion. Thrusting the pulsing stump into my mouth, I drank every particle of its life-giving blood. I was an animal who had made a kill; and as the animal will, I went at it tooth and claw. When it no longer yielded a drop, I bit the delicate neck off and chewed it up, bone and all.

Before I could stop myself, the greater part of the bird was gone. Even then I couldn't stop. I bit wolfishly into the mass of feathers, tearing at what met the tooth; whether it was bone or feathers didn't matter. Not one bone of the fowl's body escaped the mill of my teeth. Each one I smashed to fine splinters and ground to pulp and swallowed.

I ate his feet as I found them. Skin and all went down.

When I came to the head, I ate everything "but the eye-brows." His bill chewed like gristle. I plucked the larger feathers from the skin and started gnawing at the down. It resisted like a blanket, but it filled the emptiness and cheated the devils of hunger. When it was gone I wished there had been more.

When I finished my cannibalistic meal, only a few feathers here and there, and among my teeth, showed that a bird had passed that way.

Two days crept tediously past as though they marched on minutes an hour long. I trolled my fishline as ever astern day and night but received no encouragement. The sparse patches of seamoss on the hull were beginning to thin bald in spots. Birds were around and I had a few opportunities to fling missiles at them, but somehow there was no longer the former spring in my arm: my shots fell short or went awry.

One morning as I came on deck I saw a ship. When first I sighted it, I thought it was a rowboat on the horizon. But on closer inspection I made out the top of the stack and the upper reaches of the masts and booms. She was hull down, knifing directly across my bow; a big freighter pitching grace-fully into the long swells.

I had joyful visions of being towed to Samoa, to food and rest. I thought of the mast's being restepped, and resuited with sails. I could see myself provisioned anew and setting out again for Sydney, and to Mary.

She was evidently Panama bound, probably out of Fiji or Brisbane. Her superstructure was barely floating on the rim of the horizon, and she was footing it fast. Close though she was I couldn't make out her tonnage or nationality. She was still dressed in wartime gray. Any minute I expected to see her alter course and swing across wind to me.

I scaled the unsturdy mast and blinked my flashlight from the masthead. The mast labored under my weight; I climbed down. Then I raised and lowered the mainsail. All the time I shouted like a madman; I knew this couldn't be heard, but I yelled just the same. But the big ship swept on with graceful deliberation.

Suddenly I thought of a fire. Fires on shipboard are signals of distress. I rushed below and threw a shirt and a dash of the shave lotion into the bucket. I lit it from the dwindling supply of matches and carried it onto the forepeak. The ship had passed from the starboard to the port bow. It hadn't sighted me.

I grew frantic as I realized I wasn't going to be seen. I jumped and waved and screamed, and in between I did everything but sink my boat for attention. I dashed astern and changed course so as to keep in sight of the ship. A thick gray cloud of smoke blew off *Pagan's* decks from the bucket, rising about twenty feet. The mate on watch must have been figuring out his pay or telling the wheelsman what a great guy he was, because a blind man could have seen my signal. I watched helplessly as the ship grew blurry in the distance and dropped below the sea.

I stayed on the southeast course instead of reverting to south. It was midafternoon before I came across a slick indicating the passage of the ship. I changed course to east and beat upwind following in its track. There was one chance in a million that the vessel might stop or turn back. Also there was a chance the cook would dump his garbage.

When dark came on I luffed the bow into the wind and

dropped off on the port tack to my former course. I wasn't too discouraged. When you are lost, land is where you find it. I knew I would find it sooner or later; it was a matter of endurance.

The next morning early, I did something I should have done before. I painted SOS on both sides of all sails. There was no paint to do it with. I used the pitchy stagnant oil from the engine. I also painted it on the foredeck, the cabin top, and in the cockpit, in case a plane should happen over. There were only the haunting sharks or a lonely bird or two to see it, but it was there giving an international message to any craft which might pass in my absence from deck.

I studied the horizon in a slow sweep, pumped the bilges, and stepped through the hatchway.

It was a day of cancerous loneliness. I had long since finished reading the nine books aboard, and I had started through them a second time, but it was wearisome trying to read a mystery when I already knew the murderer. One of the books, however, the Bible, from which I read selections each day, became more purposeful as I reread it. It was the kind of mystery where you couldn't know all the clues, and where the more you knew, the more mysterious rather than more clear became its significance — a mysteriousness which led me to the value of faith, that gift of the Bible. Out there I needed faith, it was the only thread left to cling to.

It was about this time that the more noticeable effects of my starvation struck me fully. My wristbone I noticed first. It stood out like a Ping-pong ball. Veins which never before could be seen, but now were accentuated by shrinking arms and tightening flesh, stood out like miniature molehills. My elbows were gaunt, and my biceps like eggs. Hollows were showing in chest and shoulders; all my ribs could be counted with the eye and my stomach was a sloping valley between chest and thigh. My hips flared out sharply and a deepening cavity was evincing itself on the inside of my upper leg.

Large bony knots stood for my knees. But my feet and ankles had swelled to twice their normal size, probably from liquid seeping down from above. They were heavy, and movement about deck was laborious.

It was also at this time that the last of the moss gave out on *Pagan's* hull. A thorough search of the boat showed that the only eatables aboard were the half box of tea and the half bottle of shaving lotion.

I put a pinch of tea in my mouth each time I pumped the bilges. It helped. The shaving lotion I was keeping in case the water should run short.

The next afternoon the wind changed from east to northeast and grew rapidly in strength. This sudden shift put me on the alert and I watched sky and sea critically. I slacked sheets and for a long time ran before it, making at least two knots. But time came when the danger of being pooped was imminent. I could see a storm was on me; a mild gale was already blowing.

I worked the little ship around to where she faced up to the wind and where she was breasting the onrolling seas. I lashed the helm, unbent the mainsail and stopped it to the boom and mast, and watched her as she stood before the rising weather. She lay comfortably under jib, staysail, and jigger. I pumped her out, had a look into the wild sky, and went below, where I lay in my bunk absorbing *Pagan's* reaction to the making weather . . . and waiting.

After dark, judging from the noise in the rigging and the angle of heel, the wind came up to gale force. But so long as *Pagan* could carry sail she rode easily. I had to pump out every two hours; and it enabled me to keep a close eye on the condition of the sea and wind.

I kept my fingers crossed, hoping the wind wouldn't rise. *Pagan* in her crippled condition, I was certain, could not have weathered another hurricane, even with a hardy crew.

The hours were a nervous and physical strain I could ill afford. I lay lashed in my bunk, straining to hear and interpret every new sound. In the dead of night the little mizzenmast collapsed; I heard it go down. I trudged out on deck not realizing how weak I was till I attempted to retrieve the spindly stick from the sea. In a dozen tries I was unable to grapple it in. The strength just wasn't in my arms.

In the end I pulled it as close aboard as I could by the sheets and passed a double half hitch around the sternpost, securing it. With that effort I was overcome by fatigue. I could easily have slept in exhaustion where I lay, but for the danger of being licked off the railless deck by the sea.

I clawed my way on hand and knees into the cockpit. The bilges were in need of pumping. I could feel that need but I couldn't respond to it. I lowered my tired legs into the confined cabin and flopped onto my pitching bunk. I remember fitting my lashings in place . . . then total blackout.

When I came to, water in the cabin was higher than at any time since the first hurricane — for now I was convinced that I was in another. I was completely drenched. The blanket which I used as a mattress was a sop pad. The cabin was a din of sounds that only water in a confined space can make.

How many hours I had slept I don't know. It was dark. *Pagan* was pitching and rolling. I presumed that all sail had been torn down by winds and that heavy seas had crashed down upon the stern, flooding the cabin.

A sense of unmitigated futility swept over me, dominated me. I was ready to give up. Water was nearly washing me off the bunk. I knew I could never bail it out — I was too far gone. The hazard of going on deck to work the pump in hurricane winds was suicidal. I felt like lying back and waiting in desperation for the end.

In complete defeat one rises above fear. The mouse will fight a lion when chased to the wall. Hurricane or no hurricane I was going to pump my bilges dry. I had to; my boat would founder if I didn't. I took a heavy drink of precious water. A refreshed feeling coursed through me. Taking hold of the coamings I eased my eyes into the night to meet an amazing sight.

What I saw wasn't one of the treacherous Fijian hurricanes but a mild tropical breeze of about force three soughing out of the south. However, a heavy cross sea was running which gave *Pagan* her antic behavior. My staysail and jib were intact and the little aftermast was still trailing from the sternpost.

Above me the skies were a patchwork of peaceful stars. Only the slowly abating rollers gave evidence that a tropical gale had passed. I took heart immediately and set to on the pump.

The new southern breeze compelled me for the night to lash the stub of a tiller with my bow jutting into the southwest.

As soon as I had offered up my morning supplications I asked the Good Captain that I be excused to tend my menial tasks on deck. I wanted to get the jigger rigged and holding a pressing sail again as soon as possible.

Seas had moderated. It was simple to pluck from the easy seaway the oar used for mast; and with decks steadied by the lush breeze, stepping the light spar wasn't difficult. With my boat under full sail again, my time was my own. I pumped the bilges and went below to do my daily reading from the Bible.

With a south wind holding, the course stayed at southwest. I didn't tack to maintain a beat into the south, though I needed to make as much southing as possible, for I was still a long way from being far enough south to be under Sirius. Effects of starvation were pronounced. I gave *Pagan* her lead into the southwest. I had to. Even the little work of tacking sail was rigorous labor to me and a drain on my body moisture. To me land was where I would find it: as always my wicked intuition indulged me; it said, "Go southwest."

I hadn't eaten for five days. Five days and no food . . . and I can remember when I bellyached if I missed a meal! The sustained fast enabled my stomach juices to partially hibernate and my nights were less harassed by frightful dreams.

But the quest for food went on. I occasionally got a shot at a bird, but my strength and judgment had ebbed till I couldn't have hit the broad side of a barn if I had been leaning against it. The fishline was ever astern. But Old Death and his wary protégés snubbed it disdainfully. The sharks, now increased to some five or six in number, showed it even less attention. Their interest centered on the limping craft, and in a very strong way I felt they were particularly interested in me.

I was still navigating by the stars and sun, working ever

south till I could look up the mast and sight Sirius dead overhead. When that day came I intended to probe westward for
land . . . whatever reared above the sea.

I went on deck at daylight to be confronted with — of all
things — an island. It was no cloud I saw this time. From the
first glance there was no mistaking its identity as land.

It lay broad on the port bow: a low island, longer than it
was wide. A volcano on the summit emitted a dark curtain
of fast-flowing smoke. Its outlines were bleak because of overcast and a growing wind, which pushed a scud in from over
the horizon.

The island looked prosperous, a sure sign of habitation.
Rescue this time was certain, but I determined from the first
not to be hasty and careless, remembering that infinitely more
seamen have perished in getting ashore than have on the
reaches of the open sea. On the sea a boat can float and it is
safe. But in crossing the reefs to the lagoon or pounding
through the surf to the beach, a boat can be dashed and
its crew overwhelmed and drowned. Also, another manifest
danger to the seaman is the often unconquerable distances
necessary to travel once he is safe on shore — often over entangled, infested terrain — to find help and food. Then, too,
the hungry, thirsty, exposed seaman must remember to nibble
and sip his first food and water or run the risk of violent death
when he is most safe.

All these things I thought of as I gazed on the dark green
paradise that would soon be mine. I thought too of the huge
joy of eating again. I saw myself racing into coconut groves,
clawing down the green drinking nuts and fattening on their
soft meat and cool milk. I visualized groves of bananas growing to the water's edge and I languished on the thought of

eating and sleeping at their roots. Delicious juices suddenly flowed in my mouth as the devils of hunger prodded me.

I changed course, beating as high on the wind as possible, and kept the island on the bow, so it bore directly southeast. I made for its closest point.

Starvation and Land

I WONDERED WHAT LAND IT COULD BE. I sat before my guess-work map in the cockpit and studied the scratched-out pattern of sea and islands, and by process of elimination I checked off one island at a time until there was left only the possibility of its being some northerly point of Fiji.

It was a most difficult assumption to make because, first, I wasn't certain of the exact positions of the island groups in the area, and second, I knew little of the layout of islands in the groups themselves. It was pure speculation of the crudest kind. It was based on guessed figures of my speed and the speed and direction of the current.

I re-estimated my speed under jury rig at everything from twenty to fifty miles per day — in the end, all things taken together, I settled on thirty-five miles. Thus by figuring my speed after the hurricane at thirty-five miles a day I had covered somewhere near 700 miles in the twenty-one days before turning south. Add another 150 miles, again purely a guess, for current and various kinds of westward driftage in the nine days since pointing into the south, and I was well on toward Australia.

It was sensible to me, then, under these particular circumstances, to assume from my disproportioned chart that a line drawn south from a point 850 miles west of the Suvorovs would run through the western Fijis, and that this land on my bow was part of that group. This assumption, as anyone knows, was a mistaken one, but as I say, under the circumstances that I made it, it seemed valid.

Thus, I figured, the isle before me was the last for another 600 miles to the primitive New Hebrides Islands just east and north of New Caledonia. Making this island was a matter of life and death. I doubted seriously whether I could survive another 600 miles with a quart and a half of water left aboard and the growing burden of keeping up the pumping. But the hazard of sailing it with the hurricane season underway was the most compelling thought of all.

I was about four miles offshore; I shaped my course so as to reach up to the western point of the island. I was close enough, from the very beginning, to see tangled vegetation on the lower slopes. I thought of mangoes and pawpaws and cool, refreshing, healthful pineapples. Beautiful hunger feelings tingled through me, tickled me and tortured me, and I had to find something to busy myself with so I wouldn't think of food. I readied the anchor to be pushed off the railless decks.

There were hints of palm trees on the shore, but no sign of a village. I stood on the cabin, holding to the short mast, searching for a suitable anchorage.

Hours dragged by with torturing slowness. The sun climbed along its wonted arch to high noon. I had hoped to be in before then, anchored or beached, and on the quest for food. There was something amiss with my calculated approach. I was not closing in properly. After six hours of sailing I should have been through the reef and safe in the lagoon. Instead I was directly west of the island beating hopelessly into the wind. It was evident that my sail area was too small to make any headway. I was actually falling back from the island, losing ground.

By late afternoon wind and current had driven me well back. I climbed to the masthead searching for a sign of life to appeal to, but saw nothing. The shore line was no longer visible. The vegetation and barren upland spots began to blend as one. I was hoping that someone yet might sight me and set off. I retouched the SOS signs with the foul oil from the dead engine. Up to dark no sails broke the horizon. When night closed in, I could see no lights.

For hours I lay on the useless course blinking my weakening flashlight into the low clouds overhead and in a full circle around the horizon. There was always a chance that my spark of light might be picked up and an answering flash bob up on the horizon.

Finally, when my light grew so weak that I could hardly see it myself, I gave up. The island had completely hidden itself in the enveloping dark. It was lost to me. To tarry was fruitless and dangerous. There was nothing to do but turn back to my search for land farther west.

I dreaded the thought of having to cross the landless sea west of Fiji to the New Hebrides. That expanse seemed endless, as I envisaged it in terms of sips of water, hours of drudgery at the pump, and a wet sack. "It's your own fault," I told myself. "You didn't have to come out here, nobody pushed you out of Panama, so shut up."

I set a new course of west by south, that I felt should get me to the southern New Hebrides with good weather in fifteen or sixteen days. I pumped *Pagan* out and went below, wanting day to come so I could consult my

map. Also I cut the ration of water to less than a half pint.
At daylight I was on deck for a look at the crude chart etched
in the cockpit floor. The next few hours I spent in conjecture
over my chances of making the grade with a quart and a half
of water. There was water for eight days, possibly nine. I was
fifteen days from the New Hebrides, that is, if I could make
it in fifteen days, which meant I would be at least six days
without water. Humanly impossible.

For the first time in my life, I had a long-term look at death.
I had never before had an opportunity to look it in the face.

But now it was before me; and I had a whole week ahead
of me to get chummy with it. To my way of thinking — now —
death isn't really a dread beast unless you have time to think
about him. To be in the presence of death and to have a long-
term contract with it are two different things. You can be
torpedoed on a ship and be in the presence of death. You can
be bombed and set on fire and be in the presence of death.
You can be strafed in a lifeboat or under sub attack in a con-
voy — a lot of things can happen where you are in the presence of death.

But death in such a presence hasn't a sense of finality, or a
sense of this-is-the-end; the extreme activity and excitement
of action deprive it of that. One can't conceive of death unless
it is actually distant.

Strangely, I never once really believed I was going to die.
However I will admit I used often to stare stolidly over the
restless floor of blue ocean and ask, "Am I going to perish
alone out here on the sea?" If I thought of death seriously it
is because I toyed with an idea new to me. It never pressed
me. My desire, my strength to go on living, was too strong —
I had too much to live for. I had overcome too many obstacles.

"I am too young to die," I said . . . and believed it! My new faith in God and prayer — thus my new faith in myself — made life something I wanted badly enough, like wanting to see Mary.

Coming on deck in the morning I saw a seaman's nightmare. *Pagan* was dismasted again. Only the mizzen stood. The main and headsails were down across the decks, the shrouds, stays, and mast trailed in the water like bedraggled hair. The rigging, evidently taxed to extreme in the day of beating vainly into the wind and sea for the island, in its tiredness had collapsed in the night. The hard work of restepping the mast, of refitting the rigging, loaded my mind. Working constantly at the pump had fined me down at an alarming rate. I dreaded the work it all smacked of. But I took a sip of precious water and got started.

I dragged the old mast aboard and sawed it flush where it had snapped at the deck, and shave it flat on one side at the base for restepping; it was now only ten feet long. I shortened the shrouds and stays, and made the little mast ready to be stepped. The effort so depleted me that I was forced to lie down before continuing.

After resting I started the arduous task. I raised the mast as nearly straight up and down as strength would allow and thrust it toward the opening in the deck to step it. It missed by an inch, sliding against the cabin, overbalancing me, and crashing from my shoulder. Again I rested.

The next attempt to stand my mast found me atop the cabin staggering beneath the clumsy spar. I tried to drop it straight down into the opening. The closest I could manage the butt end of the top-heavy stick to the deck hole was six inches. My strength was gone: the exertion left me too weak to stand. I slumped to the deck and lay in a heap, puffing with short breaths.

I thought maybe if I shortened the spar it would be lighter, more manageable. I decided against it, because I needed maximum sail up. The mainsail, even on the twelve-foot mast, was nearly as small as the jigger; which looked like a pillow slip. I went below and fell on my bunk.

When I came out again I felt fresher. But in two tries to step the mast I failed miserably. The last effort missed the hole by a foot. Dejection and fatigue swept over me anew. I went below to rest. I intended to make one more try before shortening the mast.

I awakened sometime in the afternoon still weak from the labors of the morning. I took a sip of water. As it coursed down my throat, I felt a return of strength. Putting the water flask back, I saw the shave lotion. I opened it, sniffed it — it was unbearable. Throwing my head back, I downed a hearty portion of what remained of it. As I capped it, I felt an electric sort of surge through my body.

The next thing I knew I was walking over the deck and before I realized what I had done, I had jerked the mast off the deck, had pointed it up like a broom handle, and it was stepped. Everything I did in the next hour was effortless. I lashed the mast in place at the heel; set the shrouds and stays; hoisted all sail; lashed the helm alee. I felt boundless; I even felt like diving over and giving one of the sharks a bad time!

Under her shortened sail *Pagan* took more time to move. She was sluggish, but as she was driven, and as she gained her cruising speed, she tilted slightly before the southern wind. Soon I was plodding along at something less than a knot.

For the next two days I slept eighteen of each twenty-four-hour period, rising only to pump out, or to sip my drops of water, or read from the Bible. Bad dreams slacked off as general apathy set in; I was a broken robot capable of only a few simple actions.

When I finally did come out of hibernation, it wasn't because I returned to my old self. I never felt the same again after the strenuous day with the mast. Working the pump henceforth became a trial — a far cry from the days when I dried the bilges in fifty long quick strokes. Now I had to pump with one hand for a dozen strokes, then with the other. A hundred movements often failed to clear out the leakage. Halfway through each pumping, I lay sprawled in the cockpit to rest.

Each day I read the Bible more assiduously; found more and more solace in prayer and gave more time to it. I learned the Twenty-third Psalm by heart, and spoke it every rising and sleeping, and often in the night as I heaved at the pump. As well, I learned the Ten Commandments and many other Scriptures. My Bible — a gift of my grandpa when I was a boy — I had never read a chapter of. Aboard *Pagan* I read it cover to cover twice, devouring its words, searching out its comforts. I should have gone insane had I not had the comforting solace of my Baptist teaching. Men who sail small boats know the verity of the Good Captain who piloted my boat.

Atheism with me had been an old story. I picked up a good background for it at college. Later, in the war, my experiences at sea, and in particular the invasion of Algiers in 1942, strengthened my unbelief. I saw strange and bewildering things. I shall never forget the trains of wounded soldiers in

Algiers just after its capture. German, French, English, Italian, American, all together, their wounds making them brothers. Air raids, submarine alerts, and miles of white crosses — all in a few days.

Aboard *Pagan* the petty arguments of "college" atheism dissolved in the light of faith and the crucial practicality of Godly love under the touchstone of vital need and vital want. The test proves; the argument only conjectures. The test is a full measure, the argument a half measure. I smile when I meet atheists.

All my experiences of civilian life in depression America, and in the war, proved a pattern — a direct groundwork for my meditations alone in the vast Pacific. I cannot agree with Laplace that there is no need in this world for the hypothesis of a creator.

That afternoon of October 12, while I slept to fortify my thinning bones, I heard a heavy thud on the starboard hull. It felt solid enough to be the lip of a reef. I thought I might have clipped a part of it, in skirting it. I hurried feebly out on deck and looked around.

Near the bow, and on the sea surface, plowed a high sharp fin. A new fin from any I had seen before: a new arrival to the school of sharks that loafed constantly in the wake. He turned back to the stern and slid fearlessly along the hull, a foot off, pushing himself with a single effort.

He glided amidships and swung his ponderous body gruffly against the planking. *Pagan* shivered. He wandered gracefully off abeam, then came again. Seeing me moving on deck, he waddled close in and eyed me almost humanly with small pig's eyes, only a few feet away.

There we were, eying each other, each wondering how to

eat the other. He, the picture of tropical violence, and I, gone scrawny and desperate.

A most wonderful feeling crept over me. Here was my chance. None of the smaller sharks had dared venture so close. His careless nearness gave me every advantage of the harpooner. The trouble was I had no harpoon. My little fish spear would only tickle him. But I was full of ideas.

If there were only something aboard to make a heavy spear from. I knew that if I could get something big enough into him in a vital spot, he was mine. There were meat and blood enough in him to see me through to the Hebrides. There was at the very least a quart of fresh blood I could draw out of him — enough to last five days. I relished the strength it would give me. I could dry his half a ton of meat, and with plenty to eat I could make out with a quarter pint of water daily. It would be a tight squeeze: but it could be done.

In the bilge, I found an old steel file; under the forepeak was my hacksaw — rusted over, but usable; beneath my bunk lay an eight-inch strip of cold rolled steel, one inch wide, a quarter inch thick. From the workable piece of soft iron, I envisaged a wicked killing spear. How long would the making take, and how long would the shark be around? The work, as I cut it out in my mind, could be done the next afternoon if my endurance could hold. As for the shark, if he were like the others in the wake he would be hovering close astern for days.

The material I was working with was comparatively soft; however, I realized that hacksawing and filing it into shape would wear down my last reserves. The whole venture was a vast gamble — a gamble I was fortunate to have.

I marked the rough outline of a heavily barbed **spearhead**

on the section of steel. I commenced the long task of driving
the saw, stroke by stroke, along each mark. I watched the
ceiling as I worked so I couldn't see the slow progress of the
cutting. Each time I looked down I tried to be surprised at
the few hair widths I had bitten away. My thoughts turned
to the kill I would soon be making and the heavy feast to follow. Hunger juices flowed and the dryness of my throat eased.
The devils of appetite returned to *Pagan*.

It was late afternoon before I finished cutting out the
rough outline of the spearhead. I took a recuperative
sleep. Before I could work in the afternoon I had to over-
step my ration of water: I drank a half pint. But I felt it a
worthy risk, since a heavy feast of meat and blood was in the
offing.

By nightfall I had notched in four small niches on the upper part of the spearhead so it could be screwed and bound to
its handle. I was too worn and weak to begin the filing of the
spear point; that would start the next morning. I went to bed
early, to sleep hard so that I could hasten my labors on the
dawn.

But it wasn't easy to sleep hard. Exquisite hunger played
tricks with my dreams and horrible nightmares set me to rolling in discomfort on my bunk. My stomach knotted up and
wouldn't leave me in peace. It needed food, and if not that at
least something that could be swallowed. Every last edible was
gone. I thought of pages from my books — but I had tried
that before and it had created unbearable problems of the
bowels. Then I remembered the oil in the engine.

I groped out into the night, down into the stern compartment, and loosed the plug to the engine crankshaft. I drained
off what seemed a half pint of gurling liquid and returned to

the cabin. With my finger I stirred the thick gritty liquid that had seen many trips through *Pagan's* engine, and made ready to drink it down.

There are people who wonder and doubt how far a man will go when he is hungry . . . they are those, I claim, who have never been hungry. By hungry, I don't refer to the food-lessness of a day or even a week. Desperate hunger doesn't come until one has starved for at least two weeks — and this is best achieved after about a month of semistarvation.

I turned the pan up and drank deeply and quickly. My throat was outraged. My stomach revolted. I blustered and nearly vomited. My head spun in a light swim and I grew faint and drowsy. I remember settling back; and I remember the knots tightening in my stomach and the faraway ringing in my ears that seemed to come close and go away again. And I dreamed I was in the cockpit peering over my roughly hewed map. I was estimating my position anew; and when I shifted the nail and pounded it in, I found myself in Sydney Harbor. There were the harbor bridge, the skyline of King's Cross, and the Manly Ferry steaming into Circular Quay. Then I wakened; the same darkness, the same slapping of water in the bilges, the same soughing of wind in the rigging, the same feeling of a weak stomach.

Before daylight, though I felt slightly queasy, I pumped the bilges at the regular interval, then I stayed out on deck to work. In the waning dark I scraped at the spear point with my small file. Hour on hour I wore away at the weapon, sprinkling mites of steel on my swollen feet. By midmorning it showed a cruel, knife-edged point and two jagged flanges. Before noon it was a formidable weapon, heavy, unbreakable, sinister. I looked past it to the shark whose fin lazed carelessly above the water and who periodically glided up to the bilges and thwacked them sharply.

I had nothing at hand for a shaft to use as a helve for the spearhead. The last of the oars had gone into the mizzenmast. Shark spearing at the moment had priority over sailing; so down came the little mizzen.

With four heavy screws, I tightened the spearhead to the long oar handle. In addition I bound it with a wrapping of shroud wire. In the opposite end of the shaft I drilled a hole with my knife. Through the hole I passed and secured fifty feet of line, bending it to the heavy cleat at the cockpit coaming.

I was ready to spear my shark, but first I went below and slept a few hours.

The shark was off the beam basking on the surface. I stirred the water a bit. He spread the top of the sea with his heavy fin, thrusting it high, and sped straight in for me. Seeing me, he pulled up short, and gave me the once-over. We sized each other up and squared off.

With a thrust of his powerful body he moved up within a few feet of the planking. He stopped in utter defiance, nosing at the hull, loitering purposely. He turned lazily and moved a foot or two toward the bow. Exposed to me was his whole side. A greater favor the harpooner couldn't ask.

I swung the spear high up, ready to drive it down. I braced myself for the shock that would come. I saw a likely point midway between the dorsal and ventral fins. Bone, flesh, vital organs lay there — everything to bed a spear in.

I glued my eyes to his open flank, and drove the spear hard down. The blade hit what felt like rock, but it penetrated.

The shark lurched in a spasm. I was shoved upward, off my feet. I held to the spear and thrust it back. The great fish threshed and writhed. I felt the spear push deep into his flesh. My hold weakened and I lost it. I crumpled into the cockpit.

I saw the rope paying out into a frothy wake that broke beamward for sea room. He lunged at the end of the line, tautening it with a slam. He spun around — plunged, and I couldn't see him for the boiling he made, but I could feel his might as the decks jerked.

He flailed the surface white. Tail up he fought his way downward, curving back toward the boat. As slack showed in the line I took it in and twisted it around the cleat. The shark shot under the keel, coming up on the opposite bow.

When he flailed in that quarter he plunged again. I sat down watching his useless battlings against death. I knew the spear had a killing hold in his vitals. When his blood gave out — he would come to terms. I waited and watched for weakness.

In a moment I saw its sure signs. He lay on the surface wallowing gracelessly. I led the slack line between two cleats, wrapping it round and round and taking in slack whenever I found it. The shark was stirring only feebly as I dragged him in. Suddenly with explosive fury he shot to the end of the line. I held the line I had taken in so it couldn't pay out. In a moment he grew limp; I was pulling him in again. He felt like dead weight.

Then again he came to life, or so it seemed, and in an explosive movement bolted away, and then again quite suddenly relaxed. I watched him closely as I towed him in. Another shark was entangled in the line; the other shark was towing him. The other shark couldn't untangle himself.

I tried to pull in more line, to get another bite on the cleat. Then a second shark fouled himself with the line. Once more the line yanked tight. At that moment I saw everything. The sharks weren't entangled in the line. They were tearing at the carcass of my shark — eating it!

A third and fourth shark darted in to the death feast. I heaved frantically, and whenever the line showed slack, I wrapped it with mad haste around the cleat. I grew so weak I had to sit down, but I still worked at the line. Every pound of flesh the gluttonous pack was tearing off the carcass was vital to my chance of life. I was fighting for my life. I worked the great shark to within twenty feet of the rail.

One of the greedy pack bit into the tail of my shark, spinning him around in a half circle and racing with him to the bow till the line flew tight. There I could hear a terrifying snapping of jaws as the four set on him, ripping at him, and hastening to rip again. Great holes showed in my shark as he was thrust and pushed and torn.

I worked the mutilated mass of sagged flesh as close in as possible. The thing now was to hook him at the gills and somehow get him on board. I went below for the grappling hook, and hurried back.

The four sharks were jaw deep into the carcass — each thrusting back and tearing from side to side, pulling in opposite directions. The big shark was bent S-shaped. Rusty, blood-filled water nearly hid the heads of his attackers. Like hungry hogs, they were eye deep into the killed victim.

I jabbed my little barbed fish spear hilt deep into the head of the shark nearest me. He was oblivious to the sharp, cold steel. I tried to fit the grappling hook into the gills of the dismembered victim, but weakness felled my arms to my sides.

The grisly feast dropped down to keel depth; and then it dropped beneath the keel to *Pagan's* other side. The line was short, the oar caught against the keel and planking. The extreme pressure was bending it. Through the sole of my feet on the deck boards, I could feel the vibrations of the strained oar. I peered over to see what was happening.

From out of the water came a muffled snap. My oar bobbed to the surface. It had snapped off just above the spearhead.

I moved to the other beam in consternation and below me, gradually sinking into the hiding waters, was the gory feast. I watched it glimmer, and when it no longer glimmered I fell back on the deck boards and lost myself in remorse. I have never been at a lower moment in life.

I reset *Pagan* on her westward course, labored with the bilge pump, and went below. I slept all afternoon and all night.

Two days of sore trial slid past. Nothing more exciting than the change of night and day occurred. Physically I spent them as a vegetable would have, except that I pumped the bilges and stared for pained hours at the shapeless horizons. Mostly I slept or talked to myself. I was tired of the silence: I spoke to hear my voice.

There was an inevitable morning I dreaded to see come. I awakened with less than a half pint of water aboard. One day's ration. After my usual morning prayers I wet my tongue and crawled on deck to do the pumping. I discovered, as I watched the slow motion of my hand at the pump, that I had lost my wedding band. My fingers, thin as reef points, were too skinless to hold a ring.

I struggled with the pump and went below to read the Bible, but soon found that the exertion and excitement of the shark battle had overtaxed me. I was still so overcome that my feeling, my seeing, and my thinking were fogged over.

I could no longer remember what I was reading. What I read I couldn't recall, not a single thought, or a word of it. My mind was blank. I couldn't think straight. I wanted only to sit and stare out the one good porthole. In fact I got so bad that I couldn't even philosophize about the tough time I was having. And that's bad. But I managed to get out every hour and pump the bilges.

By late afternoon I had taken several sips of water to tide me through the day. There was one sip left to see me through pumping out in the middle of the night.

That night a high wind sprung out of the east. For hours I drove along before it to westward. In the early hours of the next morning it grew ungovernable. I took the last sip of water, crawled out to drop the main, and lay hove-to on the starboard tack.

Water was gone. There were hundreds of miles yet to go to land — nearly two weeks' sailing time. But there was a flame still going inside, burning on the skimpiest fuel.

A low scud sailed overhead. It left a dampness in the air but no real promise of rain. I wasn't discouraged; I knew that something would come along — either rain or an island or a ship to tow me to a safe harbor.

Later in the night the wind abated noticeably; the skies cleared. I crawled to the foredeck and hoisted the tiny main. Clambering back, I swung my boat on her former course. The effort weakened me so much that I was unable to pump out. I went below to a wet bunk. At daylight I managed to get the bilges dry. I was never able, not once, after that to work the pump long enough at a single stretch to see *Pagan's* bilges dry again. Thereafter I could only pump till I was tired, then quit.

I looked into the cloudy sky. No hint of rain. During the night I had thought of a scheme to condense fresh water from salt. I had a small oilcan with a spout. I filled it from over the side, fired the Primus, set it on to boil. The hole in the top of the can was capped so that steam could issue from the spout. If I could somehow trap that steam I would have fresh water.

I rigged a curved sheet of tin so that the steam could strike it and give off the yield, if any, in a dish. Eventually a drop fell in; I blotted it up with my dry, swollen tongue, and awaited the next.

In an hour my Rube Goldberg contraption netted many dozen offerings. A tablespoon of water for an hour's agitation and futile hope. I held doggedly on throughout the morning. By noon I was worn ragged; but my mouth was no longer dry. The worst was over till the next day. I pumped the bilges awhile and crawled into my blanket for the afternoon.

Then, unexpectedly, rain came. I heard it beating on the decks. A heavy black squall moved with the slacking wind from the east. I knew what it meant and ran on deck. I spread my woolen blanket over the deckhouse and cleaned the dirt from the cockpit.

The squall, not the first I had seen, but the first that had touched me since the hurricane, worked directly over me. Large droplets hosed down the boat. I washed the crusted salt from my skin and out of my beard. I drank hoggishly of the water standing on the decks, scooping it into my mouth by handfuls.

When the blanket was saturated, I twisted it dry, clearing it of salt. I let it soak again, then squeezed it over the bucket.

I had time to wring it twice before the squall passed; a half gallon of water. There was a gallon lodged in the cockpit. A gallon and a half of water! I felt like a king.

I put myself instantly on a ration of a pint and a half per day. It seemed wasteful to drink so much water in a day.

The high wind held for all day and night, and blew itself out with daylight when I hit the corners of two howling squalls that set me bouncing. Once they passed, I was left drifting in a flat calm.

The sun came up on a glassy sea. I said my long morning prayers, and turned to my Bible reading. But despite an increased ration of water, my mind didn't clear up. I couldn't remember what I had read a minute after reading it. I sat staring out the porthole, waiting for strength and the inspiration to pump some of the water from the bilges.

Finally I went on deck and found a comfortable spot in the shade of the mizzen and watched the sharks and dolphins. Out on the beam, flapping over the windless sea, was a cluster of birds. I thought I recognized land birds among them, but since I was at least 200 miles from land, I discarded the observation. Some of the birds came in close. A chronic exhaustion, too enervating to permit me to care about the birds, had hold of me. I couldn't move to challenge them. My dead brain couldn't produce a means to challenge them. I dared not exert myself in another strenuous gamble for food. One more physical strain and I was finished — I knew that.

I worked at the pump till I could pump no more; then went below to sleep. Sleep came simply and easily. I slept in childlike obliviousness till the rising water slopped into my bunk. Then I went out and pumped, till again I could stand no more . . . so it went.

When the calm still held the next morning I decided to cut the water ration to a pint. The calm vexed me and wore at me constantly. "Surely this afternoon there'll be a wind," I thought.

The afternoon aged. Out on the sea the birds screamed for wind. When the wind blows, the flying fish take to the air while chased by the dolphin and their other underwater enemies. During the calms, they seek other areas in which there is wind, where they have a fighting chance. Thus the wind aids many of those living in and out of the sea to thrive. The lean dolphin hadn't eaten in two days. Old Death and his boys spent most of their time discussing the weather, as did the birds and I.

The arrival of the next day, the third consecutive day of perplexing calm, was proclaimed by the plaintive cries of hungry sea birds. I came on deck not believing it possible that it could still be calm. But there it was — the sea was like a placid lake. Hardly a shadow showed on the surface. The sails were as limp as death. Not a breath stirred. I didn't like it. These prolonged calms are often the harbingers of hurricanes.

I pumped for what seemed an hour, till the water was down to the floor boards, and lowered my clublike, weighted feet into the hold to stare out from the porthole onto the impersonal sea, and fret.

When dark came and still no breeze, I went on deck to pray. I took the part of spokesman for the fish and birds. Hands clasped on the cabin, gaunt knees on the deck, and puffed feet protruding outboard — a position and state I never dreamed I would ever be in. I knelt under the stars, unhindered by the pent cabin, reciting my plaintive call for wind and the chance to fight for my life.

The morning following I rose knowing there would be wind — it was another morning of stark calm. A desolate, sun-glaring sea glowered at me as I came on deck. I took one look, murmured "Still calm," and once more cut the water ration, to barely more than a half pint.

Four days of continual dead wind. Twenty-two days since my last morsel of food. Forty-seven days since the hurricane — according to the X's on the bulkhead. And the closest land an estimated ten days away. That was the sober tally I made that morning. I tried to scribble it into the front page of my Bible with the one pencil aboard so it could live to explain in case I couldn't. But I didn't put it in: I tried, but I couldn't. My brain was foggy, the foggiest yet — I couldn't think of a suitable way so I pushed it aside, and stared out the porthole.

A slight swell was rolling in from the south, intimating that somewhere, at least, there was wind. I struggled onto the deckhouse, remembering suddenly that for the last two days I had forgotten to look for land. As usual there was no land — only the sea-fowl screaming dejectedly.

A loud scratching noise came to my ear. At first I thought it was the foot-deep water in the cabin. Then realized that it came from the planking, on the outside.

Over the rail I saw a large sea turtle scratching at the hull with a discolored flipper. He was an olive-green shade, pat-terned across the back with squares. I felt I shouldn't risk my small store of energy in a fruitless contest with him. I stared for a while at his pawings on the planks. I remembered the sea turtle I had harpooned in the Galápagos. I thought of the meat and blood in this one. I threw judgment to the winds and the fight was on.

I crept astern and found the pronged spear with which I

had formerly tried for triggerfish. I trembled with excitement as I made a lunge to harpoon the big tortoise. But my strength was gone; the spear struck, and skidded across his leathery shell. He plunged, swam under the keel, and came up near the rudder. I groped along the deck to the transom and knelt over him, sighting him along the spear.

I jabbed at him three times successively, but failed to penetrate the tough, hidelike shell. My strength was so far gone that even this effort had me puffing. As a last resort I laid the spear aside and made an attempt to pull the turtle aboard by grabbing him.

I fitted both hands under his shell and strained to raise him to deck. I was never weaker. I couldn't even hold him from swimming away. With a few movements of his flippers he made progress abeam, nearly pulling me in.

In consternation I teetered on the railless deck edge, kicking for balance, fumbling disconnectedly. If I fell in I knew I would sink like a rock, fleshless and bony as I was. Even if I could grasp the sides I wouldn't have the strength to claw myself aboard. And the sharks! I had seen what the sharks could do.

I released my grip on him in the nick of time, and avoided falling in by throwing myself flat and backing aboard with my legs flying. I ran my knee against the fish spear. Sitting up I found that one of the rusted forks had imbedded itself an inch under my kneecap. A burning pain attended it, the kind that gave strong hint of more pain to come.

I pulled the spear point out and watched a single drop of black blood merge. I couldn't afford to lose that drop of life; I wiped it off with my finger and smeared it on my tongue, and watched for more. None came. Blood was too dense to flow. I laid back on the deck, and stayed there for over an hour, too tired to stand. Finally I got up.

When I looked for the turtle he was gone. It was strange that a sea so calm could hide anything. I heard the water slopping in the bilge, and walked back to have a look. Water was over a foot deep inside, a hopeless task of pumping.

I pumped till I was exhausted, making tiny two-inch strokes, then I waded below to bed down. My knee throbbed. The bilge water babbled like jabbering women as it flowed to and fro. I eased off to sleep.

At noon, water in my bunk awakened me and drove me out to the pump. The calm still held. Birds spiraled overhead screeching raucously. In the sea, the dolphin moved in disconsolate circles. I gave up ever seeing a wind. After pumping till my arm failed to respond to my wish to lower the depth of the bilge water, I lowered my swollen feet, and puffed knee, into the flooded cabin.

At a later hour, when ordinarily I should have gone on deck to pump out, I couldn't go. I was aware of the need, but I couldn't drive myself. My knee hurt. I lay watching the up-creeping water, knowing that each minute I languished there meant heartbreaking work later. It was easier to fall asleep.

Later, with the sun dangling over the horizon, I was startled awake by water pouring into my bunk. *Pagan* was listing badly. My first thought was that I had allowed too much water to leak in. She's tipping, I thought . . . overloaded, sinking! I expected her every moment to turn turtle, and wanted to run on deck, but could only sit up slowly. I couldn't think quickly enough to decide what to do.

I climbed out of my bunk into water past my calves. Limping to deck I was amazed to see the mast heeling before a fresh wind. It was about force five out of the south, working *Pagan* beautifully, shoving her westward — and to land!

My spirits skyrocketed. Movement! At last I was on the way to land. I felt better, my old optimism returned. Consulting the map, I estimated I was about ten days from the closest land — the pestilence-ridden New Hebrides. I refused to consider how I was going to keep my boat pumped from hour to hour on my remaining margin of strength. I would wait and tackle each problem as it came.

I pumped the bilges for as long as the muscles were willing. But because my knee was swelling and pulsating, I couldn't bend it enough to go back below. That night I slept in the cockpit.

Four times during the spanking night I arose to pump the bilges. My knee grew worse and I was at a loss what to do. I bathed it in salt water, but the pressure of my fingers made it pain. At daylight, I lay on my back in the cockpit, murmuring my morning supplications. I prayed, as every day I had prayed; I ended my prayer as always, "And Thou wills it, there will be land."

I looked across the bows, and there, not three miles distant, lay an island. I could only stare dumbly. I didn't shout and I didn't jump; too many disappointments had dulled my sense of appreciation. I just looked at the lump of land colored in around its shores with fat greenery and shaping away to its flat crest with deeply graved volcanic rock.

I had no idea what land it was and didn't care. It was land. According to my questionable calculations I should have been more than a week off land — the New Hebrides. But here it was. I didn't care if it was Timbuktu or Shangri-La: it was land, and I wasn't going to miss it.

Rescue

I HAULED SOUTHWARD down the coast, skirting the wide, heavily toothed open reef, at 200 yards. The small island was a bare mile and a half away, across the reef and across the lagoon. Though I had been through the New Hebrides during the war, I couldn't tag the island.

It was about seven miles long, and looked seven or eight hundred feet high. It was volcanic, capped by a craterlike summit. Along the shore the malformed lava cliffs jumped up twenty or thirty feet, deeply underwashed by the sea. Here and there a flat depression ended in a white sandy beach, grown to mangrove and coconut trees.

My plan was to locate the opening in the reef and shoot into the lagoon to anchor before a village, or beach my boat on one of the sandy shores. I was racing against time. *Pagan* hadn't been pumped in four hours; water was rising. I was saving my strength for the bout with the short, clumsy tiller, and the struggle to get ashore.

Down the full length of the coast I ran, till I neared the southeast corner, and still I found no opening in the reef. As I closed with the point I realized the danger of going around it.

I dared not pass to leeward of the protruding fist of land. Once by, I could never work back: I remembered my failure at the recent unidentified island. Nor could I turn back and reach up the long coast. My course had thrown me in hard by the reef. I hadn't room to maneuver or the strength to do it. For one thing, the bulky mast, strapped as it was angularly across the deck, was an impediment. It dragged in the sea whenever the decks sloped, and made *Pagan* difficult to maneuver. I thought of going forward to cut its lashings, but I knew I hadn't the strength to roll it off. My strength was gone; I was unable to pump out. The water in the hold was rising. The point was a hundred yards off. I had to act . . . now. A dread decision with regard to my boat was in the balance — and it had to be made.

I suddenly realized that my battered little craft was a coffin. Kim Powell in Panama had said, "She'll go as far as you can stay with her." The prophecy was true. I was finished, but my sporty little cutter was still game for the fight.

I had no alternative but to wreck her to save my life . . . what is worse, I had no time to weigh the pros and cons of the predicament.

Rather than turn that corner to sure death, rather than go about and fight hopelessly — and vainly — up the uninviting coast, I kicked the helm hard down and raced bow-on toward the exposed reef: my last official decision as *Pagan's* captain, for now she was heading into an alley from which she would never return.

I was dressed in army khaki. Earlier, when I sighted the island, I had a quick sponge bath sitting at the rail; I combed the salt from my beard and arranged my bothersome hair, now long as a woman's, into a knot and covered it with a cap. My feet were too swollen for anything but stockings. My bulbous knee I wrapped in blanket stripping.

I had grabbed a few last things and crammed them in my pockets. Hand on the tiller, I awaited the shock.

The keel passed over several coral heads, about six fathoms down. Farther on the reef began to shoal quickly, and the sea floor was only four fathoms. I can anchor in this, I suddenly realized. At a slow-motion gait I limped forward to the anchor and made to put it over.

Partly because of my boil-like knee, but mostly because I had no strength, I couldn't begin to budge the anchor. I was nearing the reef; the sea was pounding like thunder on it. I sat down, put my feet against the flukes, and pushed with all my might; but I was helpless to move it. The din was closer. I was caught in the grip of the current, and I was being swept in to the reef. I got up, took the fluke in my hands, and strained at it. It raised a foot. I lost my balance and stumbled.

Pagan caught the swell of a roller, rode in on its back, and crashed stem-to against the coral wall. She shivered as though struck by shell fire. I was sitting near the port rail. One of her planks sprung, pointing away from the stem. I could see the water gush through it. In a moment she settled by the bow, the deck was awash, the fore scuttle covered. In no time I was sitting to my pockets in water. I could only sit and watch — the decks were lurching too much to permit me to stand.

I could hear a horrible noise as *Pagan* pounded against the reef at the beam. Only the watertight stern section was buoyant. The bow was still going down. Water was up to my waist. The next two rollers lifted the stern on the reef. I could feel the dull thud of the lead-shod keel against the iron-hard coral. The next sea combed across the bows, sweeping me against the deckhouse, where I clung to the mast. Each successive sea worked her higher on the reef, turning her broadside to the

destructive waves and tilting her at a crazy angle. The next
impact shook me from my hold. I slipped down the abrupt
incline and fell free of the boat onto the coral, only to be
overwhelmed by a sea that twisted me in a somersault and
threw me back onto shallower coral ground. I gathered myself
up, shook free of the grasping water, and somehow moved a
few feet to where it was safe.

I had backed away from my battered boat onto the dry coral
and sat cursing the bullying sea. *Pagan* was thrown up to
where the water was knee-deep. Each time a roller broke over
her she shuddered and ground her planks on the sharp coral.

Behind me the jagged reef ran for two hundred yards. I
turned and staggered in the stiff-legged way of the gaunt and
hungry to the brink of the reef. There the lagoon dropped to
a depth of nine fathoms, where a garden land of coral formations grew. Tiny fish were as visible in fifty feet of water as
in fifty feet of clear air. I shunned the water like poison,
knowing that if I should fall in, I would sink like a weight.

I lay down on the coral to rest and dropped instantly and
helplessly asleep. Hours later the rising tide, marching across
the reef, lapped against me. With the feel of water I jerked
awake, thinking it was time to pump the bilges. Seeing myself
on the crusty reef I was startled, then shocked. Then I remembered. The tide was coming in. The reef was covered.
Two hundred yards away *Pagan* was taking an unmerciful
pounding from the growing rollers.

I decided to struggle back to the boat and get the life raft.

I wobbled back to her, keeping in the less disturbed waters
of her lee. She was thigh-deep in water, and had been bowled
over several times. The little rubber life raft had been caught
beneath the boat and ground into the coral spikes. After trail-

ing astern for over a thousand miles of the Pacific since the hurricane, it ended on the coral needles.

I waded to the sloping deck and climbed uncertainly aboard, looking for something on which to float across the deep lagoon. *Pagan* was on her beam, teetering either way, likely to lob over again. Knife in hand I hacked away the stout lashings holding the thirty-five-foot mast to the deck. I jumped off and sloshed to where water was knee-deep, and looked back.

This rising sea was whamming *Pagan* and threatening to bowl her over. Suddenly *Pagan* jammed her beam into the coral and clumped over from her beam onto her decks. The hull, pointing skyward, was ghastly with barnacles and scars and loose planking.

I felt drowsy but there was no place to lie down. The growing waves were pushing me back away from the boat. Then the mast worked loose and I took hold of it. I held to it as the sea drove it slowly across the reef. When I reached the lagoon, I climbed on its heaviest part, straddling it, floating on it.

My arms and legs were dangling in the water, my head and chest resting on the hard curved surface. For a long time I lay watching the island as I floated off onto the lagoon. Finally I drifted off to a sleeplike drowse.

I awakened when the mast scraped on the soft shore. I was in a small alcove fronted with bright sand, overtowered by a beetling wall of volcanic rock. I plodded out of the water onto the white sand. I slumped into the inviting warmth and fell asleep.

The incoming tide, washing my feet sometime later, awakened me as it marched up the beach. I crawled higher on the sloping beach to the base of the twenty-foot cliff face, where

I hoped the water wouldn't reach, and dropped off again in a slumber. In a while I was disturbed again. The rising tide. Looking on the rocks I could see a high-water mark shoulder high.

The miniature cove, soon to be filled with wind-driven water, was no place to be at high tide. I could imagine the havoc of swirling waters in the bowl pushed there by the crushing tide.

Had I not been weak or my knee tender, I could easily have scaled the cliff. There were footholds and handholds aplenty. It was only a matter of simple climbing, but my arms and legs and hands were powerless.

Looking back now, I can't explain, even to myself, how I climbed those rocks. They were twenty feet high. They were sharp — no man could say they were terribly difficult to climb, I admit. At the same time I was weak — too weak to budge a fifty-pound anchor before I wrecked — yet I managed to push and pull my eighty or ninety pounds up the twenty feet of lava formation.

The first thing I did when I got to the top was to lie down for a sleep. It was a nap that lasted the rest of the afternoon and all that night. For the first time in forty-eight days I didn't have to pull myself up at disjointed hours of the night to pump the bilges. But I awakened several times from force of habit. My ears were long tuned to the creaking of *Pagan's* timbers and the myriad sounds from her watered bilges, and from wind in her sails and rigging. The absence of those sounds was as significant as those sounds themselves, and when I couldn't hear them, I could only sleep patchily.

When day broke I labored to a sitting position, feeling fresh enough to think of food and water. I was sitting in a patch of misshapen lava surrounded by thick, recklessly grown jungle, creepers, and tight trees. A mile across the lagoon I could see the remains of my intrepid *Pagan* high and dry on the shining reef. She looked frowzy and tortured. Her standing rigging was smashed away; her deckhouse gone; she lay on her beam, halfway across the long reef, pointing her naked decks to the sky.

Below me the beach of the alcove was strewn with driftage from *Pagan* — bits of chewed planking, articles of clothing, bedding, sailcloth, water kegs, spars, and shroud wires.

I searched into the entangled jungle from my seat, looking for signs of tropical foods. I had expected to find bananas, coconuts, bird rookeries, and water easily. I saw nothing encouraging — only the dense patchwork of illimitable undergrowth topped by towering oaklike trees. From near by I selected several varieties of leaves and chewed at them. They were tasteless and more dry than otherwise.

I remembered having seen coconut palms on the shore when I was skirting the reef with *Pagan*. It was my hope now to find them and eat of them till someone came along or my strength returned to where I could manage a search inland or along the coast for a village. I decided to go south and at the same time to seek for the lee side of the isle. I wondered how far I would have to go; and I wondered how far I could go.

I figured I'd better get an early start, so I wobbled to my feet. To southward, around the beckoning point that I had nearly sailed past, appeared the shortest way to the island's leeward shores. If the island was inhabited there would be a village there.

I took a stout limb for support and started on an uncertain quest over the pocked spiny lava. I ate leaves as I trudged along, and sucked the ends of broken branches for sap. A small land crab, jumping from rock to rock, darted in front of me, and I pinioned him with my stick. Taking him up, I tore him apart and sucked his bitter-tasting insides out. I chewed his plated legs, sucked the shelly mass dry, and spit it up. It gave me fresh strength and hope.

Farther along I found another crab. He too I sucked from his shell. I had come now some fifteen or twenty yards in a couple of hours. My walking was unbearably slow. I wanted to go faster. But the rocks! They were rocks such as I had never seen before. They were like an eagle's claws inverted. The island is volcanic in origin, and evidently centuries of rain, pelting upon the wearable lava, has fined it down to innumerable stalagmite-looking points sticking up at heights from three inches to three feet. They crowd upon themselves in their formation like a close forest, making a flat space — even the width of a bare foot — something to remember. I teetered among them, placing my feet carefully on the least sharp of the points and using my hands on the higher lava spires to brace myself and push myself along.

My legs were weakening and my bad knee beginning to ache. My swollen heavy feet were too much of a load to be carried much farther. Their weight was such that often I had to lift them from behind the knees over the higher rocks. I lay down among the rocks to rest. It was easy to sleep. I could have slept forever. Sleep was as effortless as thinking to an active mind. My body cried for twenty-four hours of sleep, but my judgment complained at the little distance I had traveled. I forced myself to move on.

In an hour I wended through another ten yards of rock semi-jungle. I was so tired I trembled; I was ready to quit. I looked for a spot to lie down. From out of the rocks a coral snake glided toward me, weaving in such a way that I knew he didn't see me. My parched throat watered at the sight of him. Instantly I thought of his meat and blood — food! When he was close enough I trapped him with my stick, holding it into the center of his body, pressing hard, trying to break his back. He writhed madly. I was hoping he would soon succumb. My hunger juices, whetted by the crabs and leaves, were yearning. I wondered how one went about eating a snake. I pushed against the stick the harder.

My strength began to give out; my arms trembled so that the stick moved, losing its purchase, and the snake darted into the rocks. The exertion tired me so I sat down, napping where I sat, but not for long: I felt a compulsion driving me to round the point while I had strength to walk.

Later in the afternoon, another twenty yards along, I came upon a lone coconut tree. It was short, not reaching higher than twenty-five feet, and a dozen green nuts, most delicious for drinking, were nestled in its fronds. Slapping the tree I shouted happily, and kissed it. Here I could stay eating the nuts till I grew strong again.

In a short time my joy faded to ironic discouragement. Though the life-giving coconuts were a scant twenty feet overhead, I was powerless to reach them. I knew that I was powerless to climb the tree. I threw my hiking stick at them. The shoulder muscles were so weak that my arm came out of socket, and fell limp at my side till I pressed it in again. I gave up and slept on the mound of earth at the base of the tree.

When I arose in a few hours, I searched about and found a weazened old nut. My knife, though rusted, was suitably sharp. But not the world's sharpest knife could have availed me much then. I was too weak to use it.

Nevertheless I set to work hewing at the end of the nut. After what seemed hours I had hacked through a bare inch of the outer fibrous husk. My fingers, hands, and arms ached from the clumsy work. There was an inch to go to the inner nut. But I was so weak and tired I doddered. Even as I stared uselessly at the nut I dozed. I dropped it and fell back. I slept as I had wanted to sleep, uninhibited and without moving, the rest of the afternoon, and the whole of the night.

I awakened next morning weaker than when I had fallen asleep. Beside me lay the wrinkled nut, and near by the knife. I took them up and struck one against the other with chopping, half-strength cuts. Within minutes I was tired. My hands cramped up and refused to open or close. I had only to cut through an inch of husk to find three small depressions. By punching one of them, I could reach the inside cool milk. I picked the nut up and beat it against the sharp rocks. I pounded it till my breath came in gasps, then dropped it in despair and lay back in a heap.

The third day ashore and I had seen nothing but a tortuous floor of projecting crags and confused growth. My tongue was puffed and sticky. The bad knee was turning black. Coral poisoning, picked up out on the reef, which I had been unaware of up to this point, was festering in a dozen places on my feet and legs.

I lay about a hundred paces inland. Hard by I could hear the sea pounding into the under-washed caverns along the shore. I knew I was on my last legs — and my only chance for life lay in getting back to where I could watch the water and intercept a chance passer. I struggled to a shaky stance and trudged toilsomely in the direction of the sea, stumbling and falling, oblivious of everything, intent only on reaching the dull noise of the pounding surf.

I came out upon a small alcove making an irregular half circle around a sandspit some twenty feet below me. A strong wind — sufficient, if I had been out in it under sail, to necessitate tucking in a reef — was whirling the sand in eddies along the strand. The tide was well out, revealing a bottom heavy with rocks and ledges of coral. Out on the reef, I could see no sign of *Pagan*. The sea and coral had triumphed over her. Around the shore were indications of her presence. I lay down and slept.

Sometime later I heard sounds that weren't exactly the sea. Looking from my perch I saw three small native children racing excitedly about the beach. They were bushy haired and black skinned. They shouted and screamed in high glee over the fabulous findings they were making. They were directly below me.

I leaned over the ledge, intending to shout, "Hey Joe, come here." Instead, a weird, uncontrollable gurgle rattled forth. The boys looked around, then up. What they saw was mirrored in their faces. Their eyes grew saucerlike with terror; in one motion they dropped all they had collected and ran screaming for their lives.

I was so suddenly left alone that I was afraid I had imagined what I saw. But the footprints were there — they spoke volumes in relief and peace of mind. At least someone knew that a stranger was on the island.

I lay back and slept, waking to stare at the watery point around which they had gone, as long and as often as possible. Heavy hours dragged by. The tide worked up the beach to full. Driven by the flush wind it thundered into the worn cliff base, throwing dollops of water well back into the matted brush and vine.

Finally I heard loud shouts and watched the mouth of the alcove. An outrigger broke into view carrying six young boys. They were punting her along in the shallow water. I hailed them. They dropped on one knee, the better to see me, and stared incredulously. They were a scant thirty yards away.

I could tell that they had seen few white men before. And it was apparent that the frightened children hadn't been taken seriously in their village. The gullible teen-agers had come to investigate.

I motioned them into the cove so I could be dragged from my perch in the rocks. They tried valiantly to poke the delicate-hulled outrigger into the precarious opening, but were forced to give up. The zesty wind blowing, the tide coming in, the heavy rollers breaking into the rock-ribbed cove, baffled their seamanship. Rightfully they gave up.

They smiled gamely, indicating that it was impossible to come in. They indicated that I should move out to the ledge at the fringe of the cove mouth, about forty feet from me; from there they could possibly catch me as I jumped over. If I could but win to that point, I was safe. I tried to stand, but there wasn't enough push in my arms and legs to get me off my back, and I showed them how helpless I was.

They motioned that they were returning to their village, that they would come again. I communicated to them that I was foodless, waterless — I fell back in a fainting gesture to imply that if they didn't come for me soon, it wouldn't matter if they never came. Lying back was so peaceful. I forgot they were there and soon found myself dozing.

I was shocked awake by water splashing over me. It was dark. I thought I was aboard *Pagan* in the tight cold cabin. I was saying to myself, "It's time to pump the bilges." I felt around for the tea. Just a pinch to chew while I heaved at the pump. My hand scraped across the rocks; then I remembered and looked out onto the black lagoon.

The sea was pounding against the cliffs. The tide was coming up again. A high wind was blowing and salt water was bombarding the jungle.

I supposed the natives had come looking for me, and missed me. I was too weak to sit up for long. I propped myself on my side so that I could squint through a crevice in the rocks at the sea.

The wind and water were cold, my clothes were sticking to me. I was getting properly miserable. Then I saw lights on the water. They were well off from the shore. I knew it was the outrigger come for me. Then I made it to be two outriggers, maybe three. When they pulled up even with me they stopped, and evidently anchored to study the situation.

The torches burned fiercely in the wind as the boats huddled offshore. Occasionally, when the sea and wind were momentarily slack, I yelled gutturally. They heard me, and shouted back encouragement above the brewing storm.

It was understandable that they didn't hazard their delicate outriggers in the obstreperous surf. The surge of sea over the rocky bottom would have smashed the hulls out of them. I called to them at every favorable opportunity, and when they heard, they answered reassuringly.

Hours dragged, the torches one by one were put out, and finally only one torch shone in the water. I grew panicky, thinking I'd never be rescued. The natives were evidently waiting for daylight. I was cold, wet, and miserable. Surely they were cunning enough to devise some means of getting me out before then.

I set up such a caterwaul of despondent calls that soon the boats sprang audibly and visibly to life. Several torches flared up, voices sang out, and one of the craft detached itself and moved slowly away to the north. Something was afoot.

The other boats moved in to around fifty feet off the rocks. I could see naked shoulders and bushy heads under the fires. They called good-naturedly and pointed to the north.

I called to them in Spanish, then in French, but they gave the same friendly answers, and waved their flares to the north.

Sometime later I heard brush rustling in the jungle and the snap of limbs underfoot. I threw myself down out of sight and listened. A voice called in a strange tongue and I sat up and answered. Those on the water joined in and an excited three-way interchange cropped up.

A torch suddenly swayed in view from the dark, and stopped in the air above me. An exclamation of disbelief came from behind the sputtering light. The bearer was panting heavily from his struggle with the rocks and bramble. All I could say was, "Hello Joe." I could not sit up any longer; I could only extend a hand.

I made out massive shoulders and arms beneath the light, and a bushy head. He was a tall man. His voice, husky and full of understanding, spoke soothing words, and shouted instructions to the boats. The light disappeared, and the powerful arms closed about me, wafting me into the air.

My Good Samaritan hustled me in a jiffy over the forty feet to the overhanging ledge, where the boys earlier could have saved me. I was held in hard-muscled arms while one of the boats, heavily manned with oarsmen and punters, worked up to the battered rock face. I could hear oars slapping the water furiously and the punting poles pounding at the black, shapeless cliff face to find the boat off. Instructions were loudly bandied. The craft, flooded with torchlight, was directly below, heaving to the surging seas. More words passed from mouth to mouth. This time they were desperate instructions. The prow was scraping over the charred rock. My benefactor twisted me upside down, and handed me down at the ankles. Upreaching arms folded me in and exclaimed when they felt my small girth. When I was safe aboard a yell of triumph went up from all throats. The other boats answered.

A moment later an audible crash shook the small craft. It was my benefactor, who had jumped aboard from his perch. It's a wonder he hadn't broken a leg or stove the light deck in.

I was laid on the stern of the open boat. The stanch oarsmen worked the boat off the cliffy shore. My friend came to me and covered me over with a sheet of tapa cloth. When I clamored for food and drink he offered me a baked *kumala*, a kind of sweet potato, which I took and nibbled a morsel from. The long days and nights of quiet desperation were over. The fact of food in my hands and a pot of native tea being offered me overwhelmed me. Suddenly I lost all caution. I bit viciously into the *kumala*. I chewed it voraciously and swallowed it in great gulps, washing it down with volumes of the hot tea.

I sighed and exclaimed over the food with pleasure, much to the delight of my friend, who egged me on generously, giggling happily as I bolted great mouthfuls. I knew I shouldn't be gobbling as I was; but though I tried mightily, judgment went glimmering after the first taste.

When I was gorged I lay back and fell asleep to the tune of oar beats and punting poles and the lilt of a strange language.

Tuvutha

WHEN I CAME TO, it was with the deep consciousness of the village around me. I was in a thatched hut, lying on my back. Above me were the rafters and ceilingless dome of a thatch dwelling. A ridgepole of coconut trunk supported a thick roofing of pandanus and coconut thatch, all lashed intricately in place with a coarse fibrous rope. This I realized was the hut of the man who had saved me.

I lay on a woven mat spread over a layer of coconut leaves stripped from the branch. My bed was a hard uncomfortable one. When I stirred, someone sitting at my side moved and looked at me closely. It was a native woman who showed relief at my stirring and whose eyes indicated she had tended me for anxious hours.

I had been in a coma a full day and night. The whole time she had sat patiently, feeding me in my delirium on a balm of coconut milk. My knee was poulticed in a soggy wrapping of native herbals; the offensive coral poisoning too was checked. My life was saved.

Itchica, as I learned, was the man who rescued me from the rocks. He carried me to his dark hut where care of me was given into the hands of his soft-spoken, efficient wife. She, with her woman's intuitiveness and native cunning, saw my condition at a glance.

She knew that the starved shouldn't eat as I had eaten, nor drink as I had drunk on the outrigger. She nodded her head gravely over my gaseous, swelling stomach, swollen to where the stretched skin burned, and my breaths that came in short gasps.

Even after I was saved from the rocks, she knew I might have died. The *kumalas* wolfed so hungrily, and the tea gulped, could have — but for her — finished me. With a long calloused finger she probed far down in my throat, turning and upsetting my stomach, freeing it of the unchewed lumps of heavy food and the flood of water. She put her hands on my stomach, pressed gently and firmly till the gases rumbled out of my throat and my breathing became normal.

After that I was pervaded with a sense of nothingness. But to return. When I awakened thirty hours later, staring into the strange rafters of the hut, she was still there, tending me. I owe her my life. And I owe my life to her husband, who scrambled over the rocks for me.

She is Una, an infinite woman; a woman of great kindness and understanding. Una rarely smiled or showed emotion. She wasn't exactly inscrutable for I know she felt deeply, and in small ways she showed it. She showed the depth of her feelings in the selfless care she gave me. She proved herself unforgettable in the numberless things I saw her do before I left the island. Anything she did, she did well. She is one of these rare women who accomplish a prodigious amount of work in a single day.

I was famished from my long coma. Una gave me a half shell of coconut milk and a hot broth of fish and breadfruit with a turtle egg to eat raw. Itchy (as I nicknamed Itchica) propped me up from behind as Una fed me a bit at a time.

It was difficult for me to chew even the small soft bread-fruit lumps. My jaw muscles grew so tired in a few motions that they refused to wag. My swallowing muscles too soon collapsed and I couldn't force anything down. I learned, before long, that the best way to eat was to have an hour's rest between tidbits. Then my jaws could munch again and my swallowing machinery was good for a few minutes' work.

When the villagers learned I had come to life they trooped in for a look. The hut was filled to overflowing. They sat around cross-legged, leaning toward me searchingly. I lay studying every face and feature for a clue to the land I was on. They weren't black so much as coffee colored. They were clean, healthy, powerfully built, tall, congenial. I couldn't identify them with any land I had seen in my travels.

I spoke to the soft-featured blacks, asking the name of their land. To a man, they spoke no English. I spoke next in French, then in Spanish; they looked blank and finally giggled at my efforts. I laughed and they laughed with me, and I knew we were pals.

Pointing to the ground, I asked, "New Hebrides?" No one moved. "New Caledonia?" No response. "Loyalty Islands?" Still silence. Though I knew I was far from the Solomons, I asked, "Solomon Islands?" This struck a responsive chord. Again I asked, "Solomon Islands?"

One of the old men came forward nodding his head: evidently in his long life he had heard of the Solomons. Indicating the surroundings he said, "Lomaloma."

"Lomaloma?"

"Lomaloma, Tuvutha."

"Lomaloma, Tuvutha?" The words meant nothing to me. I pressed him further.

"Lomaloma, Tuvutha i Lau," he said.

Lau I knew to be the easternmost part of the Fiji Islands. But I knew I couldn't be in Fiji. I had missed the Fijis and sailed on to the New Hebrides. But what the oldster said made me think. I could easily see the hale men before me were a far cry from the malarial, ulcerous, potbellied natives I had seen in the New Hebrides during the war.

I figured maybe I had misunderstood him. We haggled in blind alleys further. Eventually a crude chart was scratched on a box top. A finger was laid on a remote oblong dot in a string of dots designated as the Lau Group of Fiji. The island was Tuvutha; the village Lomaloma. The word impinged on me like a bolt — "Fiji!"

I stared long at the ludicrous map. To the south was Lakemba, to the north Vanuambalavu, to the west Nayau, and farther to west, the main islands of the group. The incredible fact that I was in eastern Fiji was hard of belief. My estimates of speed and position of *Pagan* after the hurricane had been immensely wrong. It made me wonder, had I been near Samoa or not? Where exactly had I been these last seven weeks during my blind searchings? I can never know. But I shall always wonder about it. At any rate, I still say I did what I thought best and it saved my life. That's the test.

Now I was isolated on a primitive island which I soon learned, from sign language and guesswork, was visited every four months by a native island trader. The copra schooner had just left a couple of weeks before. More than three months before it would come again. Three months out here on a lonely, unvisited tropic island.

Sitting in a semicircle about me and towering over me were twenty massively proportioned black men. Their faces, their voices, their attitudes, were friendly. I was sure they were peaceful people to be isolated with.

The average height of the bushy-haired men was a mite short of six feet, some of them running to six feet four and six feet six inches. They are what you would call "built like a brick jailhouse." They are the healthiest looking humans I have ever seen. Their teeth, which they never brush, are straight and beautifully white.

Ordinarily they dress only at the loins, men and women, wrapped around from the waist in the lavish sulu which extends to the knees. The women expose their breasts commonly — that is, all except the younger unmarried women, known as Marys, who almost never do. These islanders have a precocious, apt look, and a graceful stately carriage from balancing their food at the ends of poles across their shoulders and porting it over narrow jungle trails. They are broad at the nostril, thick at the lip, and their hair runs to a great halolike bushiness which is both ornamental and traditional. Their generous hearts, I soon learned, are the biggest part of them.

They represent the inbreeding of Melanesian with Polynesian and Tongan. A unique Negroid people are the result.

Here there is no malaria, no tropical ulcers, no dread European diseases. The "advantages" of civilization, happily, haven't invaded this remote corner of the world — and I hope they never do! Every indication of vital health is rampant. The greatest and often most unobtainable desires of so-called civilization — peace, quiet, security, health — are here the simplest commonplaces.

Now that Una had nurtured me through the first two critical days, my condition improved rapidly. The natural food of the island agreed beautifully with me. On the third day I was able to stand shakily; on the fifth I could walk to the door with the cane Itchy made me from *Pagan's* timbers and peer out at the village and call to my growing circle of friends.

Itchy also made me a rather imposing looking chair which I called my throne. I sat in it during the days that I waited for strength to come to my legs so I could walk. The natives sat around me in a deep circle, watching curiously anything I did. I was the first white man to stay on the island, though a few had visited it.

A large number of the natives gathered at Itchy's hut every night to puff at their hand-rolled jungle cigarettes and chat together over the dim lantern. On my third night at the village I was in good spirits for the first time since my rescue. I was coherent and able to sit unassisted in my chair. After a few jovialities they began asking me about the circumstances of my arrival on the island. To answer them was no easy job.

There were about fifteen words of English known to them and the same number of words of their language known to me — but luckily we had hands.

First I had to remind them that there had been a war; and that it was over. Then I explained that I had a wife, showing them Mary's pictures which I had crammed in my shirt pockets when I ate my wallet, and the white space around my finger where there had been a ring till I grew so skinny it had slipped off. I also told them that I was from the "island" of America, far away, of which they had heard. And that Mary was from the "island" of Australia. I scribbled a sprawling map on a sheet of paper, drawing in popular landmarks, including Tuvutha. They were astounded that their island was so small.

I showed them New York, Frisco, New Orleans; and explained the impossibility of obtaining transport to my bride of long absence from any of these places. I drew in Panama and indicated I had sailed from there aboard *Pagan*. I first impressed on them its great distance by pointing in a high, exaggerated arc out to and over the horizon. Then I took the approximate width of Tuvutha, one mile, and multiplied it many many times by flashing and closing my palms before them, at the same time tracing the path of my voyage on the crude map. Their credulity was strained, and yet I hadn't made the distance great enough: such a distance was incomprehensible to them.

Then one of them asked me what had happened to my shipmates aboard *Pagan*, and how many there had been. I hastened to explain there were no shipmates, that I had sailed alone. He asked the whys and wherefores of my thin bones and my being wrecked out on the reef, and again he asked where my crew mates were. I explained I was alone, that I had sailed singlehanded. He didn't understand and asked me if, in my extremity, I had eaten them. I hastened to assure them all that I had sailed from Panama entirely alone. Since they couldn't conceive of anyone attempting such a voyage singly, they couldn't accept explanations. The fellow still didn't comprehend.

Another came forward. He asked in most precise pantomime if I had eaten my crew members. He even went to the extreme of holding my arm and champing at it by way of explanation. At this point I am sure they all believed I was a cannibal. Not a breath was taken as all leaned on the next words I should utter. With the most articulate puppetry, I re-enacted the whole voyage, stressing particularly that I had started out solo; and even if I had had someone with me I would not have eaten him.

Episode after episode I related, right up to the night of rescue. Throughout, they were geared to attention; amazed and impressed in turn. The islander is strictly a seaman at heart. For the island in a sense is a ship perpetually at anchor. Things of the sea are deeply involved with his life. His respect for a seaman is unlimited; often the chieftains are such by virtue purely of their prowess at the helm.

My exploit struck them in a vital spot — though I am sure they couldn't see why I had done it for a mere woman. But since I was from "civilization" I am sure they forgave me this queerness. With childlike appreciation they demanded unanimously to hear the account again. So, not suspecting what I was getting into, I repeated the wild yarn, word for word, action for action.

They received it jubilantly; and wanted to hear it still again. To a man they shouted *talanoa* (story). Their simple, earnest appreciation threw me on my beam ends. To get out of the rut I seemed to have got into I insisted that they sing for me instead.

In their ready way they were agreeable.

They sang their ancient battle songs in booming, hypnotizing tones. They sang in a stately, ever-varying chant accompanied by solemn chords from a ringing triangular iron. The effect was gripping. The singers themselves were highly affected, seeming to be in a semi-trance. They sat hunched loosely forward, head down, eyes partly veiled with the profound emotion of their music. The dogs howled mournfully.

When the singing ended I thought the party was over. But then they insisted that I sing for them. This nearly floored me. Not only was I stricken with stagefright, but I'm not musically inclined. Truth is, I sing as most people scream. However, they insisted, so I prepared for a questionable debut.

The only thing I could think of was "Deep in the Heart of Texas," so I sang it. It went over big. It was a raving success. They crowded close, wanting more. I gave them next "The Star-Spangled Banner," which was a little slow for their taste, so I livened things up with "Roll Out the Barrel." This was right up their alley, so I led on with "Waltzing Matilda," an Aussie song, and tried to end the show with "Pistol Packin' Mamma." Once again they were laid in the aisles. I sang the rousing football song of the University of California (my alma mater) and before they could importune me further I gave the "all's finished" signal, and made ready to bed down. Una, seeing I was tired, took my part and the party dispersed.

The first week my stern dietician allowed me only soft foods like boiled fish, baked breadfruit, chicken skin, *kumala*, *uve* (a type of yam), turtle eggs, boiled eels, mangoes, pineapple, and papaya. I couldn't eat much at a time before my jaws tired, or my swallowing apparatus failed. Too, my shrunken stomach filled with only a few bites and before I could eat on I had to wait for digestion. I was constantly hungry. I ate as often as my complicated conditions permitted.

I took meals from a kind of table Itchy had pounded together from my faithful fore scuttle that had taken such a drubbing from head seas during the hurricane, and from which on many occasions I had stood squinting hopefully across the bows for land. Now I was eating from it!

I ate about seven meals a day, arising at least twice in the night. I had but to say "*Una, kai kai*" (food). She always stirred from her sleep uncomplainingly, elbowed Itchy, and the two of them prepared something for my middle-of-the-night snacks. Itchy lit the fire and warmed whatever Una decided I could have. Then Una would sit beside me, breaking the hot food into small bits, taking out bones, handing it to me, and speaking fast, strange words if I didn't chew well.

I always felt bad when I roused them from a deep sleep. But as it was I hadn't strength to sit, and when strength came, it was too painful to sit long because of my bony hanks. You have no idea what it is to sit or lie on fleshless bones. The Fijians don't know of inner-spring mattresses. My bed, of leaves stripped from coconut fronds, was as hard as *Pagan's* bunk boards, only harder since I had no blanket now. I felt like a ship in dry dock — shored up by my bones.

One night I attempted to climb to my feet with my cane and stagger across the room to the food shelf so as not to impose on Una and Itchy. I had a preview of what it is to be ninety. With mincing, shaking steps I got under way. Fijian children sleep where tiredness finds them. Halfway across the large room my toe touched a leg and I went reeling amidst the family of six boys. Oh the torture of being fallen on by a bony man! Judging from the squawks of the waking boys there are few things worse — like being hit by a gunny sack of wood, or worse. Una admonished me severely for not calling her. I was fed and carried back to my bed, where I slept till my intricate hunger mechanism could manipulate again.

At the end of the first week, Una and Itchy let me know that henceforth I could have any food I wanted. I promptly pointed out a small pig rooting on the common. In a short time the village boys were in wild chase, and the piglet was in the pot. Soon I was happily gnawing pork joints. Thereafter, anything I wanted was lavished on me.

From this time on Tuvutha became a shipwrecked seaman's paradise. First of all, every article of *Pagan's* gear found on the beaches or floating on the lagoon or otherwise gleaned from the reef or the sea floor was brought to me by the natives. Everything was spread out before me and what I wanted I dragged toward me, the rest I pushed back.

I kept only one of the suits of clothes and a dress shirt. My feet were too swollen for weeks to wear shoes; so I gave them to those who found them. They fitted only the small boys: the men's feet were like pillows. The remainder of my gear — several suits of khakis and an odd assortment of clothing — I handed out so that as many as possible could have an article to wear.

The pleasantest surprise came when my jewelry was returned. My silver identification wristlet, bought in England at the first of the war, and my gold wedding band from Australia, were laid before me. I was delighted. I had never expected to see them again after they dropped off my fleshless hands. The sharp-eyed divers had seen them flash at nine fathoms on the lagoon floor and retrieved them.

The *sulu,* or loincloth, wrapped about the waist and twisted under is all I wore the whole time on the island. "Going native" was fun. The Fijians got a kick out of it too.

When I was able to walk I spent my days wandering through the village, limping at half pace on my cane. At Lomaloma you don't knock, you just walk in.

I spent many of my visits in the home of the village schoolteacher. My ambition is to be a schoolteacher, so we spent a lot of time talking shop.

The village chief, Tupa, and I became great buddies also. Several times I was invited in for *kai kai* and one night I received his supreme compliment: I slept in his *koro* (house).

That night Tupa and I sat talking across the pale lantern. He prepared his native smoke, drying a greenish leaf over a smoldering coconut husk, and rolling it in dried banana stripping. Someday, he said, he was going to the island of America.

He pulled heavily on the weak cigarette with his thick lips. He had heard at Vanuambalavu, in his youth, of great hotels and their fabulous elevators that take you flying between floors in buildings higher than coconut palms. His black calloused hand rose in a quick glide; his face gleamed. He wanted to live in a hotel and take high rides.

He blew a whiff of smoke from his wide nostrils. The trains. He wanted to ride on them; he wanted to attend the theaters; eat in the great restaurants; visit the big homes — Tupa is going to do everything when he comes to America. The muscles under his black skin quivered with excitement as he told me. An infinite vision was in his eyes.

To him America will be another Tuvutha. He will go where he wants and have a good time. Americans will open their hearts to him as his island did to me.

That night before I slept, I prayed in my usual orisons

that the stately chief would never be allowed to fulfill his
naïve simple dream.

Another of my friends, the grizzled old God-fearing native
pastor, spent many an afternoon limping with me along the
beach, talking of many things. Often we dwelt on my profound experience when I refound Va Kalou (God) out on
the lonesome sea. He too had found Va Kalou in early life
in stress and storm between the islands on his outrigger.

He had been crippled as a young man in a heavy offshore
blow. He had foundered some five miles from land and had
swum to shore only to be battered by the high seas on the
coral reefs. Only Va Kalou could have saved him, so he gave
his life in service to Va Kalou. He had been educated for the
divinity in a Methodist school in Lakemba, capital of Lau.
That was thirty years ago. Over the years he managed to
hang onto ten or fifteen English words he had picked up at
the trading post, with which we discussed the religion of his
little wooden church and local gossip.

I asked him one day, because of my interest in sociology,
what the divorce rate was among the natives. I had an idea
it would be low — I knew it wouldn't be of the staggering
proportions of the rate at home. He didn't understand what
I meant. I was more explicit when I reasked. Still he cocked
his head and squinted his eyes in perplexity.

I went to the extremes of description. I explained in my
petty vocabulary and pantomime the marriage ritual. He
comprehended. I indicated ten marriages, of ten men and
ten women — Fijians of course. He nodded understandingly.
Now, I asked very carefully, at what rate — that is, how many
out of ten or a hundred — did they separate? He looked blank.

He could follow me to a point, but from there he was lost.

Then I knew the trouble. He couldn't reach me in what I sought to describe, because in his total experience no such occurrence had crossed his path. There was no such word as divorce in his vocabulary; no such custom in his island lore. He couldn't conceive of it . . . I couldn't explain it, nor could you. To his mind, marriage was marriage; and that is that. There was no divorce. People married and stayed married.

Another thing I saw in my travels about the village was the courtship ritual. There were at least three matches in the process of making that I could observe — and often the young couples were near as I hobbled about.

The young man, seeking among the village belles his choice of mate, upon finding her manages at all available moments to be somewhere within her sight. This, of course, appears quite "accidental." No matter what his preoccupation, whether it be work, play, or just loafing, most or all is done within sight of the beloved. These activities, however, are of such a nature as to impress the young lady with the young man's qualities as a possible husband.

The young Mary, by the same token, observes these advances, but of course appears not to see them. But at the same time she too turns up quite "accidentally" in his presence, rushing hurriedly about her mother's housewifely chores. This process goes on from a few short weeks to months. Then comes the final act in the affair, an ultimate test which determines whether or not the relationship shall dissolve or continue.

The young Mary, at the moment she concludes that here at last is the man in her life, in an "accidental" way allows her *sulu* to sag to her waist, or her simple cotton blouse to fall open at the front, exposing her breasts. This, the most intimate show of affection, saves the young man the strain of proposing.

The parents of the two — who all along have slyly observed developments — now, upon seeing this fullest show of affection, negotiate a marriage, which, as I learned later, soon takes place. After the marriage, the young couple separate, each returning to his respective home as formerly. On a day soon after, the whole village joins in to erect a *koro*, whereupon the newlyweds move in and set up housekeeping.

In my further travels, I met Cama, a philosopher. He too had been led to the island metropolis at Lakemba by the lure of education — to be a schoolteacher. But after two years of truck with formal knowledge and the faithless promises of civilization he returned to primitive Tuvutha. For over twenty years he had forsworn his books and his desire to bring education to his island.

Cama had a wistful face when he said the native's greatest need was to be protected from the evils of civilization. He too had a ten-word English vocabulary. But philosophers like Cama don't need an extensive word range — for they speak with ideas in the large; a universal language.

He swept his hand over the peaceful valley at the foot of the extinct volcano. What need of the outer world here? Here there is no criminality, no economic competition, no sexual perversion. The old, the infirm, never worry. Good health is unavoidable, peace has no option. If there is sickness, the jungle abounds with healing herbs. Witness my improved coral poisoning, the healing of my poisoned knee, the very fact that I was alive and not dead as all had expected.

I told him about the war, of which hints had come to the

island. He was glad to hear it was over. When I explained the devastation of the atomic bomb he was horrified. Later, the chief, schoolteacher, and pastor came to ask if this were true. I nodded gravely. They looked at me from inscrutable masks.

To impress them I explained. I used my hand to indicate an airplane, which they recognized. I whistled as I indicated a falling bomb — and then said *"Boom,"* as it supposedly struck. This too they comprehended, for they had some idea of bombs. Then I inferred that the plane was flying over the island. Raising a finger I said, "One atomic bomb," then showed it falling — explaining that it should hit at mid-island. In a motion I pantomimed that Tuvutha had been wiped out, everyone killed, the very air seared and infected. They were astonished. The old philosopher walked away shaking his head.

Another time toward the end of that first week, the five of us sat sipping the healthful coconut milk in the chief's hut. We were talking in our limited way at odds and ends. I told them of the starvation of the "islands" Europe and India. I went on to explain the shortages of England and China and Russia. I told of war shortages in food the world over.

They were in high satisfaction when I informed them that only Tuvutha, in all the world, had no shortages. They had all heard of the fabulous island of America. To their circumscribed minds all lands were islands. They couldn't believe that *kai kai* could be scarce in America. By my telling of that condition, their deformed little island became infinitely swelled with importance.

At another time, waiting to accompany a fishing trip out

on the lagoon, I described the Empire State Building, our whizzing automobiles, our skies dark with planes. I explained the movies, huge universities, and the Golden Gate Bridge. They couldn't fashion in their minds what their ears heard.

The pastor asked me if there were magnificent churches. I told him yes, but it would have been unfair not to say that the beer joints, pool halls, and night clubs were far more numerous and better patronized. Before any more embarrassing questions arose, I made adieus. They were loth to end the discussion: I was glad. Among them America's reputation by hearsay was high; I wanted the illusion to hold, so I left to go down to the lagoon beach where the outriggers were moored in readiness for the day's fishing.

A few of the village children were around to see the boats away. As yet the elders had not come from their *koros*, except for one of the Marys dressed in *sulu* and soft cotton blouse, who stood tending an outrigger, its bow resting on the beach. She helped me gain the narrow flat deck, then shoved off well onto the lagoon to tread water and await the others.

I sat facing forward, watching the activity ashore or the colorful marine world below. Suddenly something whizzed over my shoulder and plopped on the deck in a sort of receptacle near the bow — and when I saw it, I couldn't believe it: it was the Mary's soft cotton blouse!

I knew what it meant for a Mary to loosen her blouse at the front to a man — but to remove it! I gulped! And surely I must have blushed. To me there was nothing "accidental" about this: it was entirely purposive, a desperate show of intention, yet she seemed so unconcerned.

I wondered how I could say in a tactful way, to one who

didn't speak my tongue, that I was already married — happily married.

Ashore the other outriggers were pushing off to join us. Inside I stirred desperately. But as the boats glided up, I saw a startling thing. There were some seven Marys on the five craft, and all of them, after the normal manner of the married women, were undressed to the waist. Then it all came clear. The women are the chief divers, and with divers any kind of clothing above the waist is undesirable; and since fish spearing involves much underwater activity, the women — even the Marys — wear their *sulus* from waist to knees only.

The Mary on the stern was still regarding the water in a very unconcerned way. I heaved a long, peaceful breath and settled back to enjoy the trip.

Going Native

I FIRST ATTENDED the native church on my seventh day on the island. Fijians attend church three times on Sunday: early morning, afternoon, and dusk. Wednesday morning too, at dawn, is a church date. The *lalo,* or native ceremonial drum, calls the hour of church. I went clad in my wrinkled blue suit wearing socks to hide my puffed, poisoned feet.

The women enter first and sing a long mournful song for about ten minutes. They seat themselves on the floor on the left side of the room at the front. When the mournful song is finished the men come in and sit on the right. Behind them in neat rows are the boys, and to the left the girls.

The natives are a beautiful sight on church day. The halo of dark frizzy hair is combed and oiled to eye-catching perfection. Sunday-best *sulus* are broken out and short-sleeved colorful shirts are worn. Where the skin shows it is oiled with *wali wali,* an aromatic coconut oil, which makes it coppery.

The proceedings, despite the Fijians' natural religious seriousness, have a dash of humor. In the back of the room sits one of the village elders, glowering over the boys. He carries a thin, twenty-foot rod. Let one of the boys scant his sabbath duty, and he is nicked sharply on the head. The little boys, in fearful fervor, bend to their songs and prayers.

My throne was placed beside the pulpit. The pastor and

his two assistants were last to enter. The pastor was wearing my pin-stripe tan coat which he had found in the wreckage. He had offered it back — but I insisted that he keep it. It was a late collegiate cut, three buttons down the front and abbreviated lapels. The sleeves struck him well above the wristbone, and across the front it was tied with a string — since it wouldn't button around his massive chest.

Services commenced with a deep-throated, fast-moving chant accompanied by the time beat on a steel triangle. A highly persuasive prayer then ensued from one of the deacons. When he finished he mopped his tear-stained cheeks with a large white handkerchief. He prayed directly to God and not with the honeyed words or through the ears of a fastidious parish.

Another weird thrilling song was voiced up. The other deacon, my philosopher friend, poured some of the salt of his wisdom into a very moving prayer. He too wept openly as he prayed. It was strange to see these towering, heavily muscled men weeping volubly on their knees. Another song ricocheted around the close walls; and my friend the pastor advanced to the pulpit.

The sermon that followed was the most convincing that I ever heard: yet I knew not a word that he spoke. He expounded the Word in no uncertain terms. In thundering tones, with his great fists beating the pulpit, he dinned his inspired message into every rapt ear.

A final song was sung and services were concluded.

I took a stroll around the barren little room. The pulpit and two crude benches were its only ornamentation. It didn't even have a kerosene lamp on the ceiling. On one wall was a colorful whisky advertisement showing a picture of a shark. The walls and floors on the inside were unpainted. Church!

The church was about twelve years old, paid for by the natives from their copra gathering and built by the Colonial British Government.

That afternoon I enjoyed one of the most delightful treats of my whole stay in Fiji. Una had caught me an *uga vule* (pronounced "oonga vooly") or giant coconut crab. It was the first I had ever seen, like something out of *King Kong* in the miniature.

Offhand he appears to be a compromise between a crab, a lobster, and a tarantula. The width of his great claws is often more than two feet, and the plier-like, heavily toothed pincers on the end can amputate a finger. On the very stern end of the *uga vule* is a fist-sized round shell, looking like a small bag. When captured he is kept alive as a future food supply by a vine tied to this bag and suspended from a limb, or the hut ceiling. Hanging thus, claws down, he is helpless. He lives by climbing palms and cutting down the nuts from which he tears away the tough fiber, somehow breaking open the tougher nut and consuming the milk and soft meat inside.

The delicious white meat of the giant crab is a meal for three men. It is tastier than lobster. I often had lobster, or *urau* as it is called, but never when I could have *uga vule*. The meat is most toothsome when boiled, though the natives prefer it roasted in the shell over hot coals. The saclike pod on the creature's back contains a rich natural sauce which seasons the soft sweet meat.

The islanders were unusually kind and generous with food. Not a meal passed but that a dozen contributions came

in from the fires of the surrounding huts. When the fishermen returned at night from the coral lagoon, they always
brought a delicacy or two. The men who foraged each day
in the jungle invariably returned with some special fruit
or vegetable. Even the children at their play ran upon odd
tidbits in the jungle or along the sea front and brought them
timidly forth.

Whatever was offered me, I ate. I never questioned the
validity of a single bite. If I needed reassurance there was
plenty of it. The natives in their buoyant health were boun-
teous guarantors for their food. Their beautifully muscled
bodies, milky teeth, perpetually pleasant dispositions — in
general, their health and verve — were a perfect testimonial
to the fare they thrived on.

I ate baked eels and raw turtle eggs with perfect aplomb.
Boiled octopus, fish heads, and dried sea worms — no matter what, I took them all as they came. Una prepared many
odd dishes for me. Some of them looked mighty queer, but
so long as my strength grew and the wrinkles filled out. I
didn't care what she stewed up.

Whatever I wished to eat, I had only to suggest. I had but
to say *"Kai kai uga vule"* and Una strode off into the jungle,
returning in a while with one of the giant coconut crabs. If
it was eels I wanted or turtle soup, or if it was lobster or
clams, Una always took up her burlap sack and walked word-
lessly off to the lagoon. If it was a fruit or vegetable from
the jungle I wanted, Itchy or one of his six boys swung onto
one of the narrow jungle trails and soon brought it in.

On Sunday night after my first week on the island I began
to snap out of weakness. My body began to look like what a
body should look like. A padding of flesh appeared around

my thighs and I could sit down on my bones without need-
ing to support part of my weight on my hands. The cushion-
ing effect was better for sleep, too. Flesh was appearing
throughout the body, which, because of my seemingly
large hands and feet, made me look less like a clubfooted
pup.

The next morning, Monday, November fourth, I felt
strong enough to think in terms of getting off the island and
continuing my journey to Australia. I called Itchy and gave
him the lowdown. I told him I wanted to get going. He looked
grave and displeased; but he called a few of his neighbors to
sit in on the plans.

They were introduced, but the names turned out to be
unrememberable, so I just called them Joe, Bill, and Mike.
I proposed to them that we doctor up one of the outriggers
and weigh anchor for Lakemba, about forty miles away. This
they vetoed immediately. It was the hurricane season, a time
of variable winds and unpredictable calms. Too risky; don't
be in a hurry; take it easy, they said.

Itchy suggested we await the arrival of the copra boat in
January. All agreed that it would be better to wait than
venture out on the sea and made to adjourn the meeting. I
said no, and explained I hadn't seen my wife in eighteen
months, and couldn't wait any longer.

They listened as I unfolded a plan for signaling passing
ships, provided there were passing ships. My sails, though
chewed by the reef, were somewhat intact; so was my halyard and the copper block to heave the sail up with. I proposed we cut the top out of a prominent coconut tree and rig
my gear to it, so we could raise and lower the sail as a signal
if we sighted a ship.

That afternoon my ragged little mainsail was fluttering from the bald head of a conspicuous coconut palm.

In the evening the chief informed me that a ceremonial *Yangona* or native beer bust was to be held in my honor. I didn't know what he was talking about, but if it was going to be fun, I assured him I wouldn't miss it.

Shortly after, I was seated on my throne at the apex of a circle of cross-legged men on the floor of the chief's *koro*. From where I sat in my rickety varicolored chair made from *Pagan's* timbers, I looked down on the whole assemblage: a sort of king of nothing. Several weak lanterns dimly bathed the dark room. The men were in a festive mood. Elbows on knees they chatted pleasantly, waiting for the ceremonial to commence. All the village elders were present. Young boys, teen-agers, were allowed to look on from the door.

To the center of the circle walked four village girls, who sat facing me. They were to perform a *meke ta,* or dance in my honor as guest. Four more came in and sat down back to back with the others, facing away from me. Another sat just inside the doorway with the inevitable iron triangle and bar to beat time.

The faces of all were decoratively smeared with white paste. Garlands of hibiscus fiber, dyed purple and entwined with flowers, hung about their necks. Their breasts, arms, and legs glistened coppery with *wali wali.* On their wrists, ankles, and upper arms were bands of coconut frond and flowers. In their beautifully groomed bushy hair, and behind their ears, were flowers. In the right hand of each was a flower.

The time beater at the doorway started the ball rolling. The girls facing away from me sang one of the rich tribal songs and all clapped in unison. Those facing me sang with the others, at the same time waving the hands and arms gracefully in pattern. The expressive arm and hand movements were telling a story I couldn't follow, but it was beautiful and sincere. What ensued was a dance sitting down — which is the way the Fijians do it.

As the dance progressed the girls changed places several times; the singing grew to a high pitch, and more expressive and picturesque movements came into the dance. In fact, by the time they finished they had done everything possible to do sitting down, short of standing and dancing.

I arose and applauded, and insisted on shaking the hand of each performer as an appreciative gesture. Such enthusiasm prompted them to put the whole show on again. The next time I merely smiled.

Then came the *Yangona*. This comes under the title of Fijian alcoholism, without the imputation of Alcoholics Anonymous. *Yangona* is a native drink the partaking of which hasn't the distasteful results that our own similar "ceremonials" involve. The drink is evidently healthful. It is enjoyed only by the men, and then only on special occasions.

It is prepared by pounding the kava root in a hollowed log stump and mixing the pulpy root with water by hand in a large shallow wooden bowl. The pulp is strained from the water through the fibers of the hibiscus plant, leaving the water brownish and "spiked."

The leader of the singers then comes in, sitting respectfully before the kava bowl. She claps twice as a traditional expression of reverence, and a coconut shell is filled from the bowl and handed her. This she brings to me, the

guest, who quaffs it off and passes the shell back. It is re-
filled and taken to the chief. And thence to every Tom, Dick,
and Harry till the bowl is emptied. Then a new decoction is
made up. While the drinks are being passed and while fresh
bowls of the brew are being mixed, the men chatter and
banter across the circle.

Yangona has a taste that is indescribable. But there is nothing mysterious about its effect. It is heady, inducing a giddy
drowsiness. I should have quit after my second round. By
the tenth, I was all for singing "Deep in the Heart of Texas,"
and raising general hell with the boys. Shortly after, Itchy
wisely decided it was time to take me home before the party
got too rough.

The next morning I had a hangover which was nothing
more than a semi-diarrheic condition. It left me a bit shaky
at the knees. Among the healthful qualities of *Yangona* is
its action as a physic.

Una fed me lightly on breadfruit noodles cooked in
coconut milk with *vasua* or clam. I washed it down with
lemon-grass tea and had a papaya to finish with. She scolded
Itchy for leading me astray in "that den of iniquity."

That afternoon of the fifth of November was spectacular.
Shortly after lunch a cry rent the village. There was something on the horizon. A sail! Itchy and Mike came dashing in,
overflowing with gibberish and pointing to seaward excitedly.
I knew it was a ship from the cry of "*laca mota*" from the
beach, and sought my walking stick.

Itchy was impatient with my slow gait — he picked me up
in his arms and ran across the village with me as though I
were a stalk of bananas. Gione, one of his sons, brought my
throne. Sitting on the beach, I could see the sail and part

of the cabin of a copra schooner making down the coast.

Mike and Joe were working the sail. When I said "Up," they hoisted it. When I said "Down," they hauled it in. The vessel moved along till she was abeam of us. Mike and Joe agitated the sail madly. I stood on my chair waving my cane and shouting; everybody was doing something to attract attention. We screamed, we jumped, we waved. The vessel moved serenely down the coast and out of sight. I felt empty. Everybody looked disappointed, but Una seemed pleased that the boat hadn't seen the signal, and hadn't come for me. She came up and let me know that I wasn't *bula* (strong) enough to leave the island.

I concluded that there wasn't enough diversion in the sail alone to catch attention. Possibly it couldn't be seen from so great a distance; even if it could, it might not be recognized as a danger signal. I told the chief and suggested we build some brush piles on the beach to be lit next time we sighted a sail or funnel. He agreed. At his command all the boys in sight hustled into the jungle. Soon four impressive tinder heaps graced the beach.

Itchy was dead set on giving me a shave and trimming my hair. He had been agitating to do it all week, and each day I had stalled him. I dreaded this worse than tooth pulling. Many times I had seen the men shave themselves with cold water, laundry soap, and razors honed on a chunk of grindstone. Itchy was determined to get to the bottom of my whiskers. I could delay no longer.

My beard was five inches long and blond as platinum, from the constant touch of the sun. My hair had overgrown my ears and forehead, and was well down toward my shoulders. It too had been breathed on from above and was streaked with blond. It was all this blond business behind the sun-browned face that had so startled the beachcombing children that day I had peered down on them from my aerie in the rocks.

Itchy had an old pair of dull scissors for the shearing. Bill, Joe, and Mike oversaw the job. Hair flew and whiskers scraped. After an hour of manhandling and unforgettable misery I was bald-faced and near bald-headed.

Seeing myself just after being shaved was a jolt. It was a foreview of what I may be at ninety-nine. A skeleton of my real self peered back from the glass: wrinkled at the deep-sunk eyes; enlarged at the cheekbones and shallow in the cheeks; heavily veined over the forehead: bony at the jaw and throat; wide at the ears. From cheekbones to hair line was a swath of sunburned color; below was sallow flesh long hidden by my beard.

A Sail!

THERE HAD BEEN SOME TALK over the last few days of an *uga vule* hunt. Una told me that one had been planned for me. It would consist of a large party — Bill, Joe, Mike, Too-kai, and Suvi and all their family. We would leave next morning, early, to be gone for three days.

I knew nothing about an *uga vule* hunt — but I was raring to go.

At daylight I wobbled down to Itchy's outrigger and climbed aboard. Six other outriggers were assembled; families and gear were aboard. Everybody was in festal mood. The village lined the strand to wave us away. My throne was lashed aboard and we shoved off. Itchy stood on the dancing bow punting the thin shallow hull along at lively speed with a long pole. Una stood on the stern helping with the same man's job.

Later, when we changed course and the wind hauled round to aft, two heavy coconut fronds were stuck in the bow and the wind pushing against them drove us along effortlessly. Una laid aside her pole and steered from the stern with a large paddle.

The purpose of an *uga vule* hunt is to mix work with pleasure and at the same time inject the quest for food. This became apparent as the hunt progressed. As we glided over the coral bottom all eyes searched the coral shelves for signs of life.

Suddenly Itchy splashed overboard, spear in hand. Leaning over the side I watched him jerk downward through six fathoms of water, overtaking a large sea turtle that had seen us and plunged. Itchy stopped in mid-water, hovering over the turtle. His muscles tensed, then rippled, and I could see he was jabbing viciously. Then he reached for the surface with long strokes, towing his kill behind.

About two miles away from the village we nosed into a flat depression on the rocky coast. It was fronted by a white beach and planted to coconut trees. The boats pulled in and threw out their stone anchors made fast to the boat by vines. Una went ashore to stew tea for my morning meal, for I still ate every three hours. Itchy carried his copra knife, burlap bags, and axe ashore.

Mike's wife brought me some "cat's eyes," on the back of which grows a sweet-meated little animal you eat raw. I had them with *kumalas*, bananas, and tea for my morning snack.

The hunt was to take us right around the island. At each coconut patch we were to stop and gather the copra, or coconut meat. When the copra work was done the women were to pitch in and comb the area in search of the *uga vule*. Then we would load the copra and the *uga vules*, if any, and proceed on along the coast to the next open shore grown to coconut palms.

The coconut palm is the basic commodity in native life. The meat and milk of the green nut are an important liquid and food of the diet. Later, when the husk has dried and the nut matured, a coconut "cream" for cooking is obtained, as well as *wali wali* or ointment for the skin. The husk is used for fires, for smoking the *koro* against mosquitoes, and making sennit or native rope. The dried meat of the mature nut is shredded and eaten or is sold or traded as copra, about the only source of income open to the native.

The plaited fronds of the palm serve as building material for house roofs and walls, mattresses for the beds, baskets and fans. The bole is used for uprights, crossbeams, and the ridgepole in the hut.

When we made our first stop the coconut harvest was on. At a bark from Itchy the boys hurried off into the palm thicket carrying coarse jute bags. Each family worked separately, and for itself. Itchy and Una had an edge with four sons in the field. The boys' job was to quest for the brown dried nuts, and when their bag was filled to bring them in to Una. She, working with the axe, split each nut in halves with a stroke and dropped them near Itchy, seated close by.

Itchy with the double-edged copra knife in hand, twisted the white meat from the shell by a magic motion. It was tossed in a pile and later sacked. Soon the area was depleted of suitable coconuts. While the men sacked the harvest and loaded it on the outriggers, the women went deftly into the jungle in search of the *uga vule*.

Searching out the *uga vule* is an extreme test of eyes and intimate knowledge of the denizen's habits. He lives in the rocks, burrows in the undergrowth, and is difficult to ferret out and subdue. Unfortunately I was still too weak to follow into the jungle, so I missed seeing how the captures were made.

In less than an hour six *uga vules* showed up among the huntresses, so we moved on.

The fronds perched in the bow caught the wind and

pushed us off onto the lagoon. One, two, four, five, seven, nine fathoms of lucent water showed under the hull. A coral tip, or a shell, or a fish at that depth is as clear as in the hand. I liked nothing better than lying on the outrigger deck searching into the constant puzzle of the lagoon bottoms.

"*Vasua!*" A piercing cry from Una. Before I could see her, she was gone. She had dived in. I wriggled around so I could watch her spiral downward through fifty feet of water, spear in hand. Her hair streamed behind. Her vivid *sulu* flashed against slanting sun rays. She pulled up short, settled in slow motion on the ocean floor. Itchy spun the boat around.

Una's objective was a giant Fiji clam. She had spied the open lip and dived on the split second. The clam blends with the coral, as rattlers in the dust. Taking them from where they nestle in the coral can be dangerous.

Itchy had lost his first wife in a tragic episode with the *vasua*. She had hunted alone on the open reef, had thrust her hand under a partly open shell, and it had snapped on her, imprisoning her at the wrist as in a vise. And there she had perished, helpless, before the rising tide.

As Una prepared to approach the clam, to spear him at a vital spot, Itchy poised himself. Spear in hand he was ready to dive down to pry her free should any commotion indicate she was trapped. I leaned more closely to the water to see what Una would do, and to see how she would do it.

She eased over her prey, and by a soft movement slipped her spear point to the shell edge. At this point a motion of water will warn the giant bivalve and he will slap his curving shell edges closed. A crucial moment. In a second she jerked. She thrust quickly, and with a joggling motion she twisted violently. The powerful, vital muscle that clamps the lids shut was severed. Then she seemed to gather herself upward with long strokes and came to the outrigger to breathe. In a moment she dived again. This time Itchy stood poised anew with his spear. Una was still in danger. A shark might be lurking in the coral heads. Una floated onto the living coral floor, spread apart the valves of the clam, and cut away its choice meats. The shell is thick and sometimes weighs hundreds of pounds. Una swam back with the chunks of fat white flesh and heaved them on deck.

Next we stopped at a larger grove farther along the northwest shore, where we lunched. We carried away eleven more *uga vules*. That night our camp was pitched on the north point of the island on the shore of a small embayment. I slept on a mattress of pandanus strippings, in an open clearing of the grove. The stars were my ceiling, while the gentle roar of the tide on the distant reef dulled my senses.

The next morning we crowded our growing copra yield onto the shallow-draft outriggers, pushed off from under bending coconut palms growing over the water, and hauled down the uninviting windward shore.

We made two stops in the morning and one in the afternoon. Itchy and Bill conferred on whether we should attempt to make another inlet farther along before dark. They decided yes, so we loaded up and cast off, heading southeast along the cliffy shore.

Before we reached the spot, I could see it around the point ahead. The palm fronds showed over the cruel, jagged lava, near where I had been cast up. We crept up to the point and threw our frail craft into the race that swept past it; and ran with a spurt into the open bay.

There on the exposed sand was a sight I had never dreamed

possible to see. My one-time jaunty little cutter, *Pagan*, lay washed up on the beach — keel deep in sand she was, battered and splintered by her trials. She had scraped over two hundred yards of ungodly reef, floated a mile across the lagoon, and settled on the beach straight and level, with her bow pointed out to sea. There is no logical explanation for it. Nothing I can think of can explain it. She sits there today, hopelessly denuded, wrecked beyond the wildest dream of repair. It is a heavy-hearted sight.

That night I walked over to her, and rubbed her splintered stubs. Few boats have lived her thrilling life. Though her life was short under my hand, she lived it to the full and gave a full measure of service. In our trials together I had come to know my boat as a real person, and now I saw her bones captured by the sand. I felt a welling of deeper sentiment than one should feel over the riven kindlings of a hulk. I caressed her aged timbers, looked the last time over her naked frame, and walked away.

By midmorning the following day the open shores of Pagan's Cove, as I named the miniature bay, were sufficiently hunted; we shoved off. It was from this point that Itchy had embarked the night of my rescue, and groped through the dense jungle and over the ragged rock to me. We passed the sandy nook where the sea had thrown me up; down a short way was the treacherous cove where I had lain the last day and night.

Another mile and we pulled into the last inlet before reaching the village. The spot was too close to Lomaloma to have much copra, and it yielded only three *uga vules*. Here the bags of copra were unloaded and sprinkled over the flat rocks for drying in the sun. In a few days they would be resacked, and placed in special little huts near the village till the copra boat called in January. Before we departed I noticed a new activity.

The women brought long lengths of a brown vine onto the beach. All set to and cut it into twelve-inch lengths. Then on a rock or log it was pounded into wisps and bound in small sheaves. Each outrigger took a number of the pulpy bundles and pushed off. We didn't continue down the shallow coast, but put off into the deeper lagoon.

We hovered over the coral heads, watching the grottoes beneath, where sea life teemed. Presently something was seen in one of the black recesses of a coral peak. All craft hurried to the spot and anchored in a circle over it. Several heavy steel spears were cleared for action on each boat.

The sheaves of pounded fiber were dipped for a long minute and pounded again on the outrigger prows. With these the women swam down into the limpid water, depositing them at arm's reach in the dark openings. The men stood poised on the flat prows, spear in hand, tensed to dive.

Evidently the beaten vine exudes a substance which partly paralyzes, at the same time annoying, the fish. Fish, ordinarily too quick to follow with the eye, drifted lackadaisically from the caverns. The men plunged spear first on the easy prey. In two hours there was fish enough for the village. We filled out extra space with red, blue, green, brown, white, and black fish — some of them four feet long.

At dusk we pulled back once more into the bay of Lomaloma.

In the *keteketes* or baskets were two dozen fish. Also there were two turtles, a number of *uraus*, *vasua*, oysters, eels, turtle eggs, and thirty-seven *uga vules*. The village was festive.

My buddy Tupa, the chief, told me that next day there would be a village feast in my honor.

That night I felt infinitely stronger, something like my old self. The three-day outing had done it: three days of the freshest air I ever breathed, coupled with the rich meat of the *uga vule* and the life-sustaining coconut milk. The whole time I wore only a *sulu*. I lay hours in the sun. I strolled the beaches, or I napped, or I kidded with my friends — a proper combination of activities to restore health.

I looked forward to the coming feast.

The whole morning was consumed in preparation for it. First of all, the native ovens were made ready. These are ingenious devices for baking food in the ground. Broad holes — a dozen of them — about two feet deep were dug. In the bottoms, a bed of glowing coals was built up. Over the searing bed a layer of round stones was placed. The food, well wrapped in banana leaves for preservation, was placed on the hot stones and covered with sand. In three hours it was uncovered, and presto! The meat was so tender it fell from the bones.

Two hefty pigs were slaughtered and committed to the ovens. Ten chickens were baked, a hundred pounds of fish, thirty *uga vules*, *kumalas* by the dozen as well as *jaina* (bananas), *casava* (a type of yam), *mae* (breadfruit), *uvi* (sweet potato) — everything edible, cookable, and in season. Fruits such as eating bananas, papayas, mangoes, pineapple, passion fruit, and others I neither know nor could remember, were in abundance.

Young coconuts were stacked about to wash the feast down. On Tuvutha a feast isn't a feast unless there is plenty left over.

Palm fronds were cast side by side and end on end half the length of the grassy common in the village center. The food was uncovered from the savory ovens and crowded steaming onto the palms. Within the reach of all was a portion of everything.

We sat down cross-legged — for now I was strong enough and had flesh enough over my bones to sit comfortably — before the unbelievable abundance. My place was that of the guest — at the head of the table. Several leis of stained hibiscus fiber entwined with flowers were given me. In appreciation of the kindness and generosity of the whole village I wore them about my neck, despite their discomfort.

The chief nodded at me to begin. I dipped my fingers in the food within reach and all followed suit. The banquet was on. I ate of everything, as did every feaster. In the next hour we made classic gourmands of ourselves; for we ate to completion, then chatted awhile, and ate again. I grew sick of the sight of food; the very thought of it nearly burst me.

The Fijian loves a heavy eater. The more I ate the more they beamed.

The chief at last arose and gave a pained speech and sat down quickly. The pastor spoke; also the schoolteacher; and my philosopher friend of the wistful face. I was called upon to tell my story; which I did, to the uninhibited delight of all. The girls came forth and performed their gaudy sit-down dance. The chief stood and proclaimed a ceremonial *Yangona* to be held immediately in his hut, and the feast was over.

I was in no condition for a stag party, remembering the effects of the last. To show the boys I could take it, I went, but after my second round begged off and headed for a night of full sleep.

The next week was a hard one for me. I loved the island; I enjoyed being on it; but I longed to be on my way to Mary. At least I wanted to get some word to her and my family that I was safe. On the island I was caged and helpless.

I spent my days in quiet desperation. Hours I stood each day on the beach, searching past the thundering reef to the unbroken horizon. Every minute I hoped for a mast to appear.

To kill time and ease my mind, I strolled endlessly through the settlement, stopping in practically every hut.

I watched the women sitting in their lively social groups weaving intricate floor mats. I watched them beat out the *masi* of the mulberry tree for the decorative tapa cloth. I watched them weave baskets and fans from pandanus and palm leaves. I watched them prepare their foods, mother their children, make their homes.

The women have certain tasks about the village which they are more or less expected to do. However, in the easy life of nature, nothing is definitely the work of one sex or the other. They carry water, collect firewood, assist in preparing the native gardens and in their upkeep. They fish with throwing nets in the lagoons and dive for *vasua*, oysters, and *uraus*. They are the cooks, housekeepers, and family launderers. The Fijians are the cleanest native people I have ever seen. They bathe and wash clothes tirelessly. They keep tidy homes and grounds. Men and women are equally fastidious about their hair, keeping it combed out in a neat frizz.

The life of the Tuvutha native is essentially co-operative, though some of it is communal. The gardens, back in the jungle, are individually owned and planted. The heads of families and their sons work them mostly. When the natives dig their foods from the ground they replant shoots and roots immediately so there is an unending food supply in growth. The richness of the soil requires neither fertilizer, irrigation, nor plowing — merely weeding and simple planting. These jungle gardens yield lavishly.

Fruit groves, native trails, feasts, and the coconut thickets are communal properties. The chief is responsible for them. If they require attention he strolls through the village after dark calling off names and designating chores. And that's that.

Housebuilding and repairs are done after the fashion of the logrolling bees back in Texas — the neighbors all pitch in. The same for boatbuilding.

The old and infirm are easily provided for by the great abundance. Sickness, if any, is herbally treated. A doctor would grow rusty on the island.

An average day of life at Lomaloma is something like this: everyone hits the deck soon after daylight. Nothing much is done till about eight o'clock when the women serve up breakfast. It is a simple repast: usually *kumalas*, fish, boiled bananas, crabs, and fresh fruit.

The women clean house, wash clothes, weave mats. The men sharpen spears or knives, repair the house or boat till about eleven; then they round up their sons and head into the bush for rations. They return around two, laden with baskets of fresh jungle produce carried on the ends of a pole swung across the shoulder.

A medium-sized meal is partaken of. The rest of the afternoon is frittered away — maybe with a short fishing expedition, or a nap, or a social call, or helping the neighbors. The inevitable bath is fitted in.

The evening meal, just at dusk, is the main course of the day. This is the heavy meal, although no Fiji meal is really heavy unless it might be for occasional pork or chicken. The dinner is more elaborately prepared and offers more variety than the earlier meals of the day.

The evenings are spent sitting in doorways, watching the children at play, or chatting with neighbors. About nine o'clock everybody yawns heavily, lanterns go out, and night sounds prevail.

In this atmosphere of balanced tempo I fretted away my days, strolling the beach, eyes on the horizon. My ears were constantly on the alert for the cry that would go up if a sail should be sighted. My mind was in Sydney with Mary. I wondered what she was thinking. Had the long letter I left at Post Office Bay, nearly four months before, been picked up? If so, had she received it?

Unknown to me she had received the letter in early October, postmarked August from Guayaquil. But all she knew was that I had sailed from the Galápagos the last of July, bound westward.

I had expected to arrive in Sydney aboard *Pagan* by the end of September — and here it was half through November. Six weeks overdue! Mary's thoughts must have been very grim.

The morning of November 15 came around. Another day of anxiety was starting in its usual easy way; it was a good time for something to happen. It happened.

A sudden cry went up from the huts on the beach. In a moment it was resounding through the village. When I heard *laca moto,* I knew a sail was on the horizon. I hobbled toward the beach.

It was a sail all right — advancing down the coast. The craft was a motor schooner with an auxiliary sail, and she appeared to be footing it fast. Itchy and Mike began hauling the sail up and down while Bill and Joe lit the four fires and fanned them. Suvi and Tookai ran to and fro waving their fish nets. Una stood by implacable and still. A chorus of shouts went up. Everybody else was in motion.

Red flames broke from the stacks of tinder; blue smoke spiraled upward. Every eye was on the sail, which continued on imperturbably. Twenty minutes passed. The sail altered not a jot. I felt the same sinking feeling I had felt ten days before when we lost the other sail. More fuel was added to the fires.

The sail dropped suddenly out of sight. I knew it couldn't have disappeared over the horizon so soon — I couldn't figure it out. Then I realized that the boat had seen our signal, had dropped the auxiliary sail, and was coming to investigate. Her bow swelled into view, and suddenly I was jumping more wildly than all the rest.

A gang of us jumped on Itchy's outrigger and paddled out to pilot the newcomer through the reef. I made her out to be the *Lae*, a copra schooner of forty-five feet. When we pulled alongside, I went immediately aboard. The captain, a gnarled old Fijian who had seen many years in the island trade, spoke no English. But the mate, a young Tongan, had a speaking acquaintanceship with it.

In slowly spoken words I explained my circumstances and asked him if he could take me off the island. He conferred with the old sea dog, and turned to me saying yes. He explained that the boat was owned by Stockwell, an island trader and copra merchant, from Vanuambalavu. They were out weighing copra and had two islands to visit before returning north.

The ancient schooner rattled its ponderous anchor onto the sandy bottom off Lomaloma. In the friendly manner of the Fijis, the captain, mate, and crew came off with me to stretch their legs.

I walked promptly up to the hut, escorted by Itchy, Bill, Joe, Mike, and Tupa, all looking glum. Una had preceded us long before and had knowingly packed my few belongings in a battered chest given me by Itchy. She stood shaking her head, telling me not to go. My battered old blue suit was hanging ready for me by the door. I took it, stepped inside, unwrapped my *sulu*, and with Itchy's help slipped into the suit, my seedy white shirt, and a clean pair of socks. I walked back into the arena of drawn faces. There was nothing to do but say good-by and go quickly.

The next few minutes were the hardest of my life. How does one say good-by to the people who have saved his life and been the exemplars of kindness and generosity? What the natives saw was a simple handshake all round — but inside I was in a turmoil.

When I shook hands with Una she was still shaking her head and saying I wasn't well enough to go. Everyone who had been so good to me was there. Itchy was looking down at his feet and so was Tupa. Bill, Joe, and Mike were standing apart. The pastor, the schoolteacher, and my wistful philosopher friend looked straight into my eyes and smiled brave smiles. Tookai and Suvi were looking downcast. The families of all stood close around, silent. I felt as though I were doing wrong by leaving, so I hurried.

I waved good-by and hopped into the dinghy. At the last

minute Itchy jumped in, determined to stay to the last. An outrigger came out for him; more good-bys were said; more handshakes; and the anchor was dragged aboard. With the engine roaring and the old boat trembling, we made for the opening in the reef. Itchy's outrigger followed us to the open sea. That was the last I saw of Lomaloma.

CHAPTER XXVI Australia

We anchored outside the reef off Nayau, a near-by island, the first of the two to be visited, at noon. I went ashore to see the copra weighed, but as soon as the local chief heard of my sea venture, I was ushered off to an impromptu *Yangona*. First a chicken was hastily boiled, a stalk of bananas was brought in, and I ate before the large circle of smiling faces.

I told my boat story by pantomime and the addition of a growing Fiji vocabulary. Once wasn't enough so I labored through it a second time. I was told that the schooner would be shoving off soon for another village down the coast. There was time for a drink of the ceremonial kava. I took it on the run. After thanking them all for their generosity I went to the boat.

The next village was a repeat performance of the first. The worst part was eating another chicken, and more bananas.

Nayau was the island from which Itchy and Una emigrated to find their happiness. I was now in the village where they had formerly lived. I met Una's worn and aged parents, a venerable old couple married forty-two years. Itchy's father was dead but I was taken to his blind old mother. She was told that Itchy had been kind to the *kai vavalage* (white man). She nodded, smiled, and sat quiet.

That night I slept in the hut of Una's parents. Before day-light, as arranged, I was awakened and hustled off to the rattling, trembling schooner. When the sun had been up little more than an hour, we were swinging to anchor off the little island of Thithia, the last step before going on to Vanuambalavu. Off to the southwest, on the horizon, I could see the gray crater top of Tuvutha.

It appears to be the bounden duty of Fijians to be hospitable. I was hardly ashore at Thithia before the "key" to the village was given me. In part payment for the food and comfortable chair that was brought me, I told my boat story twice. There wasn't time for a *Yangona*, so I shook hands with those nearest and was rowed out to the smoking schooner.

We pulled away from the reef making a course of north for the long, twisted island of Vanuambalavu.

There is a radio station there from which I intended to send an immediate message to Mary and to my mother. Also, ships often pass there bound for Suva, main city of the Fijis, I was told. It seemed incredible that in a few hours I would be in radio contact with my wife.

We nosed our way through a perplexing maze of coral reefs and coral heads. The Fiji islands abound in them. Coming up to the anchorage before the white trading post, we let go the anchor, and it rumbled down in a wide bay active with outriggers under sail. A large village, nestling among tall palms, lined the shore.

I went off with the first boat to meet the *vavalage*, Mr. Stockwell. I found him in the warehouse under a wide-brimmed hat, in island shorts and sandals. He was weighing flowing sacks of copra boated in from the outlying isles.

I stepped up and stood leaning on my cane, watching him in the midst of his dickerings with barefoot, stolid natives. He was tanned golden, had a sturdy laugh, and though grayed at the temples he hefted the great sacks to the scales. He saw me with a jolt: it was seldom he saw strange white men.

I introduced myself, clasped his hand, and tried briefly to account for my presence. He smiled quizzically as I talked. On his face was a creeping disbelief of what I was saying. The old sea dog broke in and told of what he had heard at Tuvutha. The young Tongan mate backed him strongly.

In a widening grin of appreciation, and with an occasional "blimey" whispered hoarsely forth as I recounted my siege on the sea, Stockwell listened. At the end of the part about the hurricane he said, "Stone the crows, lad!"

I could tell he was finding it difficult to believe. But he had to believe. There I stood, my bones still prominent from the rigors of my five months' cruise; and the old sea dog and the young Tongan mate pointing out that parts of *Pagan*, from her masthead to keelson, littered the beaches and the village of Tuvutha.

Stockwell sat down and bade me be comfortable. I talked on. He sat with lips apart, his eyes never leaving my face. Suddenly he stood, and taking my arm led me into the trading post and out back to his family quarters. We sat there long hours as I went on with the account of my voyage. When I finished, his first reaction was a lengthy minute of wordless appraisal. He shook his head, smiled, then launched into a series of questions covering the whole voyage. He was keen to know about the hurricane and my prolonged search for land. Finally he said, "You've probably set a record for one man under a jury rig, if it's true you sailed a crippled boat from the Suvorovs to here."

He went on to comment on my luck in slipping into Tuvu- tha past the offshore reefs. Then suddenly he said, "This wife of yours, what's she like? I want to see the woman a bloke would sail the Pacific for." Mary is always a topic of easy dis- cussion for me; a topic of especial fluency, and one which at that moment I was able to expand upon.

At length the topic turned to Stockwell and his existence as an islander. We continued for long hours as he reminisced over over the more than thirty years he had been butting around Fiji as an island trader. He had seen the hulks of many fine craft that had met watery ends along Fiji's iron-bound coasts. I wasn't the first castaway to turn up at Vanuambalavu; and in many cases where the sea had taken a tragic toll there had been no castaways to turn up. He told of sudden hurricanes, shallow offshore coral heads, and treacherous currents. I felt fortunate to be alive, fortunate that there had been no hurricane, that somehow I had sailed past the jagged offshore reefs, and that the treacherous currents had not destroyed me.

The afternoon was wearing on to dusk, and I wanted to get word to Mary and to my people at home. Stockwell reported that the radio was broken down, that there would be no possibility of a message until I could reach Suva Bay on the main island of Viti Levu, some 180 miles to westward. But that was a problem that could wait till after dinner; he ushered me to his generous table.

Mrs. Stockwell, a charming Tongan woman, had pre- pared a doggoned good "Yankee" dinner for me. It was ham and eggs with real bread, coffee, and apple pie. I had eaten the native foods for so long that it was wonderful to eat the less healthful civilized concoctions again.

That night I slept on a soft mattress. I slept the more soundly because plans had been made as we talked far into the night to send me by launch to near-by Kanathea, where there lay a copra boat inbound to Suva.

After a Sunday breakfast of oatmeal, fried eggs, and pancakes, another welcome Yankee concession on the part of Mrs. Stockwell, I chatted with my genial host on his veranda. We awaited high tide so the launch could top the reef at a break in the island through which I was to pass en route to Kanathea. When the water was up sufficiently I made my adieus, and once again was on the move.

The little launch skirted a tropical coastline fringed with sleeping palms. The islets in the lagoon were misshapen, palm-grown and coral-bound; the breaking water from hidden reefs around them shot up from minute to minute like tiny explosions. Here was a harbor that in the old days had been a roadstead to tall whaling ships and pearlers. Now there were only a few petty copra schooners, and the likes of me, a broken-down twentieth-century castaway en route to his lady love. We passed over the shallow reef between two shoulders of land where the long island parted. Across an open stretch of reefy sea lay Kanathea. Suckling to it was the small copra ship.

A native conned us through the coral heads and soon we were tied alongside the copra boat. She was the *Tui Cakou* — "twee thakow." All steel, about 700 tons, well appointed, and fast. I swung aboard and found the captain.

The little ship was loaded to her Plimsolls and ready to go for Suva. She was waiting for Monday; but first she had to stop at the island of Naitamba for a passenger and small cargo. We lazed away the afternoon fishing from the sun deck.

Before daylight of Monday morning the bow and stern anchors were drawn in and we moved out of the tight coral lagoon. To the right was Vanuambalavu; to the left, Hat Island; and dead ahead the gray dome of Naitamba.

There was no break in the reef through which to make entrance into the lagoon at Naitamba. The ship had to laze back and forth outside the reef and the goods were to be lightered out in longboats under oar. I went ashore with the first boat to the fatly vegetabled island to fetch the passenger and his cargo. Naitamba slopes away from its high rugged end to a low gentle end resting on the water. The low coastal slopes are rich in coconut growth.

We steered in to a short cement jetty built to accommodate copra loading. On its seaward end, greeting us, stood old Gus Henning, a veteran islander and mariner of the Southwest Pacific. I lit as soon as the craft was secured and strode with Henning off to his tropical paradise built up and developed over the years from a desert isle.

I met Mrs. Henning, active and benign, who took us to her capacious lounge where I saw combined the grace of Europe and the cool quiet of the South Pacific. A Fiji Mary, wrapped in her *sulu* and in customary bare feet, slipped in with tea. I told the Hennings the long story of my voyage, only this time I didn't have the gnarled old sea dog to back me up when they questioned its parts.

A castaway's story wasn't a new one for the inhabitants of Naitamba. Many an adventurer down in his luck had passed through there. Yet, despite this, the Hennings were amazed with the difficulties I had encountered in my Pacific traverse;

and they took a heartfelt interest in my trials and my predicament.

Old Gus Henning, himself a veteran sailor of the Fijian group, and, in fact, a large portion of the Southwest Pacific, was sincerely disappointed that I had lost my brave little *Pagan*. Boats and the sea were an abiding love with Gus. He offered to return with me to Tuvutha to determine if *Pagan* could be salvaged. He wanted to see her alive again and before the wind. But I described *Pagan* as I had seen her last: her keel imprisoned in the sand, her lines broken and battered, her bones beginning to parch, and her few salvageable items prize possessions of the natives at Lomaloma.

Mrs. Henning was greatly concerned that Mary in all these months since my departure from the Perlas hadn't received definite word of my whereabouts. Many times she had fretted patiently when Gus's craft, overdue from a long passage, was making its way in. There were no radio facilities on the island or a message would have been readily sent to Australia.

The Hennings had come out from Europe after the First World War to take up plantationing. They reared a family and cultivated an island between the wars. The children left for the second war, and at its finish decided to stay on in England; the Hennings were left with an island full of memories.

Mrs. Henning offered to show me over the plantation. We toured the house. Nothing lacked that I could see. Comfortable ornamental bedrooms. A spacious lounge room; two porches — one glassed in, one open. A well-equipped kitchen. Soft overstuffed furniture; European rugs; radio; maid service by a bevy of Fiji belles. We stepped from the cool, five-room house onto a green sealike lawn which sprawled around it. Next to the house on the fringe of the lawn lay cultivated tropical gardens, towered over by imported shade trees and coconut palms.

Farther on the grounds were fenced and laid out in vegetable gardens. There were cows, horses, and pigs. In the fowl run I saw turkeys, geese, and chickens. A part of the warehouse was given over to a provisions store for the Hennings and the fifty natives who worked the island.

A world of men dream of such a hideaway: the Hennings told me it was very incomplete!

The *Tui Cakou*, with her markings in the water, was ready to sail in midafternoon. She headed out into the Koro Sea, making southwest for Suva. The Fijis are a lovely archipelago to sail through, blue islands to left and right. Through the night as I wakened in hunger and rose to have my customary nightly meals, I thought ahead and hoped for success in my quest for transport on to Australia.

Next morning the little ship was tied bow and stern to the copra wharf at Suva, and I was taking a last look at her. A tall decorative Fijian policeman came for me from the Immigration Department.

To one used as I was to our hard-boiled cops girt with revolvers or carrying clubs, the Fijian arm of the law is a study in contrasts. The weapon carried by the officer who came for me was a ready, jovial smile which completely disarmed me.

He wore the famous, well-groomed, bushy headdress. The navy-blue jacket was collarless and beautifully tailored, set off by polished golden buttons. It disappeared at the waist beneath a colorful crimson scarf, clasped by a thick leather belt buckled in front with a shining brass buckle. From under the bright scarf and reaching to the knees was a white *sulu* with a diamond-shaped hemline. From beneath the white skirt showed the powerful legs and customary bare feet. The result: the world's most colorfully attired police force.

At police headquarters I was accepted and politely passed through with unbelievable facility. In this world where international travel without a visa is next to armed aggression, it was strange not to sign half my life away to the authorities. From the highest commissioner to the lowest barefoot private, I was very patiently handled and cared for.

I was anxious to get a cable, announcing my safe arrival, away to Mary. The commissioner very considerately hurried my papers along.

The cable I sent read: "Am safe and well in Fiji. Taking first ship to Australia. Will cable. I love you. Johnnie."

Almost immediately, and even before Mary could possibly have received my cable, I received a cable from her. She had heard of my wrecking in a news flash, and had rushed a message whose very words showed that a heavy burden of dark uncertainty had been lifted from her mind.

Those words: I read them and reread them; they were a reprieve from doubt, a welcome home, an avenue to a whole new future.

The problem of where to stay while I was in Suva looking for transport was extremely perplexing, because I had six offers from people who earnestly wanted me to stay at their homes. I felt like a heel saying yes to one, since it meant saying no to five others.

Honestly, I don't know why seamen persist in getting wrecked in some of the outlandish places they do, when they can do it in a nice place like Fiji.

I finally decided to stay with young Ernie Hurley, from

Morris-Hedstrom Shipping. He was my age, married; we had much in common.

I was promptly taken in tow by the Fiji *Times* and escorted around town. They turned me up at the Yacht Club and introduced me to all the local helm talent. My picture was snapped with yachtsmen and members of the Fiji police force. I had a nice story in the paper; and I heard my name on the radio that night. But none of the publicity helped me get back to my wife, a project which was still as great a perplexity as it had been in New York — except that now I didn't have a thousand dollars to buy a boat.

My problem was still to find a ship bound for Australia. Nothing was expected for a month. Plane fare was exorbitant — besides, I was broke.

A British tramp had sailed for New Zealand two days before, bound to Melbourne via Hobart, Tasmania. I approached the Royal New Zealand Air Force, stationed at Suva, with the idea of hitchhiking a lift to Auckland. From there I could pick up the ship. Tough luck, I was told — there was no military traffic.

The American Consul suggested I contact the U.S. Army Air Corps, stationed across the big island of Viti Levu at Nandi. The next day I took passage over the dusty coastal, and partly inland, road aboard a rumbling native bus that rolled and pitched to outdo *Pagan*.

At the air base I gave the colonel in charge a sad account of my recent months. I appealed to his romanticism by bringing my wife into the story. Like all Americans in the face of misfortune, he grew softhearted. The Army can't carry civilians, but, as he put it, "a shipwrecked seaman is different."

At the moment he had nothing going to Australia until the

first of the year. But there was a "kite" in three days for Tontoota, New Caledonia. Plenty of traffic, he said, dropped in from the States and Honolulu to Tontoota; and plenty went back. But nothing much went on west. I might get to Tontoota and find myself stuck there. It might be better to wait at Nandi till January.

I had three days to mull the pros and cons of the prospective flight to Tontoota. In the meantime I continued to search for transport to Australia. I jaunted back across the island by bus to the head offices of the Colonial Sugar Refining Company. Could they put me on one of their sugar boats crossing the Tasman? No soap. All space was chartered by employees voyaging home for Christmas holidays.

I decided to gamble on the plane to Tontoota. There was a possibility I would get stuck there, but my wicked intuition, telling me as ever all would come out right, pressed me to take it. It was known that craft were flying out of there to the Solomons and into New Guinea. Possibly I could follow that track and connect with Australia from one of the northern points. Anything to keep moving in the right direction.

On the morning of the twenty-eighth of November I boarded a medium army bomber. I had just finished breakfast at Nandi, and when I lunched it was my Thanksgiving dinner, in the army mess at Tontoota. After having sat around helplessly for a week at Nandi, I traveled a thousand miles in a few hours.

I reported to the colonel at the field with a letter of introduction from the colonel at Nandi, and told him the sad story of my life on the sea. He listened considerately, but told me there were no flights that could assist me just then. I was billeted and told to stand by.

More days of fretful waiting were to follow. The day after my arrival a special letter came from Mary. She had written it more than a week before, and it had followed me by air mail from Suva and Nandi.

Mary's long months of patient waiting showed up between the lines. She had received my letter of July mail from Post Office Bay in the Galápagos. It had arrived in Sydney the first week in October, explaining my expected arrival before the last of September — in other words, I was always a week over-due when the letters had arrived! And here it was only a very few days from December!

At that time little or no shipping was leaving New Caledo-nia — nothing whatever bound for Australia. My only avenue of travel lay by air. I searched the flight schedules every day. After four days I was tempted to return to Fiji, and try from there again. The pilots dissuaded me. "Anything can hap-pen," they said. And it did.

A great four-motored transport slithered in from the sky unexpectedly. Aboard was an inspecting officer bound for Sydney via Brisbane. Five days of nerve-worn waiting was over — the next morning at daylight I would start the final lap.

At noon of December third I landed at Brisbane on the same field that nineteen months before I had taken off from to speed south to my wedding. It was impossible to believe that in less than three hours I would be with my wife again. A lot of water had flown beneath the keel since the last time.

Reporters from Brisbane papers took pictures and asked questions about my voyage. I sent a cable to Mary telling her of my arrival time in Sydney.

The giant plane lifted easily and roared over the rugged coastal terrain that was so familiar to me. We swooped on Sydney, crossing her sinuous harbor and beloved bridge, made a wide sweep of the city, and shaped up for the approach to the runway and angled down to it.

I was the most eager passenger aboard.

My gear was first to be unloaded and I was first passenger to alight. And then I saw Mary. I remember her coming toward me — and I believe I moved to meet her. For a second I saw her unfathomable blue eyes. . . . She was in my arms . . . a thousand dreams had come true . . . my trials on the sea were far away.

I can't describe that moment any more than you could. At such a time you live too fast for description in mere words. What mattered then was that I was home from the sea . . . back again with the one person who counts in this world.